DEAD
ON TIME

Also by Clifford Witting

DEAD
ON TIME

CLIFFORD WITTING

Galileo Publishers, Cambridge

Galileo Publishers
16 Woodlands Road, Great Shelford
Cambridge
CB22 5LW UK

www.galileopublishing.co.uk

Distributed in the USA by SCB Distributors
15608 S. New Century Drive
Gardena, CA 90248-2129, USA

Australia: Peribo Pty Limited
58 Beaumont Road
Mount Kuring-Gai, NSW 2080
Australia

ISBN 978-1-912916-634

First published 1948
This edition © 2022

Printed in the EU

The republication of this book is dedicated to the memory of Diana Mary Cummings, the daughter of the author. She died November 26th 2021.

The original dedication was to

DUDLEY and EIRA

"... I classified Ona superstitions under four main headings. First: fear of magic and the power of magicians, even on the part of those who, professing their art, must have known that they themselves were humbugs. They had great fear of the power of others..."

E. Lucas Bridges: *Uttermost Part of the Earth*

CONTENTS

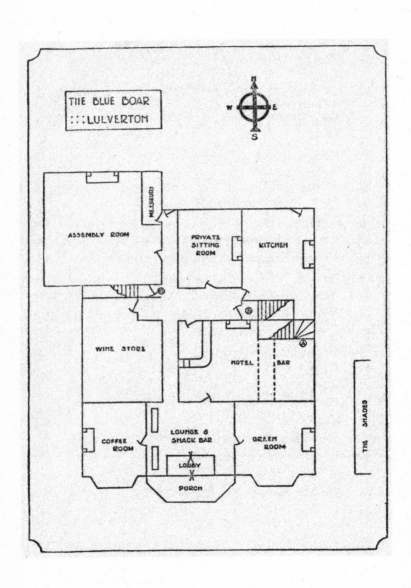

Last Orders

DETECTIVE-SERGEANT Albert Martin replaced his empty tankard on the small table by his side and sighed reflectively.

"It was good while it lasted," he said.

Detective-constable Peter Bradfield replied:

"Ada's on the way up with some more."

There was still plenty of time before the Blue Boar closed for the day. It was not long after nine o'clock in the evening of the first Thursday of the year, and the little party of men in the room above the hotel bar were thoroughly enjoying themselves around the fire.

"I wasn't meaning that, Peter," Bert explained with a happy grin on his round red face. "Not that I don't say but what another pint wouldn't be welcome, 'specially from a source that's not famous for splashin' out 'ospitality."

"You ungrateful old man!" protested Bradfield. "I bought you two pints in a row in this very pub last week. Your money was in your other suit—as it usually is."

"Ungrateful maybe, but old—no. None of your back-chat, young feller. Just 'cause the 'igher ups see fit, in their ignorance, to make you up to D.S. tomorrow, that's no reason to give yourself airs. You don't step into my shoes till I step out of 'em, don't forget, and that won't be till the stroke of midnight. Then you can step into 'em." He glanced down and compared Bradfield's feet with his own. "But I doubt whether they'll fit."

"I'll buy some cork socks," said Bradfield, which, in its lack of any merit as sparkling repartee, was typical of most occasions when old friends sit drinking beer together.

Bert Martin took no notice of his subordinate's impudence,

but went on:

"When I said it's been good while it lasted, I mean bein' in the Force." He coughed impressively. "Lookin' back over the long vista of the years, what do I see?"

Just then Ada brought in the beer, and for a busy minute that was all any of them saw. This stag-party in one of the upper rooms of the Blue Boar in Lulverton High Street was something of an event, for it was to celebrate Sergeant Martin's retirement after thirty years' service. It was only a small gathering. Besides Martin and Bradfield it included "Tiny" Kingsley, the burly superintendent of the Lulverton Division of the Downshire County Constabulary, Detective-inspector Charlton, who was in charge of the C.I.D. men attached to that division, and Dr. Stuart Lorimer, the young police surgeon, who was a close personal friend of the others. Peter Bradfield was a sunny-tempered, tall young man, smooth-haired and with a wide, flat nose. His clothes were always well cut and he wore his hat at a rakehelly angle over the right eye, as if it had been thrown on his head from a distance and had somehow failed to fall off. He was the darling of the other sex and maintained the social contacts of the C.I.D. in Lulverton. During the second World War he had been in the Royal Regiment of Artillery and had come out with the rank of bombardier. Now, as soon as his promotion came through, he would have to accustom himself to answer to "Sergeant."

These five good friends had enjoyed what Sergeant Martin had described when he had issued the verbal invitations as "a bit of a supper" and were now sitting round the fire, while outside the English climate was adhering to its New Year resolution to make things as unpleasant and damp as possible for the long-suffering inhabitants of the British Isles in general and, so it seemed to those in that unprotected area between the South Downs and the English Channel, Lulverton in particular.

Ada collected the empty tankards on the tray on which she

had brought up the fresh ones, and went downstairs again. The men went on chatting about this and that as they smoked and drank their Downshire brew. Bradfield threw another log on the fire. It was all very cosy and pleasant. Martin mentioned, with pride and satisfaction in his voice, the handsome clock that had been presented to him by his colleagues.

"Couldn't 'ave wished for anything nicer," he said.

"There's a rumour, Sarge," Bradfield told him with a straight face, "that the Maharajah of Molhapur is sending you a little memento—probably an elephant."

"Never 'eard of 'im."

Inspector Charlton said with a smile: "Then you haven't been reading the papers lately."

"The back page mostly," admitted Martin. "The rest of it's all so depressin'. What's 'is nibs been up to?"

"The Anglo-Molhapur Society are holding an exhibition in London during the next week or so, and the Maharajah and other eminent State dignitaries are parting with their family treasures for the occasion. I hope they get them back safely."

Superintendent Kingsley took his pipe out of his mouth to remark: "They say the collection's worth half a million."

"Well," chuckled the Sergeant, "I hope the old boy 'asn't forgotten 'is former schoolmate, though I think the missis'd bar an elephant. 'Andful or two of the crown jewels would be more acceptable."

Beer being what it is, Bradfield rose to his feet at this point in the conversation.

"I think that's the phone," he said.

Elsewhere in these pages there is a plan of the ground floor of the Blue Boar. The room in which Sergeant Martin was entertaining his friends was on the first floor, immediately above the hotel bar, and the door of it opened on a landing that is indicated on the plan by means of dotted lines. At one end of the landing was a wide staircase leading down into the hotel bar, part of which could be seen from the landing by looking over the wooden balustrade. At this same end of the landing was a door through which access could be gained to another flight—much narrower than the main staircase—which was used more by the staff than by residents or customers, and in particular by Ada on her trips downstairs to obtain further supplies of refreshment through the serving-hatch behind the counter in the hotel bar.

Bradfield now went down the back stairs, passed the serving-hatch and turned to the right. As he walked along the short passage, the door at the far end of it, which led in from the yard at the back of the building, opened to admit a man.

He was a tubby little fellow, somewhere between forty-five and fifty years of age. His face was as round and shining as a new penny and of the colour of a Worcester Pearmain. His bright eyes shone genially through gold-rimmed spectacles, and he wore a dark overcoat that fitted too tightly to hide his plumpness, a black Homburg hat and a thick grey woollen muffler. Hanging from his right arm was a dripping umbrella and in the gloved hand protruding from the over-short sleeve were clutched a score or so of leaflets that had not been improved by their exposure to the wind and rain.

He did not come right into the passage, but stood on the threshold, peeping round the half-opened door and looking, thought Bradfield, like a shy little cleric who has strayed into the sultan's harem and is trying to find some kind person who will show him the quickest way out.

"Can I help you?" Bradfield asked politely.

"Indeed you can!" was the eager reply. "I am not quite sure whether this is a private entrance or whether it leads into the hotel."

"It's the back door of the hotel. Which part do you want?"

"I am in search of the drinking-bar."

Bradfield turned and pointed down the passage.

"Go straight along and turn to the left. You'll find the door

4

to the bar just round the corner."

"That is most kind of you. I fear I am not very well acquainted with the geography of the place. I am extremely grateful to you."

"Not at all."

He stepped aside. The little man came right in and closed the door behind him. Before he went off down the passage he fumbled with his bunch of leaflets and managed to separate one of them, which he handed to Bradfield with the earnest injunction:

"Read it, my boy, when you get a free moment or two. I am sure you will not find the time has been wasted."

Guessing that it was a religious tract, Bradfield took it with a word of thanks. He was putting it away in his pocket when the little man said:

"Can you tell me, please, how far it is off closing time?"

"That's some little while yet," Bradfield told him. He looked at the watch on his wrist. "It's not quite five-and-twenty past nine, and they don't shut till ten o'clock."

"Splendid!" beamed the little man. "Souls can be saved in far less time than that. Thanks once more—and don't forget to read that little pamphlet, will you?"

"No, I won't forget."

"Splendid!" said the little man again, and proceeded briskly in the direction of the hotel bar, with his sodden umbrella swinging on his arm.

Within a few minutes Bradfield was back upstairs with his friends. They all sat chatting round the fire until, at a quarter to ten, Ada came in again.

"Would yer be wanting any more?" she asked in her dreary, adenoidal voice.

Ada was no beauty. Tall, sad and droopy, like a willow tree after prolonged drought, she was, at twenty-five, nobody's darling, and it did not seem likely that she ever would be, poor girl.

"Yes, Ada," Sergeant Martin said promptly, "I think we can

all manage another."

Nobody contradicted this statement, so Ada collected up the empty tankards and made for the door with a tray-load of them. As she reached it the door was pushed open with a violence that caught the tray and sent the tankards flying. Ada was more annoyed than frightened.

"What d'yer think yer up to, clumsy?" she demanded. "You keep out of 'ere! This is a private party, and you can 'op it, see?"

Clumsy had clearly no intention of 'opping it. He called Ada by a rude name and pushed her out of the way. When he lurched past her into the room and stood there swaying, they saw that it was Jimmy Hooker.

"Ah!" he said, waving a dirty forefinger drunkenly in the air. "I thought you'd still be up 'ere, sports. Thass good. Thass very good indeed."

Jimmy Hooker was what is known as a "character"; a short, sturdy, swarthy man with a touch of gypsy about him, never to be seen, even in the height of summer, in anything but a shabby tweed overcoat, a silk scarf that had once been white, and a bowler hat intended for a man with a very much larger head. Its appearance gave the impression that Jimmy had made it a better fit by packing it out with paper. If use of the razor two or three times a week qualified him for the description, he was clean shaven. His age was difficult to estimate; between forty and fifty was a fairly safe guess. Of regular employment he had none, yet to call him a spiv would have been unfair; pedlar was a better and more gentle name. When there were flowers to sell he hawked them from door to door. At other times it might be rabbits or mushrooms or firewood. Again, it might be clothes-pegs or scrubbing-brushes or puppies or white mice or bottles of hair cream. Nothing came amiss to Jimmy. In addition to his manifold business activities, he was an authority on horse-racing and had once been through the hands of the police for a small infringement of the Street

Betting Act, 1906. Everyone in Lulverton knew Jimmy Hooker. The kids all loved him because of the toys he could make out of bits of wood with no more tools than a penknife with half a blade. It was a sidelight on his character that he never tried to make a profit out of this talent; the children got the toys for nothing. They said that Jimmy always kept his scarf tightly knotted on account of a horrible picture tattooed on his neck. Most of their mothers believed this as well.

The group round the fire had all turned towards Jimmy. As Ada collected up the scattered tankards, Superintendent Kingsley said in his forthright way:

"What do you want, Hooker?"

Jimmy, who still wore his bowler, was drunk enough to be very much on his dignity.

"*Mister* Hooker to you, if you please," he slurred, drawing himself up proudly. "How'd you like it if I was to call you 'Kingsley' without the 'andle? A gen'leman's entitled to—"

"What do you want?" the Super said again.

"S'nice way to talk, I mussay. I'll ask you to keep a ci'il tongue—"

"That's enough of that, Hooker. Get out!"

Bradfield turned his head to glance at Inspector Charlton. He was frowning slightly and Bradfield guessed his thoughts. Jimmy Hooker had not come upstairs for a blackguarding match with the Superintendent. Once or twice in the past the police had had cause to be obliged to Jimmy. This might be another such occasion, and the situation seemed to call for a little more finesse than the worthy Super was displaying. Bradfield's surmise was correct, for at this point the Inspector joined in the conversation—and his voice, as someone had once described it, was as sweet as dark brown honey.

"What's the trouble, Jimmy?" he asked. "Is there something you want to tell us?"

Ada had retrieved all the tankards and had now left the room, after having given Jimmy the benefit of a toss of her untidy head and a sniff of high disapproval. Jimmy remained planted where he was, midway between the door and the fireplace. He turned his head towards the Inspector and blinked at him, as if trying to bring him into focus. Charlton's voice had great power to mollify, and for a moment it seemed that he had succeeded. But a tractable man such as Jimmy Hooker can be very stubborn when in drink. He stood glowering for a time, with his arms hanging loosely at his sides and his rough, dirty hands half concealed by the long, ragged-cuffed sleeves of his shabby overcoat, then announced:

"—ed if I will now. Find out fer yerselves."

Whereupon he turned about, rather too rapidly for his equilibrium, paused to get his bearings, then made for the door as if the room were a cabin in some storm-tossed liner. He did not close the door behind him, so Bradfield got up to do it. He looked out and noticed with some surprise that Jimmy had not turned to the left towards the staircase, but had lurched off in the other direction. Bradfield's last glimpse of him was as he went round the corner into a passage that would take him to the other end of the building. If Jimmy was proposing to leave the Blue Boar, or even to descend into the bar, he was going by a somewhat roundabout route.

As Bradfield came back to his chair the Inspector was saying to the Super:

"He must have had some reason, Tiny. He didn't seek us out for the fun of the thing."

"A man'll do anything when he's bottled. Probably heard our voices when the door was open and barged in to make himself a nuisance."

"'Fraid I can't agree with you. He obviously had something to tell us. Nothing else would have brought him upstairs." He swung round to Bradfield. "Peter, make a point of having a quiet word with Hooker tomorrow morning, will you? He'll be sober then. He usually goes into the Shades for a pint as soon as they open."

His assistant said that these instructions would be carried out and then added:

"When Jimmy swept off in a huff just now he didn't go straight down into the bar. He went the other way."

"Where does that lead?" asked the Super.

"There's a passage runs along the side of this room, sir. The front bedrooms and the residents' lounge open on to it. When you get to the far end there's another passage leading off to the right—that's to the back of the building—and at the end of this there's a little narrow flight of stairs that'll take you down to the ground floor. It comes out between the wine-store and the assembly-room."

"In other words," said Charlton, "it's a way of reaching this room and leaving again afterwards without attracting too much attention."

They were still discussing this when Ada put in an appearance with the drinks ordered by Sergeant Martin.

"Miss Betty's just called 'last orders'," she told them. "Would these be the last you'll want?"

"Yes, thanks, Ada," answered the Super. "One pint will keep us quite busy enough for the next five minutes." Ada looked disappointed at this. Customers should be made of sterner stuff. She was turning to make her sagging departure when the Super detained her.

"Just before you go, Ada..."

"Yes, sir?"

"Did you notice what happened to Hooker after he'd left this room?"

"Saucy swine, pushing 'is nose in 'ere! I told 'im somethink. Can't 'old it—that's 'is trouble. I said to 'im, 'Now, you listen to me,' I said—"

The Super interrupted her.

"How did he get downstairs again? Can you tell us that, Ada?"

"'E come by the back stairs, which 'e wouldn't 'ave done if

'e'd bin the gentleman 'e isn't."

This rather cryptic remark was occasioned by the fact that across the foot of this staircase ("C" on the plan) was a door marked in such a way that the male sex fought shy of it. The announcement, however, was some-what too prohibitive, for the staircase did not lead only to the ladies' room, which was on the first landing; it also gave access to the upper floors.

"I was standing at the serving-'atch," Ada went on, "when down 'e come, the blundering lout. 'Ooker,' I said to 'im, 'you know as well as I do that you didn't ought to use them stairs,' I said. 'And another thing,' I said. 'I won't 'ave you interfering with my customers. If you can't stop from poking that ugly nose of yours into things what don't concern you,' I said, 'then I'll 'ave to tell Mr. Collins,' I said. 'Mr. Collins 'as warned you once already about making yerself a nuisance,' I said, 'and if there's any more trouble with you, 'e'll bar you from coming in 'ere and you'll 'ave to do yer drinking at some other pub,' I said."

"What did Hooker do?" the Super asked. "Did he go home?"

"Not 'im! 'E called me somethink I wouldn't soil my lips by repeating and went back to the saloon. 'E's still there, soaking up beer like the sands of the desert.

They all smiled at this picturesque simile, and the Super dismissed Ada with a word of thanks. Just as she closed the door behind her the town clocks began to make it known, one after the other and in a variety of keys, that it was ten o'clock. The last note had not long died away when there was another interruption. Without the formality of knocking, Mr. Collins, the licensee of the Blue Boar, came into the room. Because of his likeness to the famous character in the *Daily Graphic* cartoons he was known as Pop to all and sundry.

His usual genial countenance now wore an anxious frown and he was breathing heavily.

"All right, Pop," Bert Martin reassured him. "We'll go

quietly, though I must say you're a little bit on the smart—"

Mr. Collins cut him short. He addressed himself to the Super, fiddling as he did so with the signet ring on the little finger of his left hand—a sure sign that he was worried.

"Mr. Kingsley," he said, "I've come straight up to tell you. There's been a serious occurrence downstairs. A man's dropped dead—and I don't think it was in the way of nature."

"A customer?"

"Yes. Chap by the name of Hooker."

II.

KCN

THE Blue Boar, which derived its sign from the crest of Richard III, was one of the old coaching houses. It faced due south and comprised two separate buildings, divided by a cobbled way that led to the yard at the back. The western building formed the hotel portion and had three storeys; the eastern building, which was very much narrower and had been erected at a later date, had only two storeys and was known as the Shades.

The ground floor of the Shades was partitioned into two bars, one behind the other: the public bar, which opened on to the High Street, and the private bar which had its entrance in the passage-way between the two buildings. From the private bar a narrow staircase wound up to the upper floor, which was used for storage purposes.

It is not with the Shades, but with the ground floor of the hotel premises that we are immediately concerned. Although the layout of this should be clear from the plan, a few explanatory notes are advisable. The "green room" had no theatrical associations; it was known by that name because of the colour of the cane chairs and tables placed there for the convenience of customers. The staircases marked "A," "B" and "C" have already been referred to. Just inside the door at the foot of staircase "B" was a public telephone fixed to the wall. Bar customers seldom had occasion to use this staircase. Residential guests, or those taking meals or holding meetings in any of the upper rooms, almost invariably made use of staircase "A," except when they came down to use the telephone. Unless they braved the displeasure of Pop Collins's good lady, who was in charge of the catering arrangements, and made their exit through the back door of the kitchen, the general public could leave the building by only two doors: the one at which Peter Bradfield had encountered the little man with the tracts, and the one at the front of the building. This main entrance had a pillared porch surmounted by a large plaster model of a wild boar with long tusks. This fierce-looking creature had once been a bright blue, but now the paint was sadly cracked and faded. Glass-panelled double swing doors led from the porch into the lobby, from which two more doors gave entrance into the front lounge, which was more commonly known as the snack-bar. The assembly-room at the rear of the building was used for dinners and such other functions as the weekly luncheons of the Lulverton Rotary Club.

When Pop Collins made his startling announcement, the only one who spoke was Superintendent Kingsley.

"We'll come down," he said.

They all rose to their feet. As they followed the landlord out of the room and along to the top of the stairs, he said over his shoulder:

"He's in the hotel bar. I've given orders for all the downstairs doors to be locked, including the one from the bar into the lounge."

Sergeant Martin, who had lingered to finish his beer in case he might not get a chance to go back for it, was the last to come down. As Charlton reached the foot of the staircase he turned and called back:

"Martin, see that nobody goes out this way." Accordingly the Sergeant came no further than the bottom stair, while Bradfield followed the others into the bar. There were not more than a dozen persons already there. They were clustered round a long leather-covered seat that stood against the wall opposite the fireplace. On this lay Jimmy Hooker with a cushion under his head. He still wore his overcoat, which had been unbuttoned, but his scarf had been removed from his neck and placed with his bowler hat on a nearby chair.

Between the end of the divan and the door leading into the snack-bar was a small glass-topped table. Behind the counter Betty Collins, the attractive daughter of the house, sat limply on a chair, while her mother, a very generously proportioned lady, fussed round her with smelling salts, murmuring soothing words. Betty's face was white and tear-stained; she was an emotional girl.

The door into the snack-bar and the wooden partition on either side of it were glass-panelled above a level of some three feet from the floor. This partition ran round from the corner of the green room to a corresponding point at the rear of the hotel bar. It had evidently been erected during fairly recent years in order to enlarge or enclose the hotel bar.

The polished mahogany counter formed two sides of a rectangle, with the shorter side facing the street. In this side, a foot or so from the wall, was a hinged flap to enable those behind the counter to pass through into the public space. Opposite the flap was the door leading into the passage at the rear of the hotel bar. Above a waist-high shelf across the door was a sashed window that could be raised for the purpose of supplying Ada with drinks for her customers upstairs or, when it was in use, the big assembly-room on the ground floor. This door, which opened inwards, was now hanging open. The door from the hotel bar into the front lounge had been closed and locked.

The handles of the beer machine were placed midway on the longer stretch of counter. Behind them, against the glazed partition, were shelves on which were the till, an assortment of bottles, a few packets of cigarettes and tobacco, a box or two of cigars and, in a central place of honour, a brilliantly polished brass elephant about four inches high—a souvenir brought home from India by Bob Collins, who was Betty's elder brother. To the uprights that supported the shelves were attached two measuring devices, known in the trade as "optics," in which were fixed inverted bottles, one of whisky, the other of gin. At the end of the counter nearest the fireplace was a glass case containing sandwiches and sausage rolls.

It is desirable to mention one other thing at this juncture: that a big fire of coal and logs flamed and crackled in the grate, and that the bar seemed almost oppressively warm to the men who had come down from the cooler temperature of the room above.

There was one person in the hotel bar who seemed oblivious to all that went on around him. He was seated on a high stool just to the left of the snack-stand, on the top of which lay his green felt hat. His elbows were on the counter and, with his chin cupped in his hands, he was apparently staring into space. In front of him was a small empty goblet glass. About twenty-five years of age, he was good looking, but in a pretty, effeminate sort of way, with no strength of character in his face.

His hair was fair, wavy and too long at the back, and a thin line of moustache was etched on his upper lip. He was wearing a raincoat unbuttoned down the front. A cigarette drooped from his mouth and burnt itself away without being heeded.

Superintendent Kingsley took immediate charge. He shouted:

"Everyone please stand back."

The group round the divan moved away and Dr. Lorimer stepped forward. To Bradfield, who was standing a pace or two to the rear, poor Jimmy Hooker looked very dead. His usual ruddy complexion had a horrible blue look about it and his eyes were wide open, with the pupils dilated. His limbs were tensed and drawn up as if he were still locked in a death struggle. Bradfield thought he detected a trace of froth on the lips, but was not close enough to be certain.

Inspector Charlton turned and murmured to his assistant:

"Peter, phone up for the ambulance, the photographer and a couple of uniformed men to be sent here at once."

To avoid having to unlock the door to the lounge, Bradfield made for the telephone via the staircase. As he passed Martin that vexed individual muttered:

"Nice way to finish up a party. Proper policeman's 'oliday."

"Never mind, Sarge," said Bradfield. "You'll be able to stay in bed all day tomorrow."

He went up the stairs two at a time. When he got back into the bar Dr. Lorimer was talking in low tones with Charlton and the Superintendent. As Bradfield joined this little group the doctor was saying:

"I got to him too late. It must have been a largish dose."

The Inspector turned towards the counter, on which were several glasses, some empty, others partly filled. On the hinged flap, all by itself, was a plated metal tankard. He said to Betty Collins:

"Which one was Hooker using, please?"

She shot him a frightened glance, then, without speaking, pointed towards the tankard. Without touching it he bent down and sniffed at it. Then he said to Dr. Lorimer:

"Smell that."

The doctor did so and grunted. The Super followed him and grunted, too. When Bradfield took his turn he noticed first that the tankard was empty, and secondly that it gave off the faint but unmistakable scent of bitter almonds.

III.

The Overcoat of Jimmy Hooker

NOT without some difficulty, the young man at the counter got down from his high stool, took his hat from the top of the snack-stand and a walking-stick from the corner, and set off for the door to the lounge with the caution of an amateur on a tight-rope.

Superintendent Kingsley swung round on him with:

"Get back to your seat, please!"

The young man carelessly flung his hat on the back of his head and looked the burly Super up and down with an air of drunken disdain.

"You can go to hell!" he said, taking great pains with his diction.

He lurched for the door and got his hand on the knob. The Super told him to stand away, but he remained wrenching at the knob, angrily asking why the door was locked and demanding that it should be opened forthwith. The Super sharply repeated his order, in defiance of which the young man started on one of the door panels with his heavy brown shoe. The Super lost patience.

"Bradfield!"

Before the detective could get his hands on the fellow he had raised his stick and crashed the knob of it through the glass.

Betty Collins screamed and two of the other women joined in, but not so shrilly. Mrs. Collins called out reprovingly:

"Douglas, don't be so silly!"

Bradfield had some trouble with him. He lacked Bradfield's height and weight, but he was no weakling and not too particular about using his feet. Nevertheless, he was eventually made to see reason—as much, that is, as could be expected of

17

a man in his fuddled condition— and the hotel bar quietened down again. The Super and Inspector exchanged a few murmured words, then the Super beckoned to Bradfield, who stepped across to him.

"Take him away, Bradfield," the Super said into his ear. "Make it malicious damage—and no bail. We'll question him tomorrow when he's sobered up." He turned to the landlord. "Mr. Collins, please have that door unlocked."

The potman, whose name was Fitch, had been entrusted with the task of securing all the exits from the Blue Boar. He was now stationed at the front entrance, waiting to admit the men whom Bradfield had summoned on the telephone. Pop Collins called out to him. Fitch, a stalwart young Downshireman, promptly came over with the keys and released Bradfield and his charge. The latter, unaware of the arrangements that had been made for him, was quite happy to leave the premises in the company of one who seemed quite a decent type and had, after all, stopped him from making a bigger fool than ever of himself. Heaven knew that he had already gone too far, drawing attention to himself like that.

As they walked together across the lounge Bradfield noticed several persons standing around. They were those who had not been in the hotel bar when the doors had been locked. One of them was Olive, the woman in charge of the snack bar. A second was a grey-haired, dapper gentleman of less than medium height, whose upright bearing, neatly clipped moustache and sunbaked complexion spoke eloquently of Indian Army (retired). The third and fourth were a young man and his fiancée, who had been whispering sweet nothings to each other in the deserted green room when all the excitement had started. This last couple pass out of the story, but the other two are to be referred to again later in these pages.

Lulverton High Street ran almost due east and west. Towards its western end was a main crossing equipped with traffic lights. This was known as the Centre. The Blue Boar was about eighty yards east of the Centre, on the left—or northern—side of the road. A hundred yards farther along, on the other side of the High Street, was the handsome detached building that was the headquarters of the Lulverton Division of the Downshire County Constabulary.

Bradfield and his companion emerged from the Blue Boar and turned left. The smasher of windows immediately developed a tendency to proceed in anything but a straight line, so Bradfield got a friendly grip on his arm.

"I'm a bit plastered," explained the other. "If you're going in my direction, old boy, it's twenty-three, Highfield Road."

Bradfield did not disabuse his mind on this point, and he went on after a brooding silence:

"I'll be the first to admit that I was plastered, old boy, but I wasn't so damn plastered as Jimmy. Jimmy *was* plastered. Passed out completely, Jimmy did. Fell on the floor. Pretty bad show. Man should be able to hold his drink without falling on the floor."

He gave a drunken snigger.

"Bet he's suffering from boozer's gloom in the morning. Tongue like a tram-driver's glove."

His guide steered him away from a lamp-post.

"Thanks, old boy. Nearly walked into it. Who was the big fellow? Looked like a farmer. Damn rude, wasn't he? Didn't like his tone at all, old boy. Some people have got simply no manners. Ordering me about like that. Half a mind to go back and teach him a lesson."

They reached Wrythe Street, a narrow thoroughfare leading off to the left, crossed it and went past the Grand Theatre, which was on the farther corner of it. The young man continued:

"Poor old Jimmy. Never seen him drop in his tracks like that before. ... Mustn't forget to square up with Pop for that glass. Shouldn't have done it, you know. Creating a disturbance.

Absolutely no excuse. Bit of luck old Pop didn't call the police, wasn't it? I wonder he didn't. Old Pop takes a pretty dim view of me. ...That big fellow got up my nose."

When they were almost opposite the police station, Bradfield gently shepherded him across the road. At the foot of the steps leading into the building the young man said:

"But this is the police station, old boy. We don't want to go in there. Simply asking for trouble." Bradfield told him in a few words, which he tried to make as soothing as possible, that it would be just as well if he did not argue too much, because he was going to spend the night as guest of the Downshire Constabulary, whether he liked the idea or not.

"Why?" demanded the young man—and there was a note of fear in his voice.

"For damaging the Blue Boar."

"Nothing else?"

"That's the charge."

"What'll happen, old boy?"

"You'll be up before the magistrates in the morning."

"For smashing that glass?"

"Yes."

"Just that?"

"Yes."

"All right. Lead on to the dungeons."

He was quite cheerful now. Ten minutes later he was snugly settled in a cell. When Bradfield took his last look at him through the inspection wicket he was already asleep.

★ ★ ★

Bradfield paused in the street outside police headquarters to consider his next step. His charge had given his name as Douglas Winslake. He had no identity card to confirm this statement, but there did not seem much cause to doubt it, because the last words he had addressed to Bradfield had been in the form of a request that his widowed mother should be told that he would not be home that night.

"Can I leave it to you, old boy?" he had said. "Tell her I'm sleeping at a friend's house, there's a good fellow. No need to say I'm in jug. Might upset her."

So now Bradfield was in something of a quandary. Finally he decided to seek instructions. When he arrived back at the Blue Boar the hotel bar had been cleared of customers. They were now sitting and standing about in the coffee-room, where the fire had been got going again by Fitch, the potman. In the bar the police photographer was busying himself with his camera. Inspector Charlton was down on one knee in front of the fireplace. Bradfield referred Winslake's request to Superintendent Kingsley, who brought Charlton into the conversation. It was agreed that Bradfield should go round at once to 23, Highfield Road and inform Mrs. Winslake that her son had been taken into custody for malicious damage done to the Blue Boar. Bradfield was to say nothing about the murder, but if Mrs. Winslake made any statement that might have some bearing on it, Bradfield was to make a careful note of it. Then the Super said:

"Do you know where Hooker lives—lived?"

"Yes, sir," Bradfield answered; "in a wooden shack along towards Mickleham."

"Any family?"

"There's a woman—a slatternly type with her mind fixed on gin. She's known as Mrs. Hooker and she might be, though they say it's only a courtesy title. There's no love lost between the two of them, by all accounts."

"Right," decided the Super. "When you've seen Mrs. Winslake, go along and have a word with this other woman. Break the news to her, but don't put it too abruptly."

Which, thought Bradfield, was quite funny, coming from the Super.

* * *

23, Highfield Road, was one of a row of respectable, nondescript little houses in the lower-middle-class residential district at the eastern end of the town. Bradfield walked back from the Blue Boar to headquarters and commissioned a police car. In addition to the official driver he took with him a uniformed constable, in case the presence of a witness should be necessary.

They pulled up outside 23, Highfield Road and Bradfield jumped out, leaving the other two in the car. As he walked up the short front path the radio was going in the front room, but it was switched off as soon as he had given a polite rat-tat on the brightly polished door-knocker. In a moment or two the light came on in the hall, then the door was opened by a woman. She was in the middle forties and her dark hair was just becoming flecked with grey. She looked almost too young to have a son of twenty-five. She was of medium height and build, and Bradfield's first impression of her was that she was a very agreeable person. He raised his hat and asked:

"Mrs. Winslake?"

She answered "Yes" with that expression of half-controlled vexation when callers arrive in the middle of a broadcast—as if they should have referred to the *Radio Times* before intruding.

"I'm sorry to bother you so late, Mrs. Winslake," he said, wondering whether to smile encouragingly and deciding against it, "but we thought you might be getting anxious about your son."

"No," she replied rather absently. "I wasn't expecting him just yet."

Suddenly there was a change in her. She drew a sharp breath and a look of fear flashed into her big brown eyes.

"What's the matter?" she asked quickly. "Has anything happend to him? Has he had an accident?"

He smiled now; it was time to reassure her.

"No, he's quite all right, but he's—sleeping away from home tonight."

"But I don't understand. Is he staying with friends?"

"No, not exactly, madam, but he's safe and there's nothing much to worry about. He—well, he got rather excited in the Blue Boar this evening and the police had to intervene."

"Then you're the..." Her voice trailed away.

"Yes. We thought it best to put him up for the night at police headquarters."

She stood there looking worried and uncertain for a moment or two, then said:

"Won't you come in? I'm getting rather cold standing here."

He was going to say that he did not think it necessary when she added:

"I'd like you to, please."

It was evident that she either had something to tell him or wished to extract information. On such occasions it was as well to have a third party present, so he summoned the constable from the car and they went with Mrs. Winslake into the front room. Bradfield observed that the furniture was in need of re-upholstering, but that everything was spotlessly clean and tidy. A cloth across one end of the table had been laid for a meal for one, with a plate of cut cold meat, a loaf of bread and a jar of pickles. On a trivet before the fire in the grate was a brown earthenware coffee-pot, and on the mantelpiece above it was, amongst other things, a framed photograph of Douglas Winslake in Army private's uniform. The radio in the corner was by no means of modern design. The whole room spoke of high respectability, but very modest means. He put Mrs. Winslake down as a widow who lived on a pension from her late husband's employers—a pension that purchased less and less as the post-war years went by.

Mrs. Winslake asked the two men to be seated, but Bradfield declined on the excuse that they were rather pressed for time. With a word of apology she sat down herself in one of the two worn easy chairs by the fire. There was some knitting on the arm of it.

"I asked you to come in," she explained, "because am very worried about Douglas—that's my son. He hasn't done anything—really serious, has he?"

"Well," said Bradfield with a caution that the difficult situation demanded, "as far as I know he got a little bit—er—merry in the Blue Boar and finished up by deciding to smash a window—or rather the glass panel of a door." He tried to strike a lighter note by adding with a smile, "It's not his birthday, I suppose?"

"He didn't have a fight with anybody?"

"As a matter of fact he had a little tussle with me, but nothing serious. I was trying to stop him from doing further damage. He soon saw reason."

"Was there a man called Hooker with him—a dreadful little man who sells flowers and things?"

This was getting interesting, but not without its awkward side. He temporized.

"When I saw your son he was by himself."

There was no doubt about the relief with which she received this news.

"I'm so glad," she said with an attempt at a smile.

"Douglas has been with that man a lot recently. It's been a worry to me, because he's not the kind of person I... Her voice trailed away again. She went on after a pause: "Hooker called here about six o'clock this evening. Douglas answered the door to him and Hooker was very angry and threatening."

"Did you catch what he said?"

"No. When Douglas saw who it was on the step he persuaded him back to the gate and they talked there—only for a little while. It was raining. Then the man went away and Douglas came back indoors. I heard him say as he walked up the path, 'I'll see you at eight in the Blue Boar.' That's why I was so upset when you called."

"Did your son say anything about it afterwards?"

"All he said was, 'Confound the man!'" She smiled wanly.
"Well, he actually said, 'Blast the man!' I tried to find out what
it was all about, but Douglas refused to say any more. He went
upstairs to his studio and didn't come down—"

"Studio?"

"He calls it that, but it's rather a grand word. He's a
photographer, you know."

"An interesting hobby."

"That's what it used to be, but now he's taken it up
professionally. He does weddings and things. He didn't come
down from the studio until after half-past seven. Then he went
out without any supper and said he probably wouldn't be back
till late."

"Did he mention Hooker?"

"Not by name, but there was something he said just before
he left the house. He kissed me and told me not to worry, then
said, 'I'll settle things tonight one way or the other.'"

"Was your son short of money, Mrs. Winslake?"

"We neither of us have very much."

"Do you imagine that he's got himself into difficulties with
Hooker over betting?"

"Yes, I think it's very likely. I asked Douglas the same
question this evening, but he avoided an answer."

Bradfield thanked her and brought the conversation to an
end. He got away from 23, Highfield Road without having
to tell Mrs. Winslake what had happened to Jimmy Hooker.
Tomorrow would be soon enough for her to learn that painful
fact. As he and his two companions drove through the rain
and he watched sub-consciously the windscreen-wiper swing
backwards and forwards, a little voice inside him seemed
to say in rhythm with it, "Photography, potassium cyanide.
Photography, potassium cyanide. ..."

★ ★ ★

The village of Mickleham was a couple of miles or so from Lulverton, on the main road to the west. Three-quarters of a mile out of Lulverton, on the right-hand side of the road, was the residence of the late Jimmy Hooker: a one-roomed wooden shanty standing back from the road on a little plot of land rented by Jimmy from the farmer who owned the surrounding fields. The plot had been fenced round its four sides with open chestnut paling. On that filthy January night there was not much to be seen in the way of crops, but Bradfield knew that Jimmy grew flowers and vegetables, and kept half a dozen hens and a few rabbits. By the gateless gap in the front fence was a signboard on a pole. It told the passer-by that J. Hooker had firewood and fresh-cut flowers for sale. The wording was crudely done—it might have been with a stick dipped in tar—and the board itself had once formed one end of an orangecrate.

They stopped opposite the gap in the fence. Once again Bradfield left the other two behind. He pulled out his flash-lamp and found his way up to the door of the house, which was in darkness. There was no knocker or bell, so he rapped on the door with his knuckles. He had to do this several times before there was any response. Then he heard faint sounds of movement inside, and eventually the door was unlatched and opened a crack. He waited, but nothing more happened until a shrill, jarring voice complained:

"Come in, can't yer, and close that—door!

Gettin' me out er bed! Go on—say yer didn't know it wasn't bolted! Come on in, yer drunken—or I'll catch me death!"

This was awkward. The lady of the house, having opened the door, had apparently popped back into bed. Bradfield coughed politely and said through the crack:

"Can you spare a moment, Mrs. Hooker? I don't want to bother you, but it's important."

There followed such a silence inside that he thought she must have buried her head under the bed-clothes. Then he heard her moving about. A match was struck and in due course she came again to the door and pulled it a little farther open. In her hand was a paraffin table-lamp and she was wearing an Army greatcoat over her flannel nightdress. Her feet were in dirty white plimsolls with the laces untied. Few of the fair sex could be expected to retain their allure in such circumstances, but the vast majority would surely have made a better job of it than this one. Had she devoted more of her attention to soap and water during her forty-odd years of existence and a little less to cheap face powder and gin, she might have been more attractive. Her hair, which was parti-coloured and advertised the need for a fresh application of peroxide, was done up in curlers; and she was tall and gaunt. Altogether she compared most unfavourably with the last lady upon whom Bradfield had called.

She did not ask who he was. She gave him one quick look with her watery blue eyes, and there was no fear in her voice as she said:

"I know yer, with yer pushed-in nose and yer 'at worn crooked. Yer a dick. What's 'e bin doin'?"

"I'm afraid I must prepare you for a shock, Mrs. Hooker. Your husband has met with an accident—a serious accident. ..."

He paused.

"Well, go on!" she said impatiently. "Spill it! If 'e's snuffed it, say so, fer—sake."

"Yes, Mrs. Hooker, I'm sorry to say he has."

He did not expect tears, nor were there any, yet her response took him by surprise.

"Where's 'is overcoat? Oo's got 'is overcoat?"

He gaped a bit.

"Overcoat?"

"Yes, 'is overcoat. What 'appened to it? Don't stand there lookin' as if yer didn't know! Where's 'is—overcoat?"

She was getting quite worked up. He tried to placate her.

"I'm quite sure it's safe, Mrs. Hooker. I shouldn't worry about—"

"'Ad 'e still got it on when 'e was picked up?"

"Yes; the overcoat's now in good hands. It'll be looked after by the police until it's handed back to you with his other property. I'm afraid I must ask you to come along tomorrow morning to identify your husband. If you like, we'll send out a car for you at, say, nine o'clock. Would that be convenient?"

"Gotter be, 'asn't it?" she answered with no sign of gratitude. "And don't kid yerselves. I know what's there. I don't trust you p'lice no more than what I'd trust a—"

He missed whatever it was, for she put an end to the conversation by slamming the door shut. He heard her shoot the bolts inside and went back to the car. Women, he pondered, were curious creatures and did not think along the same lines as men did, yet he could not help wondering why Mrs. Hooker should be far more concerned over the fate of Jimmy's dilapidated overcoat than over the manner in which he had met his death.

IV.

Betty Is Tearful

B Y the time Bradfield got back to the Blue Boar the body of Jimmy Hooker had been taken away to the mortuary, and the questioning of the witnesses had begun. For this purpose the green room had been requisitioned. Two of the tables had been brought into use and behind them sat Superintendent Kingsley and Inspector Charlton. On the other side of the tables were chairs for the witnesses, and against the wall Sergeant Martin sat at a table by himself, with his note-book in front of him. When Bradfield joined them, he took over the duties of usher. Dr. Lorimer had gone with the body to the mortuary.

This account of the investigation into the death of Jimmy Hooker would become unwieldy if a full report were given on the interrogation of all those who were in the Blue Boar Hotel at the time of his death. Everyone—including the young couple who had been billing-and-cooing in the green room—was closely questioned, and whatever information was elicited is set down in the pages that follow. Those who are not mentioned had nothing to tell. When all the interviews were over, those resident in the hotel were allowed to go up to their rooms; the others to their homes.

The employees at the Blue Boar were divided into two sections—hotel and bar—though there was a certain degree of overlapping and interchange of duties. The bar staff that evening comprised four persons, two in the hotel and two in the Shades. The Shades bars had been in the care of Mr. and Mrs. Robert Collins. After five years' service in the Navy, young Bob Collins had come back to Lulverton, taken, with no waste of time, a bright little blonde called Mary to wife, and was now his father's right-hand man. In course of time, he would doubtless take his place as licensee of the Blue Boar, as his grandfather, great-grandfather and great-great-grandfather had been before him. To the staff he was known as Mister Bob.

In the front lounge was the snack-bar—or, to be more exact, two snack-bars with a space between them, giving access to the coffee-room behind. This part of the establishment was looked after by Miss Olive Dove. Until he heard it that evening for the first time, Bradfield, though a fairly regular customer at the Blue Boar, had not known her surname. It came almost as a shock; it seemed so totally inappropriate. "Olive" was much more to the point. "Small and oval," says the dictionary, "with a hard stone and bitter pulp." Olive Dove, with her dumpy figure, puckish face and wide, humorous mouth, was no beauty, but her intelligence was of a very high order and the sharpness of her tongue was famous among the pub-going section of the town's inhabitants. Never, as far as was known, had she been worsted in a battle of words. She always had that swift answer to which there is no counter-attack. For all that, the Blue Boar would not have been the same place without her. She was a definite draw. The male sex came back again and again to sharpen their wits on Olive. For the ladies, who do not take so kindly to discomfiture, she had a different, more benign technique. She was about forty years of age. Twenty of these—perhaps more—had been passed behind the snack-bar in the Blue Boar.

Besides keeping the business in the family, Pop Collins (his name was Robert, too) believed in keeping the family in the business. Rumour whispered that his daughter Betty would have preferred to take up music as a career, yet she had fallen in with her father's wishes. Perhaps it was a loss to music; it was certainly a gain to the Blue Boar. Betty was just out of her teens, six years younger than her brother Bob. She was a sweet child; harsh critics might have said that she was slightly too sweet—that a touch of condiment would have added piquancy. That evening Betty had been serving in the hotel bar.

It was unanimously agreed by all the witnesses who saw Jimmy Hooker stagger back from the counter and collapse on the floor that this happened almost on the stroke of closing-time. Pop Collins, who would be expected to have a more watchful eye on the time than most of those present, put it at 10 p.m. precisely, because it was a few seconds previous to that that he had come into the hotel bar from the private room at the back for the purpose of pronouncing, politely but firmly, those imperishable words, "Time, ladies and gentlemen, *please!*" On that particular Thursday evening he had had no opportunity to make this proclamation, for, at the very moment that he came through the door, Jimmy Hooker, who had been standing by the counter flap, reeled backwards with his face contorted, his lips drawn back from his clenched yellow teeth, and his fists clutching at his chest.

Pop had left Mrs. Collins sitting by the fire in the back room. Betty had been behind the counter in the hotel bar. Bob and his wife had been draping the towels over the beer-handles in the Shades. Olive Dove had been busily clearing the white-clothed snack counters. Adenoidal Ada had been upstairs with Sergeant Martin and his guests. Fitch the potman and the kitchen-maid had been exchanging badinage in the kitchen.

When a man has had so much to drink that he can no longer stand up, there is a natural tendency among such strangers as happen to be nearby to follow the example of the Levite in the parable, and if it is not possible to pass by on the other side, at any rate to edge away as far as possible and pretend that it has not happened. The average Briton always has the fear that, if he goes to the assistance of a drunken man, an uncharitable world will immediately decide that he is no good Samaritan, but the despicable cad who got the poor, weak fellow into such a disgusting condition. Out of the kindness of his heart a respectable citizen may have been helping some intoxicated stranger up his garden path

31

when the front door has been opened by the inebriated gentleman's wife. The average Briton seldom does this a second time.

Thus it was that when Jimmy Hooker flopped down, the other customers took one look at him, then turned their eyes away. He had lost his balance and would doubtless pick himself up in his own good time. It was no concern of theirs; that was Pop's pigeon. It can be said of Robert Collins senior that he shouldered the responsibility. He pushed his daughter out of the way, threw up the counter flap and came through.

"By that time," he said in his statement, "he was lying on the floor. My first thought was that the drink had got the better of him. Then I changed my mind. I've known Jimmy Hooker for the best part of thirty years. I've seen him drunk many a time, Mr. Kingsley, but I've never seen him that pickled that he couldn't get home. I tried telling him to get up and not make a fool of himself, but if he wasn't a goner by then, it was as near as makes no matter. Mr. Goodwin was nearest, so I got him to give me a hand and we lifted poor old Jimmy on to the settle. My daughter fetched a cushion from the back room. I thought Jimmy'd had a stroke or a heart attack. It was his wide-open eyes and the froth on his blue lips that put the idea of poison into my head. I came straight up for you gentlemen, but not till I'd told Fitch to get the keys from the hook and lock all the doors."

"Thanks, Mr. Collins," said the Super. "Now, there's one other thing—cleaning arrangements. When's the hotel bar swept out?"

"We use a vacuum-cleaner. The girl goes over all the floors first thing in the morning. Then she polishes up the lino with a mop."

"The hotel bar's not swept out later in the day?"

"Not unless it gets in a bad state. People are pretty good that way; they use the ash-trays."

"Was it only done once today?"

32

"As far as I know, yes."

"Did you notice anyone in the bar today with a small glass bottle or tube?"

Pop shook his head. "No, I can't say I did."

"Did you notice any broken glass on the floor of the bar—just in front of the fireplace?"

"No. I wasn't round that side much this evening." He played with the ring on his finger. "Perhaps Fitch can tell you," he suggested.

"Was your daughter serving in the bar the whole evening?"

"Yes, except between half-past eight and nine, when I took over, so that she could get a bite to eat."

"Is young Winslake often in here, Mr. Collins?"

"He's quite a regular customer." He added after a moment: "A bit too regular."

"What's the objection?"

"He's paying more attention to my girl than I care about. She's too young yet to know her own mind. I'm not saying anything against Winslake, only I've got other ideas."

"What time did he come in this evening?"

"I don't know exactly, Mr. Kingsley. It must have been after nine, or I should have seen him. Betty'll be able to tell you, I don't doubt."

"We'll speak to her, but first we'd like to see the potman. Will you ask him to come in, please?"

Pop Collins accepted this implicit dismissal.

The potman Fitch—his Christian name was Tom—was a young man not wanting in intelligence. When questioned on the point he said that when the guv'nor had caused Miss Betty to summon him from the kitchen, he had not only secured all the exits, but had also made a complete reconnaissance of the ground floor. He was therefore in a position to report:

"The only customers not in the hotel bar was a pair spooning by the fire in the green room—not as there was much of a fire, but they wasn't worrying—and Major Wildgoose, 'oo was in the gents'. I asked them to stop where they was—not Major Wildgoose; the other two. Major Wildgoose I asked to come out and wait in the front lounge, which 'e did."

"Did you go upstairs?" asked Inspector Charlton.

"No, sir. I thought it best not to. The guv'nor might be needing me."

This matter had since been attended to by Sergeant Martin. He had carefully searched the upstairs rooms and had found nobody there. It was a slack time of the year—all the Christmas visitors had left—and there were only half a dozen residents. Four of these had been in the hotel bar; the other two—a married couple—were out visiting friends in the town and had not yet returned.

"Have you been in the hotel bar today, Fitch?" asked the Super.

"Now and again, sir. Collecting up glasses and the like."

The Super repeated the questions he had put to Mr. Collins on the matter of the powdered fragments by the fireplace. Fitch could be no more informative than the guv'nor.

The next witness was Miss Olive Dove. They felt that her evidence might prove important, for, stationed behind the snack-bar, she had been in a very favourable position to observe those who had come and gone.

"The snack-bar's not what it was," she said. "We can't get the stuff. Before the war I was worked off my feet sometimes, with the coffee-room to look after as well, but now the people don't come here any more, because we can't do the variety we could. The old days of lobster mayonnaise and twenty kinds of *hors d'œuvre* have gone. Nowadays it's grated carrot and a sardine if you're lucky. Toni's seem to be able to do it, but we can't. Where they get it from's a mystery to me."

Toni's Restaurant was along the road, on the corner where the High Street and Beastmarket Hill met at the Centre. There was some cause for Olive's covert insinuation; Toni Barucci, the fat proprietor, always had plenty of the best of fare to place before his customers.

"No," continued Olive, "there wasn't much doing this evening. Nothing like before the war—or during it, when we had the Canadians."

The Superintendent said: "We're interested in the period immediately before ten o'clock, Miss Dove. Did you notice anyone leave the hotel?"

"I can tell you definitely that nobody did—not through the main entrance, anyway. You can't see the back door from behind the snack-bar. When it gets as near to closing-time as that most people hang on till the very last minute—and won't go then unless they're practically thrown out. You can take it from me that nobody left after about quarter to ten."

"By that," asked the Inspector, "you mean that nobody left the hotel?"

"Yes, through the front door."

"Did anyone leave the hotel bar?"

"Yes, two or three men did, but they all came back again. The last of them was Major Wildgoose. Before he got back all the excitement had started. He stayed talking to me and we both stood peeping through into the hotel bar to see what was going on—till that crazy young maniac Douglas Winslake got dangerous. Major Wildgoose and I just got out of the way in time, or we might have got badly cut about."

"You mention two or three men besides Major Wildgoose," Charlton said. "Was one of them Hooker?"

"Yes. He came out of the hotel bar—now, when would it have been?... No, I can't tell you exactly. Somewhere round quarter to ten wouldn't be far out."

"Did he speak to you?"

"Yes. He was well pickled. He reeled across to the snack-bar and said to me, 'Give us some caviare and a dozen oysters, love.' I told him I couldn't serve him unless he'd brought his own paper to wrap them in."

"He didn't have anything to eat?"

"No; he'd got no room inside him for food."

"He seems to have been in a good humour?"

"Very much so."

"Did he say anything else?"

"No, he just grinned at me and went off along the passage."

"Had he been in here all the evening?"

"Oh, no. It must have been about half-past nine that he came in. He'd been in the Shades."

"Did he come in alone?"

"Yes."

"Was he often in?"

"Not in here. He usually went to the Shades. But I've seen him in the hotel bar once or twice. One evening in the summer he brought in a basket of flowers and started hawking them round. Mr. Collins told him to take his flowers somewhere else and not worry our customers. Mr. Collins is very particular about things. It's all got to be just so. He told Jimmy that he didn't mind him using the house, but he wasn't going to have it turned into a florist's. I know Mr. Collins wouldn't mind me saying that he's not quite so easy as he looks. When he starts rubbing that finger of his there's likely to be fireworks. Not that he was rude to Jimmy, mind you—and Jimmy didn't take offence either. He wasn't that sort. But don't get the idea he was thick-skinned. After he'd had a few he could be very up-stage and county if anything was said out of turn."

"You said just now, Miss Dove, that nobody left the hotel through the main entrance after nine forty-five. Did anyone come in between then and ten o'clock?"

"Yes, a few."

"Can you remember who they were?"

"Let me think. ...Yes, not long after Jimmy's arrival—three or four minutes, perhaps—Mr. and Mrs. Quentin came in. Do you know Mr. and Mrs. Quentin?"

"Yes, fairly well."

The dryness of Charlton's tone was lost on Olive Dove, but not on his colleagues. They waited for his next question; they all had cause to be interested in that precious pair.

"Did they go into the bar?"

"No, they sat up at my counter, and Mrs. Quentin had a sandwich. Mr. Quentin asked me to fetch two double Scotches. I told him we couldn't serve more than singles—Mr. Collins's instructions. I don't think Mr. Quentin would have minded, but Mrs. Quentin asked in that way of hers to speak to Mr. Collins. I went and got him and he came out to talk to them. Mrs. Quentin got what she wanted—and there's not many who can do that with Mr. Collins when he's set his mind against it—and he told me to get two doubles for them, but that must be the last."

She leant forward and added in a confidential undertone:

"Though what Mr. Collins has got to worry about beats me. There's still five and a half dozen of 'Highland Velvet' in the wine-store, according to Fitch."

"You fetched the Quentins' drinks from the bar?"

"Well, not across the counter. Mr. Collins won't have the staff doing that. I slipped along the passage with a tray, and Miss Betty passed me out the Scotches through the serving-hatch."

"Which meant that, for a short time, you weren't in the front lounge to notice what happened there?"

"Only a few seconds, though. While I was standing at the hatch I could see right through into the lounge. I didn't notice anybody go out or come in. P'raps Mr. Collins'll say the same. He stayed talking with Mr. and Mrs. Quentin while I was away for the Scotches."

"How long did the Quentins stay?"

"Not long. Five or six minutes at the outside. They couldn't have any more than the one double each, so Mrs. Quentin finished her sandwich and they went."

"Are they often in here?"

"Mr. Quentin's always in and out. Mrs. Quentin's not quite so frequent, and then usually only evenings."

"Is it a habit of Mr. Quentin's to come in round about a quarter to ten?"

"That's a difficult question. He was no more likely to come in then than at any other time. I mean you couldn't set your watch by him—not like you can with Major Wildgoose. He comes in on the dot of quarter-past nine every day of the week, winter and summer alike. He listens to the nine o'clock news summary, then comes straight round. I'd say the sun and moon weren't more regular in their habits than Major Wildgoose. He comes in for what he calls a sundowner at six o'clock—seven on Sundays—and leaves at the half-hour. Then he's back again at nine fifteen."

"Were there any late-comers apart from Mr. and Mrs. Quentin?"

"Yes; just as those two were getting settled on their stools Mr. Goodwin came in with a friend. I've never seen the friend before. Mr. Goodwin had his ordinary suit on, but the friend was in full evening dress—top hat and all. Looked like Mephistopheles."

"Was there anyone else?"

"No, nobody at all."

"And the Quentins were the only persons to leave by the front door after, say, twenty to ten?"

"That's right. And *they* went at quarter to. I know that because Mr. Quentin looked at his watch and said, 'It's quarter to. We'd better be getting along.' And they said good night and went."

"They spoke to no one besides Mr. Collins and yourself?"

Olive shook her head.

"And it wasn't until after they'd gone that Hooker came out of the bar and went along the passage?"

"Just after—only a minute or two."

"Thank you, Miss Dove. That's the end of our questions. Bradfield, ask Mr. Collins to spare us another minute, please."

Olive left the green room and her place was taken by Pop.

"Mr. Collins," said Charlton, "we've just one more question for you. Your snack-bar waitress, Miss Dove, tells us that a Mr. and Mrs. Quentin were in here this evening. I understand there was some question of their being served with double whiskies."

"Quite correct, Inspector. Whisky's very short, and I have to ration it out."

"Miss Dove has been very helpful in telling us about customers' comings and goings this evening, but there was one short period when she wasn't in the front lounge. That was when she went to get the whisky for Mr. and Mrs. Quentin. Can you please confirm, Mr. Collins, that nobody came in or went out by the main entrance while you were talking to the Quentins?"

Pop Collins shook his head vigorously. "Nobody at all."

"Much obliged to you, Mr. Collins. Now we'd like to have a few words with your daughter, if she's not too distressed."

"She's all right," said her father, a trifle grimly. "Well enough to answer questions, anyway."

When Betty came timidly in she was still very white and tears were not far away. She had a handkerchief crushed into a tight ball in her hand. Charlton invited her to sit down and she perched herself nervously on the edge of the chair.

"I understand, Miss Collins," he began, "that Hooker came in for a drink at about half-past nine and that he was alone. Was that so, please?"

"Yes. I don't remember the exact time, but it was somewhere round half-past."

"Was he in a good temper?"

"He seemed—quite happy. He'd been in the Shades first."

"But he was not really drunk."

"Oh, no—or I wouldn't have served him. Dad's very strict about that."

"He had a tankard of beer?"

"Yes, he always had a tankard. He never drank from a glass."

"Was it always the same tankard?"

"No. Some customers insist on having a special tankard and won't have any other, but Jimmy didn't mind. But once he got a tankard it was his for the evening—or as long as he was in the place."

"Was he a regular customer?"

"He didn't come into the hotel bar very much—only now and again. He preferred the Shades, where most of his friends go. I've served him in there—oh, hundreds of times."

"Do you know whether he had a particular purpose in coming into the hotel bar this evening?"

"Yes, he had."

"Can you tell us what it was?"

"After he'd been there a little time he leaned over the counter and asked very quietly whether you gentlemen were upstairs."

The Super intervened here. He wanted to know Hooker's exact words.

"As far as I can remember," replied Betty, "he said, 'Are old Carthorse and Co. still knocking it back in the attic?'"

The Super coughed and said no more. To his friends he was "Tiny," but to many others, both within and without the law, he was never anything but "Carthorse."

Betty went on: "I told him that if he meant you gentlemen, you were upstairs in the small dining-room."

The Inspector asked: "Do you think anyone overheard this conversation?"

"They might have done. There were several quite near. Mr. Goodwin was standing next to Jimmy. He very likely caught what was said, unless he was too busy talking to his friend. Major Wildgoose was standing on the right of Mr. Goodwin's friend, just on the bend of the counter. Jimmy was against the wall at the other end. He'd been there since he came in."

"Mr. Goodwin and his friend arrived soon after Hooker, didn't they?"

"Yes, about ten minutes after. They came in and stood next to him—or Mr. Goodwin did."

"Was there any conversation between Hooker and these two gentlemen?"

"I wouldn't call it a conversation, really. Jimmy had had a few drinks and when he got like that he was very talkative and friendly—too friendly for most people, especially if they didn't know him. He tried to open a conversation with Mr. Goodwin and his friend and offered to buy them drinks, but Mr. Goodwin refused—quite nicely—and turned his back on Jimmy. Jimmy was—"

"Just a moment, Miss Collins. Was this before or after Hooker had asked you about us?"

"After. When he found that they didn't want to talk to him, Jimmy got a little—well, unpleasant."

"What did he do?"

"He didn't *do* anything. He just stood there talking to me, but *at* them. You know the sort of thing?

'Some people get big ideas about themselves, don't they? White collars and clean noses. One of these days they may sing a different tune. Walking about in top hats like Piccadilly nincompoops.' Remarks like that. Mr. Goodwin and his friend pretended not to hear him. After a time he gave it up and did one of his funny little tricks."

"What sort of trick?" asked the Super.

"Haven't you seen him do them? Jimmy was very clever with his hands. He always talked with them, waving them about and making gestures with them. This time Jimmy felt inside his overcoat and pretended to bring out a snuffbox. It wasn't there at all, but he did it so well that you could almost see it in his hand. He tapped the lid, took a pinch of imaginary snuff and sniffed it up his nose. Then he put his hand back inside his overcoat, buttoned the coat up again and brushed himself down in case any of the snuff had got on him." She smiled wanly. "It was very funny to watch, and it always made me laugh." The smile faded. "Jimmy will never do it again. I almost can't believe it."

"It must have been a great shock. Will you tell us what happened after that?" This was Charlton speaking.

"He picked up his tankard and had a drink of beer. Then he put the tankard down on the counter again and said to me, 'Back in a tick. Just going to see a man. Make sure nobody half-inches my beer, love. Too many Jerry Diddlers in these parts.' I think the last bit was intended for Mr. Goodwin."

"'Going to see a man.' I suppose he meant—"

"That it was about a dog. I thought so, anyway. Actually, of course, he went upstairs to see you gentlemen, but I didn't suspect it then because any normal person would go the quickest and easiest way, which is up the main staircase. Mr. Goodwin must have thought the same as I did. When Jimmy had gone he said to his friend in a joking way that Jimmy would probably fall down the steps and break his neck."

Those two steps down from the passage into the "Gentlemen" of the Blue Boar were notorious among Lulverton's drinking fraternity. Many an ignorant or thoughtless fellow had measured his length on the floor after stepping out into space without first finding the light-switch.

Betty Collins went on: "The friend laughed and said, 'It might not be a bad thing for some of us if he did.'"

The Super brought his big body upright in his chair.

"He said that, did he? Martin, got that down?"

"Just doing it, sir," the Sergeant replied in a long-suffering tone. He did his best, but the impossible was a little beyond him at his age.

"What did Goodwin say to that?" demanded the Super.

"That he didn't know his friend knew Jimmy."

"And then?"

"The friend said with another laugh—he's got a sort of sneering laugh. It sends cold shivers down your back, sort of. He said to Mr. Goodwin that he'd only meant it in a general way—that men like that were a pest. I think he said 'public nuisance.'"

Kingsley relaxed, and Charlton resumed his questioning.

"When Hooker came back into the bar, Miss Collins, did he use the main stairs, or did he come in through the front lounge?"

"He came back the same way as he went—along the passage."

"The beer in his tankard. You're quite sure there was some in it when he left the bar?"

"Yes, it was nearly full. You see, Jimmy never let his tankard go dry. He always had a pint to start off the evening with, then topped it up with halves. I've heard him boast that he could drink down to the exact level for another half pint to be poured in without being too much or too little. As soon as he'd reached half-way he'd have it filled up again. As far as I know—and I've served him ever so many times—he never drained the tankard right down to the bottom until it was time to go home."

"Did Hooker pass the tankard over when he wanted it refilled?"

"No. Dad doesn't allow that. It causes trouble. When customers take their beer in the same way as Jimmy did—and a lot of them do, you know—we always draw another in a half-pint glass. Then they know they've got proper measure."

"Who transfers the beer from the glass to the tankard?"

"Usually I do, but some people are very funny about things. You get to know after a time." She laughed in a strained sort of way. "There's one customer who always has his beer drawn up in a pint tankard, but never drinks out of it. He has a half-pint glass and pours the beer into it from the tankard before he drinks it. I always did Jimmy Hooker's for him."

"Did anyone touch his tankard while he was out of the bar?"

"I'm practically certain no one did. I was watching it out of the corner of my eye, because Jimmy had asked me to. Jimmy had been in the corner and no one came there while he was out. We weren't very busy this evening. The rain keeps people at home."

"You've told us that the three gentlemen standing at that length of counter were—from left to right—Mr. Goodwin, Mr. Goodwin's friend, and Major Wildgoose. Was there anyone else at the counter at that time?"

"Only Mr. Winslake. He was sitting on a stool just by the snack-stand. There was nobody between him and Major Wildgoose, who was just at the bend. There was a group of three or four men standing near the fire. Mr. and Mrs. Brownrigg—the ones who keep the drapery shop—were sitting on the divan, and there were—"

"What time did Hooker come back to the bar, Miss Collins?"

"Seven or eight minutes to ten, I should say."

"Did he carry on drinking?"

"Yes. He was looking very angry and he snatched up the tankard and gulped down quite a lot."

"Did it have any effect on him?"

"No, I don't think so."

"He didn't complain about the taste?"

"No."

"Did he say he felt giddy or show any signs of it?"

"Well, he wasn't very steady on his feet, but that would have been because he wasn't sober. He certainly didn't say he felt funny."

"Was that his last drink?"

"No. When the clock said ten—which meant it was five to, because we always keep it five minutes fast—I called out, 'Last orders, please.' Several customers bought more drinks.

Jimmy was one of them. He had his usual half pint of mild and bitter."

"Which you poured into the tankard for him?"

Betty did not answer at once. It seemed not so much from reluctance as from an attempt to remember exactly what had happened. Ultimately she said:

"I'm almost sure I didn't. I usually did, but I don't remember doing it that time. I believe I pulled a half pint and put the glass on the counter in front of him. The last few minutes before closing time are always rather busy and I had other people to serve."

"Did Mr. Goodwin and his friend have any more?"

"Yes. They had been drinking halves of mild and bitter and Mr. Goodwin ordered up again."

"Did they drink them immediately?"

"I'm afraid I didn't notice."

"That half pint you drew for Hooker. Was it the last drink he had?"

Betty Collins had not been at all at her ease during the whole of this interrogation, but it was not until that moment that she showed signs of real fright. Charlton gave her time to reply before he repeated the question. She said:

"I don't really remember."

"I think you do, Miss Collins. I'm not forcing you to tell us, but if you don't, somebody else will."

This brought back the tears in real earnest. They waited for her to become more composed, but it was in a passionate voice that she at last burst out:

"He didn't do it! I tell you he didn't do it!"

It was the Super who fired the question:

"Who didn't?"

She almost whispered: "Douglas Winslake."

V.

In the Shades

"HE didn't do what?" demanded the Super.

Betty Collins looked from one man to the other; from the uncompromisingly John Bull-like countenance of Superintendent Kingsley to the more finely drawn features of Inspector Charlton. In the stony, bright blue eyes of the first she found no comfort, but in the grey eyes of the other and the lips that seemed always ready to smile there was nothing but reassurance. Most people felt that way about those two— until they knew them as well as Bradfield and Bert Martin did. That encouraging manner and deep, soothing voice of Harry Charlton were amongst his most deadly weapons in his fight against crime. It was always the same. Tiny Kingsley butted his head against the wall. It was a hard head and the wall would have doubtless crumbled in the end, but meanwhile Charlton had found a gateway a little farther along—a gateway with roses round it and "Welcome" written over it—and had reached their joint objective on the other side of the wall while the Super was still making bovine rushes at the bricks and mortar.

So it was to Charlton that Betty Collins finally addressed herself. If she told him all she knew, surely this tall, kind, grey-haired man would put everything right? All would be well. Uncle Harry would see to it. So might have run her thoughts.

Quietly he questioned her, and the Super had the good sense to keep his mouth shut. It seemed from her answers that among the customers who had responded to her last-orders call had been young Douglas Winslake, who had still been sitting at the fireplace end of the counter. He had asked Betty for two single gins. When she had supplied these in a couple of small goblet glasses and he had paid her for them, he had got down off his stool, picked up one of the glasses and, with all the care of a man who knows he is not sober, had carried it round to Jimmy Hooker.

"He did this immediately you had given him the drinks?"

"That's right. He left one on the counter by the snack-stand and poured the other one into Jimmy's tankard."

"Did you see him put anything into the glass?" She shook her head.

"He didn't interfere with it in any way?"

"No—that is, I didn't *see* him interfere with it. When I'd served him I drew beer for other customers. I didn't notice exactly what Doug—what Mr. Winslake was doing. He said when he ordered two gins, 'One's for Jimmy.' I was going to give it straight to Jimmy, but Mr. Winslake said he'd see to that himself."

"And you didn't actually see Mr. Winslake tip the gin into Hooker's tankard?"

"No. I heard Mr. Goodwin say afterwards that he did. Mr. Goodwin doesn't like Mr. Winslake."

"Oh, why is that?"

"He just doesn't like him. I don't know why. Silly prejudice, I suppose."

"Miss Collins, you have been greatly distressed this evening—more distressed, I think, than you really should be. Poor Hooker's death has been a shock to all of us, of course, but I feel that you have something else on your mind. You said just now that Mr. Winslake didn't do it, referring, I suppose, to the murder of Hooker—if it *was* murder. That's what you meant, wasn't it?"

She passed her tongue over her lips, then nodded her head slightly without speaking.

"It was a rather—spirited denial, Miss Collins, and it didn't seem really necessary, because nobody has suggested that Mr. Winslake is responsible for Hooker's death."

"No, not in words—but that's what you all think!"

"Then Mr. Winslake must have had a reason. Do you know of any reason?"

"No... no, he didn't have any reason at all."

"Miss Collins, I'm going to be frank with you. When we went through Hooker's pockets a little earlier on we found a piece of paper. On it was a list of names and sums of money. By far the largest amount was against the name Winslake. Did he ever tell you that he owed Hooker money?"

"I've never asked him about his private affairs."

"Please answer my question, Miss Collins."

"Well, Mr. Winslake does have a flutter on horses or dogs sometimes. I believe Jimmy used to take the bets and put them on with the bookmaker." She added hastily: "Not in here, of course. Dad's very down on betting slips."

The Inspector was a patient man.

"Did Mr. Winslake ever tell you that he owed Hooker money?" he repeated.

"Yes, he did, but it was only a few shillings. Never as much as fifteen pounds."

Superintendent Kingsley let loose one of his favourite broadsides.

"How d'you know it was fifteen pounds?"

He admitted afterwards that it had been unkind of him. The poor kid was a mass of nerves, and this abrupt question did nothing to calm her.

She began, "But didn't this gentleman say—"

Charlton stopped her. "No, I didn't, Miss Collins. Perhaps it was Mr. Winslake who told you earlier this evening. He did, didn't he?"

Betty dropped her eyes. "Yes."

"Good." The Inspector's smile was genial, almost avuncular. "I'm glad we've got that settled. Miss Collins, we were talking just now to Mr. and Mrs. Brownrigg. According to Mr. Brownrigg, he came up to the bar for fresh drinks for his wife and himself and chanced to overhear a remark made to you by Mr. Winslake." He turned to Martin. "Sergeant, the exact words, please."

Martin flicked through his note-book, found the place and read out in an official monotone:

"'Don't you worry your pretty little head. I'll fix Jimmy.'"

Betty gave a cry of protest. "He didn't! It isn't fair. You're twisting it round! He didn't mean it like that!" She pressed her handkerchief against her mouth.

Peter Bradfield closely examined a picture on the wall—an engraving of Landseer's "The Highland Drover's Departure." The distress of others always embarrassed him. The Inspector said very gently:

"That is what we want to find out. Perhaps you understood his meaning better than Mr. Brownrigg did. Won't you tell us? It's far better to be frank with us—better for you and better for Mr. Winslake."

"It was beastly of Mr. Brownrigg! He's a horrid old man!"

"He was only doing his duty. In a serious matter like this nobody should keep anything back."

She sat chewing a corner of her handkerchief for a time before she said:

"Everyone's against him. It's all been so difficult and—nasty. You see... Douglas is in love with me—and I'm in love with him, too. Dad doesn't like it. He says Douglas is a—wastrel. But he isn't—really he isn't. He's never had a chance. He was in the army as a photographer. He was in Burma for two years and he hasn't properly settled down again yet. I can't get Dad to see that. He's got it into his head that he doesn't like Douglas, and wild horses—"

"Did Mr. Winslake come here this evening to see you, Miss Collins? Was that his only purpose?"

Bradfield gave up a little prayer that she would tell the truth. She did.

"No; he had an appointment with Jimmy Hooker. Douglas came into the hotel bar a few minutes before eight o'clock and told me he was meeting Jimmy in the Shades at eight. He said he owed Jimmy fifteen pounds and Jimmy was pressing him for the money. At eight o'clock he went into the Shades to keep the appointment."

"When did he come back?"

"Just after I had taken over the bar from Dad. He'd served in there between half-past eight and nine. Douglas came in a minute or two later. When there was a quiet moment he told me that Jimmy had given him until Saturday—the day after tomorrow—to settle up."

"Was that satisfactory?"

"I suppose it was. Douglas seemed quite confident, though ..."

"Though what?"

"I couldn't think where he was going to get it from. He was so—so mysterious. But, of course, he'd had rather a lot to drink and it always makes him a bit funny. He sort of goes all important."

"Did he stay in the hotel bar for the rest of the evening?"

"Yes, except that he—went along the passage once or twice."

"When Hooker came in at nine thirty, did he speak to Mr. Winslake?"

"No; they treated each other like strangers—until Douglas bought Jimmy that gin I told you about."

"Thank you, Miss Collins. Now, there's another thing I want to ask you about. In the pocket of Hooker's overcoat we found a leaflet—one of those religious pamphlets that are distributed at street corners. Screwed into a ball on the floor of the hotel bar was a similar leaflet, which rather suggests that somebody came in this evening and handed them round. Can you help us there?"

The girl was plainly relieved to have the conversation directed away from Douglas Winslake. Bradfield remembered the tract in his own pocket and how it had come into his possession.

Betty answered: "Yes, it was Mr. Pickwick. That's not his real name, but it's what a lot of people call him behind his back. A little round man with a beaming red face. He's ever so religious—holds meetings in the streets. I believe Douglas's mother is interested in his work, but Douglas hasn't got any patience with him."

"What time did he come in this evening?"

"I really can't remember exactly. It was before Jimmy— that's all I'm sure about. I know it because he left before Jimmy arrived. I remember thinking when Jimmy came in that it was just as well Mr. Pickwick was out of the way, because Jimmy could be very rude to people like that, and it's always embarrassing to have to listen."

"How did the tract get into Hooker s pocket?" This was the Super's question. He addressed it to Inspector Charlton more than to Betty Collins. Charlton replied:

"He probably buttonholed Hooker when he was in the Shades. These tract-distributors go from bar to bar up one side of the street and down the other. We'll check that later."

"Anyway," said the Super, "he left the hotel bar before Hooker came in. What did this man you call Pickwick do in here, Miss Collins?"

"He went round offering tracts. Some people took them; others refused them."

"What about Winslake?"

"I'm afraid he was rather rude to the old gentleman. I told you he didn't like him. He says he's a hypocrite. Mr. Pickwick wanted him to take a tract, but he wouldn't. Then Mr. Pickwick gave him some advice about keeping off strong drink. What was it he said?... 'The road may be easy, but it's the swiftest way to hell.' Douglas told him to save his advice for his pious pals. He wasn't very sober or he wouldn't have been so rude, because, after all, Mr. Pickwick *is* a friend of his mother's. Mr. Pickwick sighed rather sadly and gave it up. Before he left he raised his hand like they do in church and said, 'God's blessing on you all.'"

51

"Coming back to Hooker, Miss Collins," Charlton said, "you told us that a short while after he entered he asked whether we were in the building. You also said, I think, that other customers might have heard him say this. Do you think that Mr. Winslake heard him?"

Betty shook her head decisively.

"No, I'm sure he didn't. He couldn't have—he was too far away. Jimmy leaned right across the counter and almost whispered in my ear. He obviously didn't want anyone else to catch what he said. I think Mr. Goodwin might have done, though. He was very close."

"And then, as you mentioned, Hooker tried to start a conversation with Mr. Goodwin and his friend. He made some remark about 'too many Jerry Diddlers in these parts.' Might that have been intended for Mr. Winslake's benefit?"

"I don't think so. ... No, it couldn't have been. It was meant for Mr. Goodwin and his friend. It was what they call a parting thrust."

"Did Mr. Winslake ask where Hooker had gone?"

"No. I expect he thought the same as I did."

"Did he mention Hooker when he was away?"

"Yes. That's when he said—what Mr. Brownrigg told you: that he'd fix Jimmy. But I'm quite certain he didn't mean he was going to poison him. It followed on what we'd already been talking about. I can't imagine that Douglas meant anything more than that he would manage to scrape fifteen pounds together by Saturday."

"You yourself were not so—optimistic?"

"Truthfully, I wasn't. I'd have asked Dad for it, just to help Douglas over, but he'd have been certain to refuse."

"Mr. Winslake's manner was mysterious. That's what you said, I think?"

She nodded.

"Did it suggest to you that Mr. Winslake was going to raise the money in some way that he wasn't prepared to tell you about?"

"Perhaps he's got a friend who—"

"Please answer my question, Miss Collins."

"But it might hurt Douglas."

"Not if he's innocent."

Betty had her hands clasped on her handkerchief,. She said in a resigned voice: "I suppose I must tell you. Douglas was so secretive and—well, sly—that it left me feeling very worried about what he was going to do. But whatever it was, it wasn't murder." Her eyes filled with tears and she looked piteously from one to the other. "Was it?"

"Let us hope not, Miss Collins," was Charlton's grave reply.

★ ★ ★

Before the next witnesses, Mr. and Mrs. Bob Collins, were called in, Bradfield took the opportunity to report to his superiors on his talks with Douglas Winslake, his mother, and Mrs. James Hooker. The Super, who liked things to be straightforward, was pleased with what Bradfield had to say. He declared that if they had not yet a cast-iron case against Douglas Winslake, it would not be long before they had. If Charlton had any ideas he kept them to himself.

Bradfield also described his meeting at the back door of the Blue Boar with the gentleman referred to by Betty Collins as Mr. Pickwick. He pulled the tract out of his pocket and glanced through it.

"It says, 'Preacher—Zephaniah Plumstead.' Zephaniah! What a name!"

Charlton said: "One of the minor prophets, I expect. He must be rather proud of it, because it's printed in bold type. We've seen that tract already, you know."

"Would Zeph be Mr. Pickwick?" asked Bradfield.

"It's highly likely," said his chief. "Now please bring in young Collins—and we'd better see his wife at the same time."

Bob and Mary Collins were much easier to deal with than Betty. Bob had been serving that evening in the public bar and the vivacious fluffy-haired Mary in the private bar behind it. They had both some interesting things to tell. It should be explained first that, although there were two bars in the Shades, separated by an eight-foot high partition, the serving space on the other side of the counter ran the whole depth of the building. The central partition extended across the counter, so that customers on each side of it could not see each other. The most significant feature of this partition—as the police were to find out when they came to examine it—was that it did not fit flush against the wall of the building. There was a central window in the wall—it looked out on the passage between the Shades and the hotel premises—and the partition had been brought as far as the narrow sill, so that half the window was in the public bar and half in the private bar, with a four-inch gap between the window frame and the end post that supported the partition. The sill made a useful shelf on which customers in both bars could place their glasses. Close to the private bar side of the partition was a small round table with a mahogany top and cast-iron base of the ornamental type much in favour in the public-house of Victorian times. A few chairs made up the furniture of the private bar. In the public bar were wooden benches and a dart-board.

Bob Collins was a sturdy young man of the same short stature as his father. He had no claim at all to good looks, but had the pleasantly breezy manner of those who have gone down to the sea in ships. He was able to confirm that Jimmy Hooker had come into the public bar a few minutes before eight o'clock, had ordered a pint of mild and bitter in a tankard, and had stood talking to him until the arrival of Douglas Winslake. Neither of them had shown any signs of intoxication and, as Winslake had taken the pint of mild and bitter that Bob had drawn for him, he had said, "First today." Jimmy Hooker had wanted to pay for the drink, but Winslake had insisted on paying for it himself—and for a half pint to top up Jimmy's tankard. Winslake had remarked with a laugh that he had "managed to prise a rupee or two out of the aged parent" before leaving home.

According to Bob, Hooker and Winslake had not remained at the counter, but had moved towards the window, away from the other customers, where they had carried on a conversation in such low tones that Bob had not caught a word of it— "Not," he added, "that I had any cause to listen. It was their business, not mine." All Bob could say was that Jimmy Hooker gesticulated like a man wth a grievance—something more angry than the motions of his arms and hands that normally accompanied his remarks—whilst Winslake's manner had been apologetic. The pint pots had been refilled several times—a pint for Winslake and a half for Jimmy—and the alcohol had had the usual effect on them both, more so on Winslake, for he had drunk two halves to his companion's one. With this loosening of their tongues, they had omitted to keep their voices down as much as before, and Bob had overheard a phrase here and there. The conversation seemed to have been confined to racing and the relative merits of various horses.

"Was there any suggestion," Inspector Charlton asked, "that Winslake had lost fairly heavily recently and was proposing to get it back by more gambling?"

"I should say not, Inspector," was Bob's reply. "Rather the opposite. I won't guarantee they were his exact words, but I heard him say with a beery laugh, 'You needn't worry. I know a surer way than the nags, Jimmy.' Then Jimmy said, 'It better be.'"

The public bar had been filling up by this time and Bob had become too busy to give much attention to Hooker and Winslake. He caught one thing, however—a single word spoken by Hooker. It seemed that Bob, for the purpose of collecting up empty glasses, had lifted the counter flap and had passed through to the customers' side of the bar. Jimmy and

Winslake were still standing in the same place, now with their heads together in confidential talk. As Bob had reached past them for the glasses on the window-sill, he had heard Jimmy say, with a questioning note in his voice, "Cowhanger?"

Bob confirmed that Winslake had left Hooker at about nine o'clock.

"Was it a friendly parting?" asked Charlton.

"There you've got me. Winslake just went. One minute he was there; the next minute he'd gone. If I remember rightly, he called out, 'Cheerio, Bob!' to me, but whether he gave the soldier's farewell to Jimmy I don't know."

"How long was this after Hooker had mentioned Cowhanger?"

"Quarter of an hour—twenty minutes. Can't be too certain. Jimmy stopped in the public till about halfpast nine, then said he was going into the hotel bar—and off he went."

"During the time that Hooker was in the Shades, Mr. Collins, was anything said about Sergeant Martin's supper party?"

Young Bob looked sheepish.

"I'd better confess, Inspector. I said jokingly to somebody—old George Barney, the gamekeeper, as a matter of fact—that he'd better watch his step this evening because a social gathering of high police officials was being held upstairs in the hotel."

His little wife giggled. "That wasn't what you said."

He turned to frown at her and she made a face at him.

"All right, then," he conceded. "I called you a bunch of dicks."

The Inspector smiled. "Quite mild. I've been called far worse than that. Did Hooker overhear your remark, do you imagine?"

"I'd say definitely yes. It raised a bit of a laugh and several chaps repeated what I'd said."

"Was this after young Winslake had left the bar?"

"Yes, it was just before old Pickwick appeared on the scene. You know him, don't you? The hot-gospeller. I can't think of his right name, except that it begins with a 'P,' the same as Pickwick."

"Plumstead?"

"That's it. He was in here about quarter-past nine, maybe a minute or two after. He was pushing out Sunday school tracts to anyone who'd take ' em. He gave old Jimmy a proper sermon, all about the horrors of drink and where it would get him. 'My poor fellow,' he said. '*This* stuff will bring you nothing but grief and disillusion. Keep away from it. It's an easy road, but the quickest way to hell.'"

Bradford had not seen Mr. Plumstead in action, but this seemed a fair imitation: the unctuous voice, the restraining motion of the hand.

Bob Collins went on: "I thought Jimmy was going to tear him off a strip, but he just laughed and pulled a half-crown out of his pocket. He shoved it at old Pickwick and said it was something towards the kiddies' outing. The old boy smiled like a Cheshire cat, he was so pleased. He got out a little book of printed receipts and wrote Jimmy one out. As soon as he was gone Jimmy screwed it up and chucked it on the floor."

"Did Mr. Plumstead hand Jimmy a tract?"

"Oh, yes," Bob answered with a laugh. "I'd forgotten that. I don't know if you know, but poor old Jimmy was damned clever with his mitts. They were never very clean, but they were one of the most expressive pairs of mitts I've ever seen. He took the tract from Pickwick and said, 'Thanks, sport.' I thought he was going to put it away in his pocket, but instead of that he cupped it in his left hand as if it was holding two penn'orth of chips, then reached out into space with his other hand—and you could almost see the vinegar and salt as he sprinkled them on. Then he held the paper out to old Pickwick with 'Try one, sport. Just cooked and done to a turn.' Everybody laughed and old Pickwick said Jimmy must have his little joke."

"What happened to the tract? Did Hooker put it in his pocket?"

"Yes. He told old Pickwick it would make good light bedtime reading and pushed it away in the pocket of his overcoat."

"Thank you, Mr. Collins. Now, to come back to Winslake. When they were talking together, did you notice whether anybody else showed any interest in what they were saying?"

Bob shook his head, but his wife said:

"I can tell you something. You know in the private bar there's a table near the partition? Well, there were two people sitting there—a man and a woman. She had her back to the window and they both had Scotches that the man had come up to the counter to buy. He wanted doubles, but I said he couldn't, so he had singles. He took them back to the table and they began to talk to each other."

"What about?"

"I don't know. I didn't listen, but it must have been just ordinary small talk, 'cause they didn't lower their voices, although there were other people in the bar. Then out of the corner of my eye I saw the woman give a little shake of her head—sort of, 'Be quiet for a minute. There's something I want to hear.' The man stopped talking and they both sat listening, at the same time trying not to look as if they were. After a little while the woman leant forward across the table and whispered something to the man. He shook his head as if he didn't at all agree with her. They had quite an argument across the table. What it was all about I don't know—I couldn't catch a word of it. Then the woman got up and left. When she'd gone the man moved himself to her chair. He stayed about another five minutes and then followed her out."

"Neither of them came back again?"

"No. That was the last I saw of them."

"Do you know their names?"

Mary Collins shook her head. "I know them both well by sight. They use the Blue Boar quite a lot, but they're more often in the hotel bar than the Shades."

"Can you describe them to us?"

"The man's fifty-ish. Short and—not exactly fat, but, solid. Black oily hair thinning on top, but thick and curly at the back. He was wearing a dark grey overcoat and an Anthony Eden hat, which he put on the shelf under the table. I'd say he was Jewish. Too many rings for my liking. The woman's a slinky type and not so young as she used to be. Expensive fur coat and a nice hair-do. She looks like something out of a spy thriller. She talks la-di-dah, which is more than her mum and dad probably did."

Long before she had finished they all knew whom she meant. It was beginning to look as if—not for the first time in their professional lives—they had come up against Mr. and Mrs. Oliver Quentin.

VI.

The Great Desro

A DA of the Adenoids was the next witness. Her second name was Mullings. Her pernicious affliction of the nose caused havoc with her "ms" and "ns" and there is a strong temptation to turn these into "bs" and "ds" in the setting down of her evidence. This has been resisted. As has been mentioned, Ada was tall, sad, droopy and twenty-five.

In the execution of his duties, Peter Bradfield had often been called upon to play the gallant to serving wenches, in order to wheedle scraps of information out of them, but, as he declared afterwards, he would have stopped short at Ada. He was ready to make sacrifices in the cause of justice, but... not Ada.

When Ada had left the upstairs room after her first brush with Jimmy Hooker, she had come down staircase "B" with the tray of empty tankards. These she had taken into the kitchen for Tom Fitch to wash and return to Miss Betty in the hotel bar. At this point in her testimony Ada made some remarks of a slanderous nature on the subject of Fitch's association with the kitchen-maid. Ada had taken the empty tray to the serving-hatch and was in the process of obtaining five full tankards, when she had heard some person making a noisy descent of staircase "C." The door had then been opened, Jimmy Hooker had appeared, and there had followed Ada's second brush with him, details of which she had already reported to the police party. This, said Ada, had been before five minutes to ten, because, as she was going up the stairs a few minutes later with the tray of drinks, she had heard Miss Betty call out, "Last orders, please!"

"And Miss Betty's always careful about not serving after time, sir. Mr. Collins is very partic'lar, 'specially since that trouble at the Bunch of Grapes. Not but what the Bunch of Grapes didn't ask for it. Why, when I was working there before the war—"

"Yes, quite," Charlton interrupted her. "Tell me Ada, did you see any strangers in this place this evening—anybody you've not seen in here before?"

"No. Well, there was old Plumstead. You couldn't call 'im a stranger, 'cause everyone in Lulverton knows 'im, but I never seen 'im in 'ere before. Probably drinks like a fish in that there tin tabernacle of 'is in 'Ighfield Road. Meddling old 'umbug. Sort of man yer read about in the Sunday papers. I've got no time for 'im, coming in 'ere interfering with people's drinking. 'E ought to find somethink better to fill 'is—"

Charlton stemmed this flood with difficulty.

"When did you see this gentleman?"

"'E's no gentleman. Got all 'is fancy talk listening at the key-'oles of 'is betters. Yes, I sore 'im, the old rattlesnake."

She would have sat brooding over this if Charlton had not repeated his question.

"When was it you saw him?"

"Dunno, sir. Somewhere round arpar snine. 'E 'ad a bunch of them religious tracks in 'is 'and. I come downstairs from serving you gentlemen and there 'e was standing by the door of the wine-store, looking as if 'e didn't know where to go and wouldn't reckernise it when 'e got there. I asked 'im what 'e wanted. 'E gives me one of them smiles what makes you look for the 'alo round 'is noddle, and says 'e's looking for lost sheep. I told 'im this was a pub, not a farm; and 'e tears me off another smirk and says, 'Yer must 'ave yer little joke, mustn't yer, my dear?' *Me*—'*is* dear! Not likely, the old—"

"What happened then?"

"'E was looking for customers to give a track to. I told 'im where the bar was and said 'e'd better look out fer Mr. Collins. 'E said 'e'd bin in there already. 'Well,' I said, 'that's the lot. If yer want any more sheep you'll 'ave to go somewhere else,'

I said. Then 'e says 'good night' as if 'e was talking to 'is rich aunt and goes out through the back door. That was the last I seen of 'im and it'll be all the same if—"

"Thank you, Ada. We shan't want you any more just yet. When you go out, please ask Major Wildgoose to come in."

★ ★ ★

Alexander Wildgoose, widower and retired major of the Royal Engineers, had all the hallmarks of a lifetime spent abroad. He had the abrupt manner that comes from years of ordering other people about. One felt, on meeting him, that if he ever needed anything, from a cup of tea to a clean shirt, the first word to come to his lips would be "Bearer!" He must have found life in post-war England rather trying.

He had not much to tell the police. He had come into the Blue Boar at precisely quarter-past nine and, as he informed them curtly, was still waiting to leave. He had not been present in the hotel bar when Hooker had dropped dead. These statements were in accord with the evidence already given by Olive Dove, the snack-bar waitress.

"Were you acquainted with Hooker, sir?" Charlton asked.

"Knew the man by sight. That's all. Type of man shouldn't be allowed in the hotel. Plenty of other places for him to get a drink. Brings the tone of the place down."

"We gather he made a nuisance of himself this evening."

"Damn nuisance. Almost told him to get out myself. Would have done if he'd tried it on me. Trouble is men of his kidney can't hold their drink. Must make themselves objectionable. Or sing. Damn bad form. All a question of training. That other puppy. Couple of hours on the square. Every day for a month. Knock the nonsense out of him. Do him the world of good."

This staccato delivery reminded Bradfield of a Bren gun being fired in the "short, sharp bursts" laid down in the drill

manual. He presumed that the other puppy was Douglas
Winslake. The little major's next remark confirmed it.

"Damn nice girl just throwing herself away. Father's duty
to stop it before it goes too far. Told Collins so myself. Useless
young *sharabi*."

Bradfield had no idea what that meant, but conjectured
that it was something uncomplimentary in Hindustani. The
Super said:

"Who are you talking about, Major? Winslake?"

"Of course. Couldn't be anyone else, could it? Damn rotten
photographer. Took pictures of my elder girl's wedding. Drunk
when he took 'em. Must have been. All out of focus. If it hadn't
been for his mother I'd have refused to pay the bill. Best place
for him is the colonies. Lives on his mother. Splendid little
woman. Too soft with him, though. Holds his hand. Roughing
it. That's what he needs. Engaged to my second girl at one
time, you know. She broke it off. Very glad when she did."

Inspector Charlton asked the next question.

"We've been told, sir, that a couple of minutes or so before
closing time Mr. Winslake bought Hooker a drink. Did you
notice?"

"Definitely. Just as I was going to the toilet. Chota peg gin
and another for himself. So interested, stayed to watch the
performance."

"Can you tell us what happened?"

"The girl gave Winslake both drinks. Winslake got off
his stool. Picked up one glass. Lurched round with it to the
flower-wallah and tipped it into his mug. Far as I could tell,
Winslake trying to make it up after some sort of quarrel. Lot
of damn drunken talk about dear old pals. Thought he was
going to kiss the feller."

"What did Hooker do?"

"Scowled at him. Told him to go away." A smile flashed for
an instant across the sun-tanned face. "Not in those words,
though. Foul-mouthed feller—Hooker."

"And Mr. Winslake took the hint?"

"Yes. Went back to his stool. Suppose so, anyway. Didn't wait to see him get there."

"As I expect you know by this time, sir, we have reason to believe that Hooker died from potassium cyanide poisoning. We are trying to discover how it was administered. Have you any ideas?"

Major Wildgoose stroked his small moustache.

"Winslake, you mean? I'd say no. Dealt with men all my life. Tough characters, some of them. Wouldn't say Winslake had the guts. Not openly like that. Might've done it when no one was looking."

"Did you watch him as he took the gin round to Hooker?"

"Yes. Thought he was going to spill it. So did he."

"He didn't put anything in the glass?"

"Wouldn't go into the witness-box and say he didn't, but damn smart work if he did."

"How did he hold the glass—by the stem?"

"No. Over the top of it. Thumb and fingers round it."

"Just before this happened, sir, Miss Collins—the barmaid—served Hooker with half a pint of beer. Perhaps you can—"

"Saw her do it. Soon as she called 'last orders,' Hooker wanted to be first served. Trying to get a chota Scotch myself. Several others waiting as well. Two fellers next to me waiting for mild and bitter. Man with the loudest voice always gets preference. The girl drew three halves of mild and bitter. One for Hooker."

"Did she pour the beer into his tankard?"

"No. Can vouch for that. She put the three glasses on the counter, then got me my Scotch."

"What happened to the glasses of beer?"

"Men next to me pushed one along to the flower-wallah and started drinking their own."

"Can you remember which of the two men handed the glass to Hooker?"

"The one on my immediate left. Feller in dress clothes. Stranger to me. The other was young Goodwin, feller that lost his arm in the war. Reached across Goodwin and said, 'This is yours, I think?' to Hooker. Hooker said, 'Bit of civility makes a nice change'—or something like that. Don't recall the exact words."

"Was it Hooker who poured the beer into the tankard?"

"Not absolutely certain. Probably did. Can't imagine the others would have done it. Been trying to freeze him off."

* * *

Bill Goodwin was a personal friend of Bradfield's. He was manager of the Grand Theatre, Lulverton; a man in the late twenties, tall and broad shouldered, with fair hair and a magnificent moustache of the type that has come to be associated with Flying-Officer Kite. Before the war he had played young leads in repertory. In September, 1939, he enlisted in the R.A.F. and just a year later was shot down over Kent by a Messerschmitt. He successfully baled out, but that was his last flight as fighter pilot, for his right arm was so badly injured that amputation became necessary. In due course he was invalided out, but young leads with artificial limbs were not much in demand, so he transferred to the administrative side of the Drama. In 1946 he was appointed manager of the Grand. As has been mentioned, this old-fashioned music-hall stood on the eastern corner of Wrythe Street, a narrow turning out of the High Street at a point almost equidistant from the Blue Boar and the police station, on the other side of the road.

Goodwin's companion in the Blue Boar that evening was, according to the beautiful visiting-card that was handed to Superintendent Kingsley with a flourish, The Great Desro. His name in private life was Desmond Roberts, which accounted for the Desro, but the adjective was not, perhaps, so easy to defend. Bradfield, for one, had never heard of him until he had seen the play-bills for that week's variety show at the Grand. He was a long, lean, cadaverous man, somewhere in the early fifties, with sunken cheeks, sparse grey hair brushed straight back from a high forehead, a thin, pointed nose, and a wide mouth with lips twisted in a permanent sneer. Unlike Bill Goodwin, who was wearing his workaday clothes, the Great Desro was in full evening kit, complete with dress overcoat and crush hat—evidently his stage attire. The traces of grease-paint on his face told their own story.

The two of them—Goodwin and Roberts—were interviewed at the same time. Charlton did the questioning.

"I think, Mr. Goodwin, that you and Mr. Roberts came in here together at twenty minutes to ten. Was that so?"

"More or less," Bill Goodwin agreed in his deep, hearty voice. "I can't be too certain. Call it that."

"Do you agree, Mr. Roberts?"

The Great Desro's lip curled even more than it did in repose and the tone in which he replied to this question was no less sardonic. But neither appeared to reflect his mood. Charlton got the impression that Desro could not have commented idly on the weather without seeming cynical about it.

"Yes," he said, "I would put it at twenty to ten."

"You see," explained Goodwin, "Roberts is appearing this week at the Grand. He's the last turn in the first half, so when he'd done his little piece on the stage this evening he was as free as air till the glad morrow and decided that he could do with a snifter. I was of the same mind, so we put on our bonnets and shawls and stepped along here. I'm beginning to wish we hadn't."

"Yes," agreed Charlton, "it's not a very pleasant business." He turned to the other man. "What is your line, Mr. Roberts?"

This friendly inquiry was not very well received. Mr. Roberts drew himself up with some hauteur, as might Toscanini or Gigli when asked the same question. It was Bill Goodwin who replied hastily:

"He's the celebrated illusionist. Surely you've heard of the Great Desro?"

This eminent prestidigitator evidently felt called upon to give some proof of his powers. He moodily made a pass with his talon-like fingers and extracted a half-crown from the void.

"Why, of course!" the Inspector lied manfully. "Foolish of me. Are you here for just the week, Mr. Roberts?"

"One week only. Last week the Southmouth Empire. Next week the Palace of Varieties, Whitchester. Then Blackpool, Leeds, Brighton. ..."

He gave an airy gesture. What were engagements to the Great Desro? They fell into his lap.

"Was Hooker in the hotel bar when you went in?"

"Yes, he was leaning on the counter," said Goodwin. "He was in the corner, just by the flap. Major Wildgoose was farther along, and round in the other corner was that fellow Winslake."

The last three words were pronounced in a tone of disapproval that Bill Goodwin did not attempt to conceal.

"You knew Hooker, Mr. Goodwin?"

"There weren't many people in Lulverton who didn't. Jimmy was an institution. I'm sorry he's gone—damned sorry. We'll miss him, you know. He had a personality all his own. Ever had him try to sell you a posy? He'd fiddle with the flowers, spread them out and hold them up in front of you, and under your very eyes they'd grow bigger and more luscious. The value would jump from a tanner to half a guinea." He changed to the hoarse, wheedling voice that they all knew so well. "'There y'are, sport. Every bloom a winner. Take some 'ome for the lady. 'Bout time yer bought 'er somethink. Two 'alf-crahns to you, with a bit of fern thrown in.' Yes, Jimmy could have sold a packet of hair-curlers and some saucy post cards to a bald bishop. Poor old Jimmy."

"He tried to start a conversation with you and Mr. Roberts, didn't he?"

"Quite right. I had to be a mite terse with him. Jimmy was all right when he was sober, but when he'd sunk a few noggins he was a pest. Roberts and I hadn't come to the Blue Boar to listen to Jimmy, but for a quiet drink, so I gave Jimmy the cold shoulder. It peeved him quite a piece. He got on the old class-war stuff. Roberts's fine raiment didn't improve matters. Jimmy got the idea that Roberts was one of the idle rich."

A sepulchral grunt shook the emaciated frame of the Great Desro.

"Do you agree with other witnesses that Hooker left the bar for a few minutes at about a quarter to ten?"

"Yes. When he got tired of making funny remarks about us he staggered out to the jakes. He was gone so long that we began to think he wasn't coming back, but he did."

"What happened to his tankard while he was out of the bar?"

"Well, before he went he asked Betty in a more than somewhat pointed fashion to keep a watchful eye on it, the theory being that as soon as his back was turned either Roberts or I would swipe it. We made titanic efforts to restrain our evil natures and both managed to avoid taking a swig at it. Joking apart, Inspector, I can give you the definite assurance that nobody touched it during Jimmy's absence."

Mr. Roberts was equally positive on this point.

"And there's another thing," added Bill Goodwin. "As soon as Jimmy came back he stuck his nose into that can and accounted for probably half a pint in one go. Which rather disposes, doesn't it, of any suggestion that the beer was already doctored? If somebody did slip knock-out drops into the can—especially cyanide—it must have been done after that, mustn't it?"

Inspector Charlton always preferred asking questions to answering them, so now he put another.

"When Miss Collins announced 'Last orders, please,' you and Mr. Roberts asked for two half pints of mild and bitter, I believe?"

"Absolutely correct. I must say you're well informed!"

"Will you please tell me exactly what took place, Mr. Goodwin?"

"How do you mean? There doesn't seem much to explain, really. It was my shout, so I asked Betty to repeat the dose. She drew two halves of mud-and-blood and put them in front of us. I passed her the money, and that was that. Before we'd finished them poor Jimmy Hooker folded up on the floor."

"Did he order a drink at the same time as yourself?"

"I believe he did, now you come to mention it. Can *you* remember, Roberts?" The other man nodded. "And he was very noisy and insistent about it, too, as if he was the only one in the bar who wanted a drink before they closed."

"We've been told, gentlemen, that when the barmaid drew—"

Goodwin interrupted him with a laugh in which there was less than his usual good humour.

"Have a heart, Inspector! Barmaid's a bit brutal, you know!"

"Miss Collins, then," Charlton said without visible annoyance at the rebuke. "When she drew your drinks she drew a third glass of mild and bitter for Hooker. It seems that she put the three glasses on the counter in front of you gentlemen and that you passed one along to Hooker. Can you confirm that, please?"

It was Desmond Roberts who answered first.

"The barm—the young lady put them all close to me. I picked one of them up and reached across Mr. Goodwin to place it alongside Hooker's tankard."

"What did Hooker do?"

"He said a little politeness made a pleasant change and tipped the beer into his tankard."

"Did he drink any of it—immediately?"

Bill Goodwin said: "Yes, he did. He lifted the can, said ''Ere's 'ow!' and took quite a quaff at it. Then young Winslake tottered round from—"

Charlton held up his hand. "One moment, Mr. Goodwin. Mr. Roberts, do you agree with Mr. Goodwin that Hooker drank from his tankard as soon as he had poured in that half pint?"

"I agree entirely."

"Thank you. Now, Mr. Goodwin, you were going to tell us about Mr. Winslake...?"

"Yes. When Roberts and I came in he was sitting at the counter, pie-eyed as a newt, making a fool of himself ogling Betty Collins. Just after Betty had given us our drinks Winslake ordered two straight gins. I wondered what he was up to. He got off his stool and took one of the gins round to Jimmy. Jimmy gave him a dirty look, but it didn't put Winslake off. Before Jimmy had time to say him nay, the gin was in the beer. Winslake——"

"What happened to the gin glass, Mr. Goodwin?"

"There you have me. I didn't notice."

Mr. Roberts said he had not noticed either.

"Did Mr. Winslake say anything to Hooker?"

"Yes. Something on the lines of, 'One for the road with *me,* Jimmy. Let's not fall out. Still dear old pals, aren't we?' But Hooker had a chip on his shoulder and wasn't in the market for a tearful reconciliation. In the vernacular, he told Winslake to——off."

"On the testimony of people we've already questioned, Mr. Goodwin, it appears that earlier in the evening these two men met to discuss a business matter and that it was satisfactorily settled before either of them came into the hotel bar. Would you say from their manner during the incident you have just described that this was likely?"

"I certainly wouldn't! Jimmy Hooker showed anything but pleasure, and, on the face of it, Winslake was trying to make peace by buying him a gin. I say on the face of it..."

They waited for him to go on, but instead he flicked his lighter with his left hand and applied the flame to his big briar pipe.

Charlton prompted him. "You were going to say..."

Goodwin puffed at his pipe, then took it out of his mouth. He said:

"You people are interested in facts, not theories. It's no business of mine to air my views, but if you want my opinion here it is: Jimmy Hooker was drinking out of that can without any harmful effects right up to, the time that Winslake shot the gin into it. When Jimmy took his next sip he fell dead. I ask you..."

As he was shrugging his shoulders the Inspector asked:

"Was it a sip?"

"I led you astray there. When Winslake was on the way back to his stool Jimmy picked up the can and downed it, with no heel-taps. Then he banged it back on the counter in a final sort of way and was presumably just about to depart when things began to happen to him. He tried to grip the edge of the counter, saying he felt giddy. Then the real spasm took him and his hands went to his chest as if he was suffocating. ... Perhaps I'm talking out of turn, Inspector, but I know Winslake. He's a rat. He drinks too much and he bets too much, and he's playing fast and loose with the sweetest—no, let's not get emotional. You know what Winslake does for a living—when he's sober? Stop me if I'm wrong, but I believe potassium cyanide is used as a fixer. Surely an enterprising young photographer might be prompted to use it for another kind of fixing? So tempting, you know. There's the bottle on the shelf in the dark-room. A swift bit of fingerwork with that glass of gin—and it's curtains for Jimmy. Jimmy knew something. Winslake—"

"Why do you say that, Mr. Goodwin?" There was a sharp note in Charlton's usually composed voice.

"Why? Well, I'm not stating it as a fact—I'm only assuming so. I don't know whether you fellows have noticed it, but Winslake's been running round recently with some pretty tough babies. D'you know a man called Kochowski?"

Charlton did not, but he answered, "Which one?"

"He's a Pole, I believe. Man of about thirty and a thoroughly bad type. Thick black hair as nicely looked after as a floor-mop, and a nose like a hungry vulture's. He came to me for a job a year or so back. I didn't like his looks and showed him the door. I thought he was going to go for me, but he stalked out. He's got a bouncing sort of walk, as if he was on springs. A friend of mind in Southmouth told me afterwards to steer clear of him. Last week I slipped into the Bunch of Grapes for a quickie, and there in the corner were Kochowski and Winslake looking as if they were plotting to blow up the Town Hall." He gave an awkward grin. "Perhaps, as I said, I'm talking out of turn, but you may like to know these things." He knocked out his pipe on an ash-tray. "Seen anything of the Quentins recently?" he asked casually.

"Are we still on the subject of tough babies, Mr. Goodwin?"

"Just a sort of idle question. Thought you might have bumped into them. They were in here this evening—and earlier on, somewhere round about quarter to nine, I was standing in the theatre entrance, snuffing in a lungful or two of fresh air, when Quentin went past. He was in the devil's own hurry to get somewhere."

"Which way was he going?"

"He'd come from this direction and was making for the other end of the High Street and points east." He shrugged his shoulders again. "Maybe he was taking the longest way home."

VII.

Cowhanger

WHEN all the interrogations were at an end, there was a police conference round the fire in the green room. This was attended by Superintendent Kingsley, Inspector Charlton, Sergeant Martin, Detective-constable Bradfield and Dr. Lorimer, who had come back from the mortuary just as all the witnesses were going off to their homes or to their beds upstairs in the Blue Boar.

"Well," said the Super, opening the proceedings, "where do we stand? Lorimer, I take it you're satisfied the fellow was poisoned?"

That efficient young medico finished polishing his horn-rimmed spectacles with his handkerchief.

"No question about that, Kingsley," he said in his usual brisk, unhesitant manner. "He died from asphyxia—a cutting off of the supply of oxygen to the body tissues, caused by hydrocyanic acid and the cyanides. In this instance it was potassium cyanide. I've carried out the silver nitrate test and found definite traces of the poison. It was unquestionably a large dose, because of the speed with which it killed him. Smaller doses might take anything up to an hour. Hooker was dead when we got to him, and that can only have been a question of minutes."

The Inspector asked: "How long does it take for the symptoms to develop, Lorimer?"

"With hydrocyanic acid the effect is immediate—loss of consciousness and muscular power, then convulsions and death. Pot. cyanide is a little bit slower in its action. It might be anything from two to five minutes before the symptoms become evident. The first to develop are giddiness and great difficulty with the breathing. Then you get the same seizures as you do with the acid. The face goes blue from lack of oxygen in the blood, and the jaws are probably tightly clenched. Yes, there's no doubt the unfortunate Hooker died from pot. cyanide poisoning. Have you found out how it was done?"

"Not yet," Charlton told him, "but we've narrowed down the possibilities. Hooker was drinking from the same tankard all the time he was in the hotel bar. I can't see how the poison could have been administered except by means of the tankard—unless he committed suicide by putting the poison directly into his mouth, which seems extremely improbable. It was Hooker's custom, when he had gone down to the half-way mark in his tankard, to have it filled up again. At five minutes to ten—or a very short time after that—Hooker had a fresh half pint in the tankard and started drinking it at once. This had no effect on him—no immediate effect, that is. The first symptoms did not become evident until ten o'clock. I think we can take that time as definite. Collins, the licensee, who is a very reliable and methodical man, gives that as the time when he came into the bar from the back room to make sure that no drinks were served after closing-time. The first thing he saw was Hooker in the preliminary grip of the poison. That means that the poison must have got into him between nine fifty-five and nine fifty-eight."

Stuart Lorimer gave a boyish grin.

"Not so fast, Charlton! Medicine's not a pure science it's an art. You can't go having a man poisoned and then expect to work out your case on the lines of a railway time-table. Poison's like most other things; it has different effects on different people. Five grains of pot. cyanide will bring quick death to ninety-nine out of a hundred, but there have been cases of complete recovery after even larger doses. The great thing, of course, is to start treatment *pronto*: large draughts of ferrous sulphate and water, artificial respiration, atropine hypodermically to stimulate the breathing." He shrugged his shoulders. "There are lots of things you can do, but there was no chance this time. The fellow was dead when I examined him."

"That was at five past ten," said Charlton, then added with a smile: "Or perhaps you wouldn't like to commit yourself as to the exact time?"

"Sarcastic hound," Lorimer answered without heat. "Yes, it was ten five precisely when I examined him; and all I can say with certainty is that it was a case of acute poisoning and that the quantity of cyanide was sufficiently large for the symptoms to have developed within five minutes after administering. If a man's life hangs on whether it was administered at nine fifty-four or nine fifty-five, I wouldn't hold to one or the other." His voice became less tersely official as he appended: "If it's any help to you, I think it's highly unlikely that more than five minutes elapsed between the taking of the stuff and the appearance of the first symptoms."

"That's rather better. Tell me another thing, Lorimer. How big do you imagine that dose was? I mean, what would be the physical size of it?"

"Anyone plotting murder would be influenced by two considerations: first, he mustn't use too little, for fear his victim didn't snuff it before treatment could be instituted; and second, he mustn't use too much for fear his victim detected it by smell or taste. I'd say that, given a murderer with a certain amount of pharmaceutical knowledge, the dose would be in the region of five grains. If you can imagine five grains of cyanide compressed into tablet form, it would be about the size of an aspirin tablet— perhaps slightly smaller. You know the appearance of cyanide, don't you? It's a dull white—rather like peppermint cream. It's usually supplied in shapeless lumps, which vary in size according to how much they've been broken up. Some manufacturers supply it in round tablets. While we're on the subject, there's one other thing about pot. cyanide: it's dangerous stuff to touch with the bare hands. People whose job it is to deal with it wear rubber gloves and use tweezers as a general rule."

"That's an important point. I've been wondering how our homicidal friend set about his work. Goering and Co. kept theirs in tiny glass capsules, but I can't see Jimmy Hooker tamely agreeing to crush one of those up with his teeth, however drunk he might have been. The only alternative is that it was brought along here by the murderer in some handy container, from which it was unobtrusively transferred to Hooker's mug. What sort of containers can it be kept in, Lorimer?"

"Principally glass. In the laboratory or chemist's shop it's always in stoppered bottles. In this case I favour a small glass phial."

The Super suggested: "One of those little tubes you buy lighter-flints in."

"Yes," nodded Lorimer, "if you powdered the cyanide first they would do very well. The fellow could have got the cork out in readiness, held the phial between his fingers, and then, with a quick movement of his hand over the tankard, shot the cyanide into the beer."

"Or the gin," added the Super grimly.

"Yes, Tiny," agreed Charlton, "as you say, the gin. Let us consider the gin. I know that you think Douglas Winslake did the murder."

"*Think?* I don't just think, old man—I'm certain. Get that gin glass analysed, and if they don't find traces of cyanide on the inside and Winslake's finger-prints on the outside, I'll..."

"Take me to see the Great Desro?"

"No," growled the Super, stifling a yawn with his big hand. "Pay for yourself."

"Let us," repeated Charlton in the pompous manner that he knew could always be depended upon to rile his superior, "consider the gin. Let us—no matter how much we all want to go home and get to bed—let us ponder on the probabilities. We will assume that, for some pressing reason, Winslake decided to do away with Jimmy Hooker. Being a professional photographer, he had a supply of potassium cyanide ready to hand. He placed five grains of this in a suitable receptacle, which he slipped in his waistcoat pocket, with a view to introducing it into Hooker's drink. Winslake was not unacquainted with Hooker and was doubtless well aware that it was his habit to drink nothing but mild and bitter—and from a pint tankard, which he replenished from time to time with half pints of the same brew. Now, the essence of good poisoning is that the person who administers it shall not afterwards be identified with the crime. Unobtrusiveness is the motto of your efficient poisoner."

He looked at them in turn.

"But what do we find here? Winslake had an audience of fifteen—fourteen customers and one barmaid—I beg Mr. Goodwin's pardon; fourteen customers and Miss Betty Collins."

"A little bird has told me," murmured Peter Bradfield, "that Bill doesn't want Betty to be a sister to him."

"So I should imagine. Well, here we have Winslake with fifteen pairs of eyes on him—or liable to be on him if he attracts attention to himself. We take it that Winslake is not anxious to finish his life at the end of a rope, so he wants to avoid the glance of those thirty eyes as he goes about the business of murdering Hooker. To achieve this object, Tiny, he makes a point of getting as far away from his victim as the counter will allow. Then he buys two drinks, poisons one of them and, in the sight of all present, carries it round and pours it into, Hooker's mug. That is what is known as unobtrusiveness. I wonder why he did not have a small boy walking in front of him blowing a trumpet, or carrying a banner reading, 'Mr. Douglas Winslake is about to commit murder.'"

The Super tossed his head like an irritated bull.

"All right! All right! No need to overdo it. Winslake was drunk. He wouldn't have thought about little things like that. All he wanted was to get Hooker out of the way."

'I'm the first to agree that Winslake was drunk when he bought Hooker that gin. In fact, if he hadn't been drunk he wouldn't have bought it. But he wasn't drunk when he left home, was he, Peter?"

Bradfield answered "His mother didn't give me that impression. She told me that he spent some time upstairs in his studio—"

"Getting the poison ready," threw in the Super.

"He came down about half-past seven and left the house without waiting for his supper. He kissed his mother and told her not to worry. He'd been in the house since before opening-time, and unless he had the odd flagon of hooch hidden away in the studio he must have been sober when he left home."

"Right," said the Inspector. "That was the last Mrs. Winslake saw of him, so if he took this hypothetical phial of cyanide away from his studio, he must have taken it with him when he left at seven thirty—when he was sober. Now, a man who sets out with the deliberate intention of committing murder lays all his plans beforehand. He may have to alter them to fit unforeseen circumstances, but in broad outline they remain the same. We'll assume that it was Winslake's intention to murder Hooker by poisoning his drink. Between eight o'clock and nine there must have been a number of opportunities to do it without anyone else noticing. Winslake took none of them, nor did he attempt to make himself scarce after the poison had been put in. No, he waited until we'd come down from upstairs, and then attempted a dramatic break-out. How much easier—and how much more likely—it would have been to stroll across to Hooker with his own drink, casually move the tankard a few inches nearer to Hooker, at the same time allowing the cyanide to drop into it in the way suggested just now by Lorimer, then finish his own drink, wish Hooker good night and fade gracefully away before the poison had time to get busy on Hooker's protoplasm." The Super rubbed his chin thoughtfully.

"Hm," he said at length. "I see what you mean. I think there's something in what you say. Yes, I was a bit hasty. I'll give you that, Harry. Winslake didn't do it. Now let's hear you tell us who did."

Charlton did not accept this invitation. Instead he said:

"Mark you, I'm not saying that Winslake was not concerned in this business. I'm sure he was, but not in the actual murder—except, perhaps, as an accessory before the fact; he may have supplied the poison. We'll have a look round that studio of his tomorrow. ...As for Winslake's part in the affair, on the evidence of the paper in Hooker's pocket—supported by the testimony of Betty Collins—he owed Hooker fifteen pounds. How this debt was incurred we don't know yet. Probably betting. His mother has told Peter here that when Winslake left home this evening his last words to her were, 'I'll settle things tonight.'"

Bradfield finished it for him: "'...one way or the other.'"

"Thank you, Peter. He was also overheard saying to Betty Collins later in the evening, 'Don't you worry your pretty little head. I'll fix Jimmy'. Those two phrases were both clearly concerned with the debt of fifteen pounds; that is to say, he had every expectation of coming to some satisfactory arrangement with Hooker. I refuse to believe that Winslake intended to murder Hooker just for the sake of fifteen pounds. Hooker couldn't have done anything to him if he'd defaulted. Winslake could snap his fingers at Hooker. Admitted that Hooker might have made himself unpleasant by going to the boy's mother, but I don't believe he was that sort."

"Agreed," said the Super. "I've known Jimmy Hooker for years. He was a rascal all right, but he had his code. He might talk you out of your last penny, but he wouldn't pick your pocket—nor would he have dunned a woman for her son's gambling losses."

"Then that's settled. Now—still on the subject of the fifteen pounds—the evidence is conflicting. Betty Collins says that

Winslake told her that Hooker had given him until the day after tomorrow to pay up. Yet, according to Goodwin, Jimmy didn't show any signs of an armistice when Winslake gave him that gin. Goodwin was of the opinion that the fight was still on."

"Winslake lied to the girl," the Super suggested, "just to keep her from worrying."

"Possibly, Tiny, but I consider it's far more likely that Hooker did give him till Saturday to pay. Hooker and Winslake were together in the public bar of the Shades until nine o'clock, when Winslake left Hooker and came into the hotel. If he'd not succeeded in coming to terms with Hooker, wouldn't he have kept away from his girlfriend until he could bring her better news? No, I firmly believe that Hooker's change of front can be traced to the same reason as that which brought him upstairs to interrupt our party, just as I also firmly believe that he was murdered to stop him from squeaking—and it wouldn't have been the first time that he'd given us the timely *verb. sap.* They were too late to keep him away from us, but they got him before he could talk. A great pity..."

"*I* know," said the Super wearily. "You needn't go on."

"Everything about this murder suggests urgency. They had to close Jimmy's mouth in a hurry. Given time to plan, no killer in his right mind would take the risk of poisoning another man's drink in a pub. There were much safer ways of getting rid of Hooker. They could have done him to death on his way home; clubbed him or run him down with a car. But that would have been too late. By that time he would have spilled the beans. Jimmy knew there was a bunch of dicks upstairs in the hotel—and so did they."

He lighted a cigarette and threw the match in the fire.

"This is my theory: Winslake and Hooker met together in the Shades this evening to discuss Winslake's debt of fifteen pounds. Winslake wanted time to pay. He asked Hooker for two days to give him the chance to find the money. Hooker retorted—this is only suppositional, of course—Hooker retorted that if Winslake couldn't pay today he wasn't much more likely to be able to pay on Saturday. Winslake said he had some money coming in then. Hooker, knowing Winslake's financial position—a cheapjack photographer sponging on his mother and she with little enough herself—demanded to know how this miracle was to be worked. By that time the beer was beginning to have its loosening effect on Winslake's tongue and he let Jimmy—his dear old pal Jimmy, who was no plaster saint himself—he let Jimmy into a little secret. What that secret was we must make it our business to find out. For our present purpose we can assume that it was some shady transaction planned for the near future—between now and Saturday—from which Winslake would profit sufficiently to pay Hooker his fifteen pounds. This may be the reason for Hooker's attitude towards Winslake when they met each other later in the hotel bar. For all his faults, Jimmy Hooker wasn't a crook, and he may have voiced his disapproval of Winslake's method of raising funds; or, to take the less charitable view, he may have advised Winslake not to go on with it because it was too dangerous. Winslake was seemingly in no mood to listen to wise counsel, yet, knowing that he had antagonized Hooker, who might become a menace, he tried to make peace with him by standing him a drink."

This made quite an impression on the Super.

"I think you've got something there, Harry," he conceded.

Charlton went off on another tack.

"When Hooker and Winslake were talking together in the Shades there were, immediately on the other side of the partition, our old friends Mr. and Mrs. Oliver Quentin, bless their little hearts. Belle Quentin, whose ears are as sharp as her tongue, eavesdrops. The evidence of Mary Collins, young Bob's wife, doesn't leave much doubt about that. We mustn't presuppose too many things, but I'm willing to bet you a fiver that Belle Quentin overheard young Winslake letting the cat out of the bag."

"They couldn't have done the poisoning," the Super said. "The Dove woman says that when they came into the hotel later they stayed in the snack-bar and didn't go anywhere near Hooker. Besides, they left at a quarter to ten, and if they'd monkeyed with Hooker's beer before they went he wouldn't have lived till ten o'clock."

"I quite agree. I'm not saying Quentin actually did the job, but I am insisting that he had something to do with it. Where was he off to in such a hurry when Goodwin caught sight of him? That must have been a minute or two after Quentin had left the Shades. Quentin's a thoroughly bad egg. You know as well as I do that he's been cocking a snook at us for years. I've sworn to get him before I'm put on the retired list. Perhaps this is my big moment. If I can catch him for murder instead of for black marketeering, so much the better. We must find out first what little game he's now engaged upon. Obviously young Winslake's, in it as well."

"The only clue we've got," said the Super, "is Cowhanger."

"Yes," Charlton agreed after a thoughtful pause, "Cowhanger."

★ ★ ★

They were all feeling badly in need of sleep, but the conference continued. Charlton said:

"I'm proposing to tread very carefully with the Quentins. We don't want to scare them. If we lie low they may venture to carry their little scheme through. As you probably know, they live in Vanbrugh Road, which is a turning to the left, up near the top of Beastmarket Hill as you come away from the Centre. The house is called Capri and it's on the corner of Vanbrugh Road and Beastmarket Hill. Facing it, on the farther corner of Vanbrugh Road, is a house called Colstonfields, which has been taken over and turned into offices by the Downshire Education Committee. All the houses in Vanbrugh Road are in the mansion class. I've been inside Capri, and the only luxury I didn't detect was a marble swimming bath. I've been on the phone to Hartley and given him instructions to keep close watch on Capri tonight, making a note of everybody who comes and goes. When dawn breaks he can retire into Colstonfields and continue his vigil from a front room on the top floor. I've told him to arrange this with Whitby, the divisional executive officer of the Education Committee."

"Good staff work," applauded the Superintendent.

Detective-constable Hartley was another of Charlton's assistants. In addition to Sergeant Martin and Bradfield, Charlton had the services of Hartley and another young man whose name was Emerson. It was his habit to refer to Bradfield, Hartley and Emerson as the Three Musketeers.

Dr. Lorimer now remarked: "Charlton, about tankards, glasses and the like. I shouldn't waste any time over getting them examined for cyanide. It's very volatile."

"That's in hand," the Inspector assured him. "We collected up all the things that might have been used and sent them off to the public analyst." He turned to Bradfield. "Peter, was Winslake searched at the station?"

"Yes. We didn't find anything interesting."

"Nothing that could have been used to hold a small quantity of cyanide?"

"No; just the normal things that people carry about with them: a pocket-book with a few papers and some of his business cards in it; a small amount of cash—one and tenpence, to be exact; a propelling pencil; a handkerchief; a large Player's packet with five cigarettes in it; a box of matches—and that's about all."

"No petrol-lighter?" asked the Super, his mind apparently still on flint-tubes.

Bradfield shook his head. "No, sir."

"While you were away, Peter," his chief explained, "we discovered a patch of powdered glass on the floor. It was just in front of the fireplace, about six inches away from the fender. It might have been a little glass tube crushed by somebody's foot. We looked for a cork, but didn't find one."

"Thrown on the fire," decided the Super.

Charlton went on: "We collected what we could off the lino and it's gone with the other things to the analyst. Collins said that the servant goes over the floor with a vacuum-cleaner every morning, which means that the glass was dropped there some time today—or rather, yesterday. It might have been dropped by anybody. None of the staff can tell us anything—or won't. It seems more than a coincidence to me. People don't usually throw that sort of thing on the floor when they've finished with it."

The Super did not agree. "Oh, yes, they do," he said, "when it's someone else's floor."

"These days," Bradfield thought to remind them, "lighter-flints are more often sold in paper packets."

"I quite agree," the Inspector nodded, "but that type of corked tube is still used for a number of other things. Lead re-fills, for example."

"Winslake had a propelling pencil," the Super said alertly.

Charlton mastered a sigh. "I thought we agreed, Tiny, that he didn't do it?"

"Only provisionally. We can't write him right off until we've weighed all the evidence. Apart from that, Winslake might very well have put a new lead in his pencil while he was sitting up against the counter and thrown the empty tube away. Quite innocently done, but it would explain the powdered glass on the floor."

He sat back in his chair and looked pleased with himself. The Inspector abruptly changed the subject.

"You've got your ear to the ground, Peter, and know more about the secret history of Lulverton than most of us. How would you think Hooker was placed financially?"

Bradfield considered this. "It's hard to say. On the face of it, he led a hand-to-mouth existence, but he might have had something tucked away in the old oak chest."

"Not there," Charlton said with a smile. "He evidently didn't put very much trust in Mrs. Hooker. When we searched him, Peter, we found he was a walking safe deposit. The lining of his bowler hat was packed out with five-pound notes wrapped in greaseproof paper. There were twenty of them. That overcoat of his was fitted out with poacher's pockets in a big way. We found notes of various denominations to the value of well over five hundred pounds. Jewellery, too: four rings—two diamond, an emerald and a magnificent black opal. Then there was a gold watch, and in his tie a pearl pin worth a small fortune."

"No wonder he kept his scarf well done up," said Bradfield. "The local kids all thought he was hiding something frightful tattooed on his neck. When I saw Mrs. Hooker earlier on she was more worried about what had happened to his overcoat than to Jimmy. This explains it. Who'll be the recipient of all this treasure?"

"That we must find out," Charlton answered. "Hooker didn't seem the kind of man to worry about making a will, but there may be one somewhere. Perhaps the woman knows."

"Perhaps she does," Bradfield agreed, "but I'm willing to wager she doesn't tell you where it is if it's not to her advantage to do so. More money, more gin—that's the way *her* mind works."

"How did she behave when you told her?" asked the Super.

"Without so much as a sigh of regret. She was far more interested in the overcoat."

"Did his death come as a surprise to her?"

Bradfield described to them exactly what had taken place.

"There's no doubt," he added, "that when I knocked on the door she thought it was her wandering boy returned. If she'd been putting on an act for my benefit, I'm sure she would have worked up a bit more grief."

★ ★ ★ ★ ★

They came back to the murder. The big question was: Who did it and how?

"I'm convinced," said the Inspector, "that the Quentins had some hand in it. I'll be bitterly disappointed if they hadn't. The man—or woman—we, have to look for is their accomplice— the person who slipped the cyanide into Jimmy Hooker's beer. Who had the opportunity to do this? Who was near enough to the tankard during the critical period? Hooker was standing with the glazed partition immediately on his left. We've examined the partition carefully and made absolutely certain that there is no way of reaching an arm through it from the passage; so the cyanide didn't get into the beer from *that* direction. Most of the customers were not standing anywhere near Hooker. The condition he was in would have had the effect of keeping people away from him. Nobody's very anxious to get involved with a drunk. On the weight of evidence we can rule out all but a few of those in the bar when the crime was committed—or, to go further, those who were in the bar between nine thirty and ten o'clock. Assuming that the poison was not self-administered, we are left with"—he enumerated with his fingers—"one, Winslake; two, Major Wildgoose; three, Goodwin; four, the not so Great Desro; and five, Betty Collins."

Bradfield felt he ought to protest: "Betty? Surely you can leave *her* out. Why, I'd sooner suspect—"

Charlton raised his hand. "Compose yourself, Sergeant Bradfield—yes, it's after midnight, so you can consider you're promoted."

"And don't forget the 'mister' when talkin' to *me*," added Martin, who had not dozed off as his attitude might have suggested.

"At the moment," said Charlton, "we're not concerned with suspicion, but with opportunity. Did Betty have as big an opportunity as anybody?"

"Yes," Bradfield was forced to admit.

"Then please be quiet. That's the trouble with you young chaps—one pretty face and you lose all your critical judgment. If there's an attractive woman in the case, Peter, don't let it influence you one way or the other. Never let your personal feelings get the better of you. A detective is a machine; he should never be guided by human prejudices."

He was gently pulling his assistant's leg. Bert Martin and Dr. Lorimer were both grinning like a couple of village idiots at his discomfiture, and Bradfield was tempted to remind his chief of an occasion some years before, when Charlton had signally failed to practise what he was now preaching; an occasion when he had so far forgotten his professional detachment as to deliver a telling rap with his fist on the dimpled chin of a witness who had incautiously made some offensive reference to one such "attractive woman in the case"—the charming girl who subsequently became Mrs. Harry Charlton. The victim of this vicious straight left had been the poisonous Oliver Quentin.

Inspector Charlton's lip twitched.

"I know exactly what you're thinking, Peter," he said. "That's why I'm warning you." He glanced at the signet ring on his little finger and added in a tone of quiet satisfaction: "You can still see the scar where it caught him on his blue jowl. But let's get back to the business in hand. Winslake, Wildgoose, Goodwin, Desro, Betty—those were the five who had the opportunity. Before we go any farther we must consider the time factor. The first symptoms began to appear at ten p.m. Lorimer gives the poison from two to five minutes to take effect, which means that Hooker swallowed the fatal dose between five and two minutes to ten. On the evidence of Betty, Hooker was back in the bar, after having gone upstairs to speak to us, by seven minutes to ten at the latest, and immediately took a long pull at the beer he had left on the counter. Nothing happened—not for seven minutes, anyway. It's a reasonable assumption that the poison was not put in his beer until after he had returned from upstairs. Two minutes later, at nine fifty-five—or, allowing Betty time to serve them, at, say, nine fifty-six, another half pint of mild and bitter was poured into Hooker's tankard. Hooker attended to this himself, but the beer was passed along the counter to him by Desmond Roberts."

"The famous conjuror," remarked Dr. Lorimer dryly.

"Yes, the famous conjuror. Almost immediately afterwards—we can put it at nine fifty-seven—in went the gin from the glass in the hand of young Winslake. Three minutes later Jimmy began to show signs of acute distress."

"So," said the Super, "if it wasn't Winslake, it must have been Roberts."

"'Last week the Southmouth Empire,'" recited the Inspector. "'Next week Whitchester. The week after that Blackpool. ...' It would seem that the Great Desro has not many roots in Lulverton. We must find out whether he's had any contact with Quentin during these last few days."

"This Goodwin fellow," said the Super. "Is he keen on the Collins girl? Know anything, Bradfield?"

"I hinted at it some time back, sir. I think it's highly probable. He nearly said too much while he was being questioned. I do know he's a bachelor and a very sound man. I've known him socially for years. He lost his arm in the Battle of Britain. He'd make Betty a darned good husband—which is more than Master Winslake would."

The Super hid a yawn behind his hand.

"We'll have to have a long talk with Winslake in the morning," he said.

VIII.

Breakfast from Toni's

O N the corner where the High Street and Beastmarket Hill
met at right-angles at the Centre was Toni's Restaurant.
The Centre was the commercial heart of Lulverton, and Toni's
was consequently a popular rendezvous. Among the other
services that it rendered to the public was the supplying of
refreshments to business men and tradespeople who were too
tied to their desks or counters to slip out for morning coffee,
lunch or the afternoon cup of tea without which the wheels
of industry cannot smoothly revolve. The townsfolk were
well accustomed to the sight of trays of covered dishes being
borne away from Toni's Restaurant and taken into premises
in Beastmarket Hill, the High Street and sometimes as far
afield as the blocks of offices adjoining the Public Library, at
the other end of the High Street; and they were accustomed,
too, to the young men in shiny-peaked caps—with "toni's
restaurant" in black letters on a yellow band—whose task it
was to deliver the meals and bring back the trays and empty
cups and dishes.

Those at police headquarters, who were on occasions as
busy as most, frequently availed themselves of this service, so
it was not an unusual occurrence when, a few minutes after
seven o'clock in the morning following the events recorded in
the previous chapters, a tray was carried up the steps and into
the building by a whistling youth whose "toni's restaurant" cap
was set at a jaunty angle on his fair, curly head. The rain had
ceased during the night, but the day promised to be overcast
and miserable. It was not yet daylight.

It was through the swing-door into the room marked
"Inquiries" to the left of the vestibule that the tray was
conveyed and set down on the counter, on the other side of

which Police-constable Marryat, the reserve man, sat reading the morning paper. He glanced up and asked:

"Who's that for?"

The youth grinned back and replied: "One of the guests— name of Winslake. 'Is mum was afraid 'e mightn't get no breakfast, or p'raps be given somethink what didn't agree with 'im, which is more likely."

"None of your lip," growled Marryat, and rose to his feet to go to the door of an. inner room, which he opened and poked in his head to say: "The boy's brought breakfast for Winslake, Sarge. O.K.?"

The duty sergeant, whose name was Harrison, came out of the room and made his heavy way across to the counter. As he did so the lad inquired eagerly:

"What's 'e in for?"

"Ask no questions," replied Sergeant Harrison as he inspected the tray, "and you'll be told no lies."

He had a nasty cold in the head and was not in a very good temper. One after the other he lifted the aluminium covers from the two plates that shared the tray with a cup of coffee without a saucer. One plate held porridge and the second a mixed grill of bacon, liver and tomato. Marryat looked over his superior's shoulder.

"Liver," he said with immense distaste.

"Good fer yer, yer know," said the youth. "Chock full of them vytermins. Bring the roses back to yer; cheeks, it would."

"Who's to pay?" asked Sergeant Harrison.

"That bin seen to. The old lady settled it with the caff."

"Which old lady?"

"Winslake's mum. She didn't want 'im ter starve."

"All right," said the sergeant. "We'll see 'e gets it."

"Okey-doke. I'll be back in 'alf an hour fer the tray."

He jerked his cap to an even more incredible angle, stuffed his gloved hands into his raincoat pockets and elbowed his way through the door. His parting words were:

"I'd try an 'ankerchiff fer that cold if I was you, Sarge."

As the door swung to behind him, Harrison growled:

"Saucy young b——. They're not being brought up right these days. Fourteen street lamps in less than a month. I'd give 'em catapults if I got the chance. Get this along to Winslake."

The gay young man did not keep his promise to return. He was not seen again that day in Lulverton police headquarters; and before the half hour had elapsed Douglas Winslake had eaten a spoonful or two of the porridge and had died of potassium cyanide poisoning.

★ ★ ★

By everyone employed in Lulverton police headquarters, that Friday was long remembered. To say that Superintendent Kingsley was furious when he heard the news would be a timid understatement. He charged round the building like a Spanish bull with its shoulders bristling with *banderillas*. Sergeant Harrison, that unhappy man was called all kinds of a fool for not having been more careful. When the Super gave him a moment to put in a few words, he explained that he had had no cause for suspicion; that he had come on duty without knowing what had been afoot in the Blue Boar the night before; that, as far as he was concerned, Winslake was held on a minor charge; and that it was not unusual for breakfast to be sent in to prisoners by their thoughtful relatives.

"I took off the covers, sir, and made sure that there was nothing going in to the prisoner that 'e didn't ought to 'ave—tobacco, strong liquor and the like—and I—"

"You've got a nose, haven't you? Didn't you take the elementary precaution of sniffing the food?"

"Er—no, sir. 'Aving no suspicions of foul play, I didn't, sir."

"But dammit, man, don't you know the smell of cyanide?"

"Yes, sir—bitter almonds. But I wouldn't 'ave noticed it with this 'eavy cold."

This conversation was taking place in the Super's room on the ground floor of the building. P.C. Marryat now knocked on the door. He was still thanking his lucky star that he had not acted on his own authority. When he had obeyed the sharp order to come in, he announced:

"There's a trunk call from London, sir. It's the *Daily Mercury,* and they want confirmation of the—er—occurrence."

The Super frothed up to the boil again.

"Good God! Who's been talking? Is this some more of your work, Harrison?"

The sergeant looked appalled.

"*Me,* sir? Oh, *no,* sir! Not me, sir! Somebody in the town must've got wind of it and put it round."

Marryat was anxious to get out of the room; it had an unhealthy atmosphere. He asked:

"Will you take the call, sir?"

The Super scowled at him.

"You can tell the *Mercury* to go and—no, put 'em through. I'll tell 'em myself."

★ ★ ★

While the Super was speaking to the *Daily Mercury* and discovering, to his great relief, that the inquiry related to the poisoning of Jimmy Hooker and not to that morning's disaster, Inspector Charlton was pursuing investigations with the help of Sergeant Bradfield.

Their first call was at Toni's. While they stood in the restaurant, waiting for the waitress to fetch the proprietor, Charlton idly picked up a jelly-graphed menu from one of the tables. He had glanced down the items and replaced the card against the cruet before the proprietor emerged. Mr. Toni Barucci was fat, fifty and bronchitic. He was an Italian Jew and had the fleshy dewlap, the trimmed moustache and the frizzled hair of Alexandre Dumas *père*. At first sight one would have said that he tucked his table napkin into his collar at meal-times, but a subsequent glance at his waistcoat would lead one to the opposite conclusion.

Charlton introduced Bradfield and himself to Mr. Barucci, who immediately became fussily attentive, and having given brisk, unnecessary instructions—in a brand of English all his own—to the waitresses and the bored blonde who was polishing her fingernails in the glass-fronted cash desk, shepherded the two detectives through a door marked "Private" into a little room that was half office and half storeroom. He supplied two seats by throwing various articles on the floor to the accompaniment of testy remarks about other people's untidy habits, spun the revolving chair at the roll-top desk so that he might face his visitors and dropped into it with a grunt, his feet only just touching the floor. Then, with his ringed fingers—like uncooked chipolata sausages in Court dress, thought Bradfield—interlaced across his paunch, he said:

"Now, gentlemen, may I do for you something?"

"Yes, Mr. Barucci," Charlton answered. "Did you supply any breakfasts this morning?"

"Why, yes. We have always early customers, opening at seven o'clock for the comfort of—"

"I don't mean breakfast on the premises, Mr. Barucci, but food sent out on trays. Did you provide any such meals this morning?"

"With not any faltering, I shall say no. Yet I shall ask my wife."

He separated his hands and got them on the arms of the chair, but a gesture from Charlton relieved him of the exertion of rising to his feet.

"Who deals with the orders for outside catering?"

"If they are given by the *telefono*, myself either Mrs. Barucci will take them." He jerked a fat thumb over his shoulder. "You shall see the instrument on the *scrittorio*. In this apartment the staff are not permitted. If a customer does not employ the *telefono,* whoever puts an order in the restaurant, it is the young lady in the cash-box who writes it on a fragment of paper and shall hand it to myself either my wife."

"So that no meal goes out without the knowledge of you or Mrs. Barucci?"

Mr. Barucci moved his head up and down vigorously.

"Thus entirely."

"Is a Mrs. Winslake a customer here?"

The big head stopped, in mid-nod.

"Mrs. Winslake?" He gave an airy wave of his hand. "I cannot say. She may be. We have much customers."

"Yet the name is familiar to you, isn't it, Mr. Barucci?"

The proprietor looked aggrieved.

"You demand concerning Mrs. Winslake," he complained. "I inform you. Whether you demand concerning the name Winslake, I shall tell you yes. *Mister* Winslake had been the customer, but he is the customer no longer. I am obliged to tell to him, 'Mister Winslake, I am a poor man. You do not pay yesterday. You do not pay today for your food. Tomorrow, the day next to tomorrow, you shall not be attended by my young ladies. Do not return, Mister Winslake, for the door shall be fastened on your face.' That is how I tell to Mister Winslake."

Mr. Barucci's stern expression denoted that he was not a man to be trifled with. He went on:

"And was I not exact? Do I not listen concerning an event last night? Does not the word 'assassin' pass from mouth to mouth?" A thought seemed to strike him. "Shall this be the motive of your visitation?"

The Inspector answered this question by asking another.

"How many young men do you employ to deliver meals to other buildings, Mr. Barucci?"

"Two. That is all. I could give occupation to more, yet I cannot acquisition them. And now today, if things were not already sufficiently worse, one of these *giovanotti* does not come."

"Is he ill?"

A lift of the heavy shoulders. "I am ignorant. We have received no messages."

"Can you describe him?"

"He is not short, neither is he long. His name is Stanley Dilks."

"Fair, curly hair?"

"Fair, yes, but no, it is not curly. Whether he shall maintain the hairs brushed with neatness, which is that which he does not, it shall be direct. Yes, each of the hairs shall be as direct as an arrow. 'Stanley,' I tell him, 'with your hairs not brushed with neatness, how shall you hope——'"

"And the other boy?"

Mr. Barucci was not annoyed by this interruption. He buried his face in his chins and gave a deep and somewhat wheezy chuckle.

"When I shall say to you that he is named 'Ginger' by his friends, you will not demand more concerning his hairs, won't it?"

"I should like the address of Stanley Dilks, if you can let me have it, Mr. Barucci."

"This I can reply out of my brain. His home is at Mickleham. He inhabits a *casetta,* a——how is it told of in English?" He looked round the room in search of the right word and found it lurking in a cobweb in a corner of the ceiling. "A cottage—yes, that is it. With his mother and father he inhabits a cottage. From Mickleham he comes on the *bicyclo,* yet today we have seen no *bicyclo* with Stanley sitting so happily in the pedal."

He shook his head slowly.

"Perhaps the poor *giovanotto* has encountered an accident."

Charlton and Bradfield exchanged glances. Both were inclined to agree with Mr. Barucci. Charlton said, changing the subject again:

"Those distinctive caps of yours, Mr. Barucci. What happens to them after the boys' work is finished for the day? Do they leave them here?"

"No, they take them to their homes. I do not lift objections.

It is a good advertisement for Toni's."

"Do you keep any caps in reserve?"

"The caps, no, but some of the bandages I have, which was done for me by the great merchants at London. Six they have did for me at a price of—"

"Can you lay hands on the other four?"

"Thus entirely," said Mr. Barucci, "but first I must find them. Till then I cannot lay hands on them."

He kicked out with his feet so that the chair swung and he faced the desk. Grunting with the effort, he bent down and pulled open several drawers one after the other, pawing their jumbled contents and making things fly here and there, like an eager dog digging for a bone in a pile of salvage. At last, with a yelp of triumph, he pulled out a flat cardboard box, spun himself in a half-circle back towards his visitors, pulled off the lid of the box and, with a flourish that the Great Desro might have envied, pulled out and held aloft four yellow cap-bands.

"Thus," he said.

"Thank you, Mr. Barucci. Now can you please tell me what on was your breakfast menu today?"

Mr. Barucci laid box and bands aside, re-clasped his hands across his middle and sought inspiration in the corner where the cobweb was. Then he recited:

"Grilled *aringa*—herring, won't it?—scrambled egg on toast, sausage and potatoes fried, bacon and tomatoes from the tin can. With these there is porridge or cornflakes, toast and *marmellata*."

"Was liver on the menu today?"

The little man shot him a sharp glance.

"Liver? We cannot obtain always liver. Last week we shall have it." Up went his shoulders again, "Next week we did not. We do our very good for customers."

"I'm asking about today, Mr. Barucci. Did you serve liver for breakfast this morning?"

"Why shall you demand? Tell that to me."

"Please answer my question. I've seen from one of your cards that liver *was* on the menu and—"

"Whether you see the card, why shall you place the question?"

"Because I want to know if liver was actually served today. Sometimes a menu-card is not accurate."

"At Toni's everything are accurate. I forget—that is all. Yes, there was liver, yet it was good liver. Toni does not sell wicked liver. I tell to the butcher, 'Mister Williams,' for that is his name—'Mister Williams,' I tell to him, 'this is wicked liver you try to sell to me I will not purchase liver even though it shall be but a little piece wicked. A little *look* wicked, a little *stink* wicked—and Toni does not purchase.' That is how I tell to Mister Williams."

Charlton had been doing his best to break in. He now managed to say:

"Yes, quite, Mr. Barucci. Now—"

"Never the wicked liver at Toni's."

"Please don't think I'm suggesting that all was not as it—"

"The wicked liver, no."

"Your restaurant has a splendid reputation in—"

Mr. Barucci's hackles were up.

"Finest food, finest cooked, finest served—that is the catchword of Toni's. Always for customers the kitchen shall be there for inspection. I shall explain the kitchen to you now and you shall see for ourselves."

He got out of his chair and made for the door with the grace of an insulted sea-lion.

They followed him into the kitchen, where they were introduced to Mrs. Barucci. After they had been persuaded to examine the kitchen, other offices and the back yard—all of which were tolerably clean by certain standards, if not perhaps the standards of the Ministry of Health—Charlton was able to confirm with Mrs. Barucci that no meals had been sent out since lunch time the previous day. A swift inspection of the white-metal trays and dish-covers—all with "Toni's Restaurant" stamped on them—and of Mr. Barucci's knives, forks and crockery, was sufficient to satisfy Charlton that, though the lad who had brought Winslake's breakfast to the police station had worn a "Toni's" cap-band, none of the breakfast things had come from that establishment.

There followed a short interview with a ginger-headed boy, whose every freckle was an earnest of his truthfulness. He was able to produce his yellow-banded cap and was ready to swear on oath that it had not been out of his possession since he had left home that morning. Mr. and Mrs. Barucci and members of the staff all confirmed that the boy had arrived at the restaurant at a quarter to seven—his official time—and had been helping in the kitchen between that hour and eight o'clock, when he had been sent out on an errand by Mrs. Barucci. There was general agreement that, although he had taken his cap off while indoors and hung it with his overcoat on a hook on the kitchen door, there had been no possible opportunity for any person to remove it, and subsequently replace it, without having been detected in the act by any of the staff and, in particular, by Mrs. Barucci, who had been in the kitchen the whole time and, further, did not seem the sort of woman who missed much.

As the two detectives left the restaurant and made their way along the High Street, Bradfield said:

"We shall be going to discover what has occurred to the *giovanotto* on his *bicyclo,* won't it?"

"Thus entirely," agreed his chief.

IX.

Mr. Zephaniah Plumstead

BEFORE Charlton and Bradfield could start off for Mickleham village in the Inspector's big black Wolseley to investigate the cause of Stanley Dilks's absence from duty, Mr. Zephaniah Plumstead called at police headquarters. He was received by Charlton in his upstairs office. Bradfield was in attendance.

"I have learned with distress," said this plump, applecheeked little man who looked so much like Mr. Pickwick, "of the unhappy fate of young Douglas Winslake."

"Oh, yes?" was Charlton's guarded answer.

"And I am wondering whether I may be allowed—ah access to him. Can that be arranged, please?"

"Will you tell me why, Mr. Plumstead?"

"Why? For no other reason, I can assure you, than to solace and comfort him."

Peter Bradfield, who was standing behind the seated visitor with his elbow on the metal filing cabinet in the corner, glanced meaningly at Charlton, but there was no change of expression on his superior's face.

"Douglas has indeed behaved foolishly," Mr. Plumstead went on, "but he is young and"—he threw out his chubby white hands—"well, we ourselves were both young once, Inspector. May I, then, be taken to him? I promise to stay only a few minutes. I ask this concession because now is the time—while he is in low and chastened spirits and the hand of every man may seem to him to be against him—now is the time when the glorious call to a new and higher way of life may not fall on deaf ears."

"I'm sorry, Mr. Plumstead, but I must disappoint you."

"Oh, dear. Are your regulations as strict as that? If they are, I feel I have to criticize the authorities for denying prisoners—

what a hateful word!—the benefits of spiritual consolation. Is the crime of this young man so great that he must be kept in solitary confinement? Granted that he became inebriated and created a regrettable disturbance—"

"Mr. Plumstead, I was coming round to see you this morning. Now you are here, I'd like to ask you a few questions about last night."

"Yes, indeed. I shall be pleased to help you all I can, although I have little to tell. Poor Hooker! Such a wasted life! That he should take it in the way he did—the wretched and pitiable means of escape provided by self-immolation—is a matter for the deepest—"

"Can you produce evidence that he committed suicide?"

"Evidence? May we rather call it intelligent supposition? I cannot—I *will* not attach credence to the vile rumour current in the town that Douglas introduced poison into Hooker's— ah—alcoholic refreshment."

The Inspector smiled rather bleakly.

"The police are not concerned with 'intelligent supposition,' Mr. Plumstead. We are interested only in facts. Have you any facts to support this suggestion?"

The little man shifted in his chair and fidgeted with the handle of his umbrella.

"You are getting me into a corner, Inspector," he protested mildly. "As to what happened in the Blue Boar Hotel last night, I am dependent entirely on hearsay.

I have been told this morning—"

"By whom?"

"By the man Fitch—I think that is his name—who is employed as potman. I chanced to fall in with him in the High Street. Fitch informed me that Hooker had—ah—met his death by potassium cyanide poisoning. At this reference to potassium cyanide I instantly remembered a conversation I had recently with Mrs. Winslake, who, as you very likely know, is the mother of Douglas."

Bradfield took his elbow off the filing cabinet and straightened himself. Charlton said:

"Please go on, Mr. Plumstead."

"I am privileged to enjoy the friendship and confidence of Mrs. Winslake. Since the sad death of her husband the poor lady has been grievously in need of spiritual encouragement. I have endeavoured in my humble way to supply that need. Mrs. Winslake is a regular attender of our prayer meetings."

"Where?"

Mr. Plumstead smiled. "The building is at the end of Highfield Road, in which the Winslakes have their home. It is erected on some waste ground and is known locally, somewhat scornfully, I fear, as the tin tabernacle, by reason of its being constructed of corrugated iron. At one end of it there is a little room—no more than a cubby-hole—in which, for want of other accommodation, I have been compelled to make my home. I have a camp-bed, and a paraffin stove for cooking, and I make do as best I can. The so-called tin tabernacle and all for which it stands are my life, Inspector. Mrs. Winslake is an ardent worker for the cause, although she is not what is known as a "church-goer". The day before yesterday I had occasion to call upon her with some tracts that she had been good enough to promise to deliver from door to door in that district."

Mr. Plumstead here beamed upon the Inspector, and his eyes twinkled merrily behind his spectacles.

"Perhaps I may be permitted to strike a personal note. I am, alas! a lonely widower. My beloved wife departed this world many years ago, and I have reason to hope—if I may mention this in confidence—that Mrs. Winslake, herself a widow, will one day consent to fill her place. But that is by the way. I come to graver matters. During the course of our conversation on Wednesday afternoon Mrs. Winslake honoured me by seeking my advice on the subject of her son Douglas. She expressed herself seriously concerned about him. One is forced to admit that Douglas has been—ah—a disappointment. It is

to be expected that young men will kick over the traces"—
Bradfield had his elbow back on the cabinet—"but Douglas
has carried this process to an extreme. He drinks too much
and is too fond of gambling with money that is not his to
devote to such a purpose—or, for that matter, to spend on
himself in any way at all."

Charlton said patiently: "You were going to tell us about
potassium cyanide, Mr. Plumstead."

"Yes, that deadly salt. Before I come to that, Inspector, I
should stress that on Wednesday the possibility of murder
or suicide was very far from the minds of Mrs. Winslake
and myself. Potassium cyanide was incidental to and not the
main theme of our talk, which concerned itself with the
deplorable Hooker and the highly undesirable friendship that
had developed between him and Douglas. In referring to
this, Mrs. Winslake mentioned an incident that did not seem
important at the time, but has since assumed a terrible—ah—
significance."

Peter Bradfield stirred impatiently and passed a hand back
over his sleek hair. Why didn't the wordy old idiot get on with
it?

"It seemed," Mr. Plumstead continued serenely on his course,
"that earlier in the week—I am uncertain of the exact day,
although Mrs. Winslake did mention it at the time—earlier in
the week Mrs. Winslake, having occasion to speak to her son
on some domestic or personal matter that need not concern us
now, ascended the stairs and went without knocking into the
room that Douglas uses for his photographic work—a studio
with a little dark-room partitioned off. On her sudden entry
Douglas spun round with what his mother described to me as
an expression of extreme guilt on his face. He was standing at
a work-bench against the window. On the bench was a bottle
with its glass stopper lying alongside; and on a sheet of paper
which had been laid on the bench was a small heap of some
white, lumpy substance. Douglas held in his left hand a glass

phial, and in his right hand a pair of tweezers, with which he was engaged in transferring some of the smaller pieces of the chemical to the phial."

Mr. Plumstead paused dramatically, gazed at the Inspector, then turned in his chair to see what impression this had made on Bradfield.

"There was nothing in this action to cause Mrs. Winslake the slightest apprehension; it was an operation that could be regarded as quite normal in a professional photographer's pursuit of his calling. What *did* disturb Mrs. Winslake was her son's embarrassed air, as if he had been caught in the performance of some culpable act. 'Why, Douglas!' cried his mother, 'you look quite frightened!' He answered that she had startled him by her unexpected entrance. Then he went on— and I want you to pay particular attention to this, gentlemen— he went on to explain that he was supplying some chemicals to Hooker."

"Did he give a reason?"

"Yes: he told his mother that Hooker required the stuff for the purpose of exterminating insects, and"—Mr. Plumstead chuckled with sudden glee—"that is not an unlikely reason, when one considers the insanitary conditions that doubtless prevail in the Hooker household!"

"You say 'chemicals,' Mr. Plumstead. Can you be more precise?"

"Assuredly. According to his mother, Douglas casually mentioned the three letters K, C, N. I think I can say that this meant little to Mrs. Winslake. It had no more impression on her than, for example, D.D.T. It is highly likely—in fact it was clear from her remarks to me—that she was not aware that KCN is the chemical formula for potassium cyanide. Well, gentlemen, that is all I can tell you. It is not what I believe is known as direct evidence, yet it may give you some guidance. As for myself, I cannot escape the conclusion that, having gained possession of the poison, poor, misguided Hooker—

made desperate by some private worry of which we are not aware—deliberately swallowed enough of it to end a life that had become an insupportable burden to him. I put it to you, Inspector: had Douglas intended to administer the poison to Hooker, would he have to let his mother so far into his confidence?"

The Inspector grunted in a way that might have meant anything, then asked:

"Did Mrs. Winslake give you any idea of the size of this phial?"

"No, but I imagine that it was not very large, because Douglas would not otherwise have been picking out the smaller pieces of the chemical."

"Thank you, Mr. Plumstead. Now perhaps I can take a little more of your time. Yesterday evening you; were in the Blue Boar Hotel, weren't you?"

There was a sudden change in Mr. Plumstead. A fanatical gleam came into his eyes—a proselytizing fire into his voice.

"I seek out the Evil One," he declaimed, "not in the places that are of high repute, but in those where I am most likely to find him—the public-house, the race-course, the dog-track, the slum. When I come face to face with the Evil One, or witness the mischievous works of his base myrmidons, I raise my voice against them. If there are souls to save, they are in the dark places, the haunts of sin, the grim strongholds of wickedness, the—"

Charlton had to stop him.

"I quite understand all that, Mr. Plumstead. Was it on such an errand that you went into the Blue Boar last night?"

"It was. I took with me some of those same tracts as I handed to Mrs. Winslake on Wednesday. Who can tell what good may be done by a tract? The mind seeking diversion, the sheet idly picked up, the thoughtless eye glancing at the words, then the sudden gripping of the attention, the message of—"

"What time did you get there?"

"Really, it is difficult to remember. A quarter-past nine—perhaps a few minutes either way."

"You went first into the Shades?"

"Why, yes. Who could have told you that, I wonder? Yes, I first visited the Shades, a name that goes back to the time of the Prince Regent, when the notorious Mrs. Fitzherbert—"

Bradfield looked round for some blunt implement, but Charlton had pulled up Mr. Plumstead.

"Very interesting, sir, but time is short. You went into the Shades...?"

"And distributed tracts in the two bars."

"Hooker was in the public bar then, wasn't he?"

"Yes, the poor fellow was already under the influence of drink. I fear it was to that and not to any natural instinct of generosity that we must attribute his action in handing me half a crown as a contribution to the funds for the children's outing that I am organizing with the co-operation of Mrs. Winslake and other good friends."

Charlton and Bradfield both thought this was rather unkind; Jimmy Hooker would have done anything for children.

"When I had finished handing round tracts in those two bars and having a few words with those who would listen to me, I emerged into the passage-way between the two buildings. In my search after souls to be saved I have ventured many times into the Shades, but up to last night I had never been into the hotel portion of the Blue Boar. As I came out of the private bar I decided on an impulse to remedy this omission. I turned to the right and proceeded along the passage-way into the back yard. Then I saw a door, which I opened with some diffidence, not quite knowing where it would lead me. Just inside was our young friend here." He turned to Bradfield with a smile. "He was kind enough to direct me to the hotel bar. When I got in there the first person I saw was Douglas."

Mr. Plumstead sighed deeply.

"He was in a lamentable condition of inebriation. I went

across to him, to persuade him to come away— to go home to his mother, who was waiting for him." He shook his head with great sadness. "Douglas would not listen to me. Satan was in his heart. He made a harsh, unfeeling remark to me. I saw that he was too drunk to—"

"What did he say?"

"I shall not lower myself by repeating it word for word, but he described me as a particular kind of hypocrite and told me that my company was objectionable to him. I had no alternative but to leave him. That is one reason for my presence here this morning. I wish to say to him when he is sober the things—the beautiful, everlasting truths—to which he would not lend his ear when he was steeped in liquor. I firmly believe that no sheep has strayed so far from the fold that he cannot be brought back into it. Nevertheless, I left the Blue Boar Hotel in a very downcast frame of mind, for *this* was the young man who might one day be my stepson."

"Did Hooker come into the hotel bar while you were there, sir?"

"No, I had left him in the Shades and did not see him again. Indeed, I was surprised to hear that he met his death in the hotel bar."

"When did you leave the Blue Boar?"

"On my arrival in the hotel premises, your assistant was able to inform me, after reference to his wrist-watch, that it was just short of five-and-twenty minutes past nine. I should say that I was not in the building more than five minutes, so you can safely assume that I was on my way to the next public-house down the High Street the Bunch of Grapes, is it not?—by half-past nine."

"You left by the same door as you came in, didn't you?"

"Quite so. I went out of the bar and proceeded down the passage. I had paused to conjecture whether there might be other drinking bars or rooms where persons might be assembled when I was accosted by a young woman on the hotel staff—an extremely impolite young person, I am sorry to say. But I am not unaccustomed to that, Inspector. On the rough road that I have chosen to travel one meets with many rebuffs. Yet I shall go on—"

The passion of the zealot had come back into his voice. It was like a recurring fever. Charlton said firmly:

"Thank you, Mr. Plumstead. I need not keep you any longer."

The plump little gentleman went as limp as a marionette when the showman relaxes the wires.

"Please forgive me," he said with a smile that had more sadness than humour in it. "Sometimes a fiery spirit surges up within me and I speak with a voice that is not my own."

X.

Mrs. Hooker Has a Caller

JIMMY HOOKER'S widow had been brought into Lulverton to identify the body. When this had been done she was escorted to police headquarters to be interviewed by Charlton. Bradfield, on catching sight of her in her powder and paint, her imitation leopard-skin coat and the scarlet scarf tied round her head and knotted on top, decided that she looked a shade less attractive than she had done in an Army greatcoat over a flannel nightdress.

There was only one thing that interested her that morning while she sat in the chair so recently vacated by Mr. Zephaniah Plumstead.

"What about the things what was found on 'im? I'm not standin' fer any funny stuff, mister. I want it back, every penny—and the joolry. Don't think I didn't know 'e'd got it, the skinflintin' old , keepin' me short and makin' me live like a pauper without two brass farthings to call me own."

"I'm afraid we shall have to get things a bit more straightened out before we can—"

Her shrill voice went all hoity-toity.

"Oh, yer do, do yer? And 'ow might yer suggest I'm goin' ter live while yer makin' up yer minds? Do what many another innercent girl's 'ad ter do? I've lived straight, I'ave."

He tried to pacify her.

"We shan't be unreasonable, Mrs. Hooker," he smiled.

"Before you leave I'll see that you're supplied with some cash. Do you know whether your husband left a will?"

"Not 'im. Wouldn't 'ave nothink to do with slisters, 'e wouldn't. Didn't trust 'em. But it all comes ter me, as 'is legal wife—and don't think I 'aven't got the marriage lines at 'ome ter prove it, mister. When a man snuffs it, all the money goes to 'is wife—that's what the lore says."

Charlton murmured something about letters of administration, but he might as well have addressed himself to the filing cabinet, which Bradfield was once again adorning. He gave it up and changed the subject.

"If I may, Mrs. Hooker, I'd like to ask you one or two questions while you're here. When did you last see your husband alive?"

"Yes'd'y mornin'. 'E 'ad a couple er kippers for 'is breakfast, then orf 'e went, and I never set eyes on 'im agine till just now in the morchry."

"Do you know of any reason for his death? Had he any enemies?"

"Enemies? Not 'im! Too soft, 'e was—to everybody 'cept 'is wife, 'oo've worked meself to the bone with sewin' and cookin' and cleanin'—and never a thank you." She brooded over this, then added: "Nice b—"

"Did Mr. Hooker ever say anything to you about an insecticide?"

Her laugh had a piercing quality that made them both wince.

"You *are* a funny feller, ain't yer? What's that got ter do with it? If yer want a strite answer, it's no."

"You didn't notice a glass tube in his possession during the last day or two?"

She frowned in puzzlement, then looked at him with suspicion in her weak eyes.

"Are you tryin' ter put somethink over on me, mister? I don't like the smell er this. Whatcher gettin' at?"

Charlton leaned forward across the desk.

"Mrs. Hooker, you know that your husband was poisoned, don't you? The police are endeavouring to find out how it was done and who did it. I'm not 'putting something over on you.' All I want you to tell me is: Did you see your husband with a glass tube? You may have noticed him take it out of his pocket, or something of that kind."

She shook her head. There was silence in the room for a moment or two. Then she asked:

"What does this poison taste like?"

"Why do you ask, Mrs. Hooker?"

"Does it dry on yer tongue like an iron tonic?"

"I'm afraid I can't tell you."

"Well, is it a slow job, or do yer swaller it and go straight out?"

"The effects are usually very sudden. Have you any reason for wanting to know?"

"I was just wonderin'... No, let's ferget it." She played with the cotton gloves on her lap before adding darkly: "I wouldn't 'ave put it past 'im, though."

★ ★ ★

They would be going past Mrs. Hooker's home on their way out to Mickleham village, so after she had been given ten pounds and had signed a receipt for the money, Charlton offered her a lift. This she accepted without a word of thanks and was duly deposited outside the shanty.

The two detectives drove on to Mickleham. It was only a tiny village centred round the Mickleham Arms and it did not take them long to find the cottage of the Dilks family. A woman answered the door. In her neat healthy, aproned motherliness, she offered a refreshing contrast to Mrs. James Hooker.

"Mrs. Dilks?" Charlton inquired, raising his hat.

"Yes," she replied. "You're the police, aren't you? I suppose you've come about the accident. We're still waiting for the doctor."

Charlton professed to know more than he did.

"How is he?"

"The poor boy's had a nasty shaking, but there's no bones broken."

"May we see him?"

"I wouldn't think it'd do any harm."

She drew back to allow them to enter the cottage. In a little sloped-ceilinged room upstairs they found young Stanley in bed. He had a bandage round his head and one of his hands was tied up, too, but his answering grin was cheerful enough when his mother said:

"It's the p'lice, Stan. They want to put you some questions."

"Can you tell us how it happened?" Charlton asked with a smile of encouragement.

"Yes, sir. I was on the bike—it's a smashing bike, sir. Twenty-two and a half upright frame, lustre finish."

"You were cycling to work, I suppose?"

"That's right, sir. I'd gone some way when—"

"What time was this?"

"'Bout twenty past six, sir."

"Right. Go on, please."

"I saw the lights of a car. Very bright lights they was sir. They dazzled me. I kept well to my side, but when the car was right on top of me like, it swerved out and went smack into me. The next thing I knew, sir, was when I come to."

"Were you still in the road?"

"No, sir. I was down in the reeds with the bike on top of me."

This part of the road was several feet above the level of the surrounding marshland. The causeway ran straight for about a quarter of a mile. When higher ground was reached, the road avoided a wood by veering off to the left and skirting round it before resuming its fairly direct course for Lulverton.

"It's the bike, sir," Stanley went on unhappily. "Maes alloy bends and extension. G.B. alloy brakes. And now it's a—"

"Could you have been thrown there by the force of the collision?"

"Yes, I should think so, sir. You know the bit I mean. There's nothink to stop you going over into the reeds."

"Did someone find you?"

"No, sir. When I come to, I couldn't think where I was or what'd happened. Then things began to come back to me, but I felt very dizzy and funny. I pushed the bike off me and got up. The glass and bulb in the electric lamp was broken and I hadn't got any matches, so I couldn't see what I was doing prop'ly. I tried to get the bike up on to the road, but it was all bent and the front wheel was buckled nearly double, by the feel of it." He shook his swathed head and added with melancholy pride. "Twenty-seven high-pressures. I didn't feel up to moving it, sir, so I left it where it was and walked 'ome. It was a real smasher, sir. B.17 sprint saddle, stainless—"

"Yes, it's tough luck on you, but maybe it can be repaired. What happened to your cap?"

"I don't know, sir."

Mrs. Dilks said: "He wasn't wearing it when he got back, though he 'ad it on when he went."

"Wonder what old Musso'll say," speculated her son.

"Stan, I've told you before. You didn't ought to call Mr. Barucci that. The war's over and we don't want no more unpleasantness. Mr. Barucci's a very nice gentleman, though 'e *is* foreign, and I won't 'ave you calling him by rude names." She turned to Charlton. "You must excuse him, sir. You see, the cap wasn't Stan's to lose. It belongs to Mr. Barucci, who Stan works for."

"P'raps it's in the ditch with the bike," suggested Stanley.

"We're going straight back to Lulverton," Charlton told him. "We'll have a look for it. Can you tell us any more about this accident? You probably didn't see much, but did you hear the engine? Did it sound like a big car or a small one?"

"I'd say it was a big one, sir—and 'spensive, too. It didn't rattle."

"Was it some distance from you when you first saw the headlights?"

The boy—he was only about fifteen—screwed up his face in thought.

"Yes... It's a straight stretch just there, where the road crosses the marshy bit, and ..."

"Yes?"

"There was something funny about it, sir. You know the bend by the coppice? Well, I didn't see any swing of the lights as the car came round it. And it didn't come towards me as quick as it should have. I don't think, when I first saw the lights, that it was moving at all, sir."

"And as you drew nearer to it, it started up?"

"That's right, sir."

Charlton smiled as he said: "Almost as if some desperate criminals were lying in wait for you!"

Stanley considered this.

"Not likely," he said, then appended sombrely,

"Worse luck."

"Stan!" cried his mother. "The things you say!"

★ ★ ★

They found the bicycle in the reeds. It was so badly damaged that it was a wonder its rider had survived with no more than a few minor cuts and bruises. They made a very careful examination of the machine and of the ground around it; and they could not agree with Stanley Dilks that he and his bicycle had been flung off the road by the car. From the condition of the front wheel, they deduced that the collision had been almost head-on; that the car had been swung right across the road into the cyclist's path; and that he would not have been thrown far enough to his left to have gone over the bank. It seemed more in accord with the evidence that, after the collision had taken place, the occupant—or occupants—of the car had transferred the unconscious lad and his bicycle to a place where they would be less likely to be noticed by passers-by.

The cap with the "Toni's" band was not to be found, either in the road or in the reeds below. Their search, however, was far from profitless. On the margin of the road were scattered fragments of glass, too large and thick to be from the electric lamp on the machine, which was also shattered. They decided that these fragments must be from one of the headlamps of the car, and carefully collected them together for further examination later.

One other clue they found. On the clip that secured the lever of the front brake to the handle-bar of the bicycle, they discovered green traces, as if the sharp corner of the clip had scored some enamelled surface.

"As soon as we're back in Lulverton, Peter," instructed Charlton, "get that comely nose of yours down on the trail and see if you can trace a big green car in these parts early this morning. They probably used it to deliver Winslake's breakfast and waited round the corner, ready to whisk away Dilks's substitute as soon as he'd done his job. Ring up the Yard and get them to send out a call for a big green car with scratched paintwork and a smashed headlamp—probably both on the off side; and find out whether any cars were stolen last night in this neighbourhood."

"What coloured car is the septic Quentin's?" Bradfield asked.

"Anything but green, Peter. Our Oliver has more sense than that. Which reminds me, I must have a chat with him this morning."

He removed the scraps of enamel from the brake-lever clip and put them in one of the small envelopes he always carried; and, having hidden the bicycle in the reeds, to be collected later, they moved off towards Lulverton. As they drew near to the late Jimmy Hooker's shanty, they saw that someone was standing at the front door. Before they drew level, the door had been opened and the visitor had disappeared inside, but not soon enough to avoid recognition by the two C.I.D. men.

"Well, well!" said Bradfield. "Perhaps my old eyes deceived me, but did you see who that was?"

"Certainly I did," replied his chief calmly. "That king of prestidigitators, the Great Desro."

* * *

Mrs. Winslake had already been informed of the fate of her son. When Charlton got back to Lulverton with Bradfield, he left his assistant to start inquiries about the green car, and went round himself to 23, Highfield Road.

He took with him this time the second of the Three Musketeers, Detective-constable Emerson, a young giant of a fellow with the strength of Hercules and the heart of a child.

The bereaved mother opened the front door to them and invited them into the front room. After expressing his sympathy in her loss and his regret that it was necessary to trouble her so soon with an interrogation, Charlton went on quietly:

"Your son's death is undoubtedly linked with the death of James Hooker. Let me tell you what happened last night, Mrs. Winslake. At eight o'clock the two of them met in the Blue Boar Hotel and had a confidential conversation, in the course of which your son gave Hooker certain information. We don't know yet what he told him. Whatever it was, it was overheard by certain other people and, within a couple of hours, Hooker was dead—poisoned. Fifteen minutes or so after Hooker's death, your son was taken into custody—not for being concerned in the poisoning, but for creating a disturbance. I'm afraid he was rather drunk."

"Poor Douglas."

"At seven o'clock this morning, a lad arrived at the police station with a tray of food. He told the duty sergeant that this meal had been ordered by yourself."

"No! It wasn't! Please don't believe that! The thought of it never entered my head."

"That's what I imagined. On the tray, with other food, was a plate of porridge. This had been treated with the same poison as had been used to kill Hooker—potassium cyanide." He paused for a moment before adding: "The chemical formula is KCN."

Mrs. Winslake replied absently: "Oh, yes?" Then, as if his remark had suddenly registered in her brain, she said sharply: "Did you say KCN?"

"Yes, madam."

"And that's cyanide?"

"Yes."

"What does it look like?"

"Usually dull white lumps, rather like opaque washing-soda. Amongst other purposes, it's used for—photography."

She looked at him with frightened eyes.

"No, no! It can't be true! He wouldn't have done it! It was for insects. He told me so." Her voice rose. "Tell me it isn't true! You don't believe it, do you? ... Do you?"

"Believe what?"

"That Douglas poisoned that man and then committed suicide."

"I think I can reassure you on that, Mrs. Winslake. The police are of the opinion that both of them were murdered by some third party. You mentioned insects, Mrs. Winslake. Can you tell me why?"

"You frightened me. It's terrible enough for my son to die, but ..." She left the sentence unfinished.

"I've never been happy over Douglas's friendship with Hooker. My son was easily led astray, and I'm sure Hooker wasn't honest. Men of his type rarely are. Yesterday evening Douglas went out—it was about half-past seven—and his last words to me ..." Her lips trembled. "The last time I was ever to

116

hear his voice. He said that he was going to settle things one way or the other. What is the name, please, of the very nice young man who called here afterwards? The tall, smiling one?"

"Detective-sergeant Bradfield."

"Well, I told him about it. I didn't know then that there were going to be such dreadful consequences."

"Sergeant Bradfield has reported your conversation to me, madam. I understand that your son didn't mention that it was Hooker he was proposing to settle with?"

"No, but I guessed it must be, because earlier in the evening Hooker called here. I couldn't hear what it was all about; Douglas was careful that I shouldn't. He took Hooker down to the front gate and stood talking in the rain with him. All I did hear was as he came indoors again. He called out that he would meet Hooker at eight in the Blue Boar Hotel."

"Thank you, Mrs. Winslake. Now, about these insects ..."

"Yes, I ought to tell you, I suppose. Douglas has—had a room upstairs that he used as a photographic studio. I don't usually disturb him while he's working, but the other morning—"

"Which morning?"

"Let me think ... Monday. Yes, it was last Monday morning. I went in to talk to him. I wanted to ask him whether he was going to be in for lunch. He was putting some of this stuff—this cyanide—I never guessed we had such deadly poison in the house—he was putting it in a bottle with a pair of tweezers. He—"

"It was a bottle, not a glass tube?"

"Yes, it was one of my aspirin-tablet bottles, with a screw-on metal cap. Douglas told me it was for Hooker, who wanted to use it as an insecticide."

"You're quite sure it was Hooker?"

"Yes. He distinctly said, 'It's for Jimmy Hooker.'"

"I hate having to ask you this, Mrs. Winslake, but do you think your son was telling the truth?"

Mrs. Winslake looked worried at this.

"Oh, I don't know," she said uncertainly. "I scarcely know what to think about anything. It's like some horrible nightmare. I thought he was telling the truth, because there didn't seem any reason why he shouldn't be, but since ..."

He waited for her to continue, but she sat looking down at the carpet in heart-broken silence. After a while he said:

"Did your son appear startled when you went into the room? Do you imagine that he would have been better pleased if you hadn't come in just then?"

She looked up at him and nodded without speaking.

"May we see this studio, please?"

"Yes, of course."

The house had only two floors. The studio was a small room at the back. In a cupboard over the mantelpiece was, amongst other things, a glass-stoppered bottle. It was three-quarters full. On the label was printed in large capitals "POTASSIUM CYANIDE" and below, in smaller letters, "98–100% Double Salt." In the right-hand bottom corner appeared the word "POISON." This was printed in red and enclosed by lines of the same colour. The name of a London wholesaler was evidence that the poison had not been bought from a local chemist.

Charlton said: "I'll take this away with me, if I may?"

"Oh, do," she answered in a tone of great relief.

She found a piece of brown paper in which to wrap the bottle, and the three of them went downstairs again. When they were back in the sitting-room, Charlton said: "Again I must say how sorry I am to trouble you with all these questions, but these routine inquiries can't be avoided or deferred."

"That's quite all right, Inspector—Charlton, isn't it? Do ask me anything you want to know."

"Apart from Hooker, were there any other of your son's associates of whom you—disapproved?"

"No, I don't think so." Her lips tightened slightly. "Except, perhaps, the Collins girl at the Blue Boar. I didn't encourage that, although poor Douglas seemed very fond of her. He was once engaged to such a nice girl. Phyllis Wildgoose. Do you know her? Major Wildgoose's younger daughter. The Major is a widower, and I was very pleased when Douglas told me of the engagement. Then—something happened and it was broken off. I don't know why. Douglas would never talk about it. Nor would Phyllis, her father told me. The Major and I were very disappointed."

Charlton had got out his note-book. He referred to it before he asked:

"Did your son know a man called Kochowski? I believe he's a foreigner, probably a Pole."

"He's never mentioned him. He may have known him, of course, without telling me about it. Douglas was sometimes a little bit—secretive."

"Have you ever received the impression—especially recently—that he was concerned in anything—well, I must be frank about it—anything illegal?"

"Good gracious, no! Douglas would never think of it! He may have been rather—irresponsible, but he was always a very honest boy. Even when he was at school he—"

"Was his photographic business profitable?"

"Not very, but he's only been doing it since he came out of the Army—as a profession, that is. He hasn't had time to work up a connection yet."

"Did he make enough to keep himself?"

"Er—no, not really."

"But you were in a position to help him?"

"I gave him all the money I could afford. It was understood, of course, that he would pay it back when he'd got the business going properly."

"Did he borrow any money from you before he left home yesterday evening?"

"Yes: a pound until tomorrow morning. One of his customers was going to settle his account then and Douglas

119

said he would be able to repay me."

"Did he give you the name of this customer?"

"I don't remember that he did."

"Was it a Mr. Quentin?"

"No, I'm sure it wasn't, although Mr. Quentin was a friend of his. I've never met Mr. Quentin, but Douglas used to speak very enthusiastically about him. He was extremely kind to Douglas. I should think he's a rich man. He and his wife live in one of those big houses in Vanbrugh Road. Douglas used to go there sometimes to cocktail parties. Mr. Quentin was a good friend to my poor, darling boy."

He looked across at her with grave, grey eyes.

"Mrs. Winslake, my duty compels me to put this question, but you need not answer it if you would rather not. Was your son concerned in the black market?"

She avoided his glance and looked down at the worn carpet again.

"I don't know what you mean exactly by 'concerned.' A lot of people get things in the black market—quite respectable people, too—but they don't make their living by it. Douglas couldn't have been concerned—as you put it—because he never had any money, and men who deal in that sort of thing always have enough to spend on enormous cars and—"

"I'm afraid you're evading a direct answer, Mrs. Winslake. Did your son bring home at any time food or other goods that he could not have obtained through legal channels?"

She sighed unhappily.

"I suppose I'll have to tell you. Yes, he did, but only little parcels of things—and half the population in the British Isles are doing the same—"

"What things were they, madam? I'm not trying to convict you out of your own mouth, but to find out who killed your son. Was it food?"

"Mostly. Butter, bacon, sugar, perhaps a tin of corned beef— things like that. Once it was some whisky."

"Can you tell me the brand?"

Without answering, she rose to her feet and walked across to the sideboard. From this she produced a bottle, which she held out for him to examine the label.

"'Highland Velvet',"he read aloud. "Make a note of that, please, Emerson. Mackinnon's 'Highland Velvet.' Thank you, Mrs. Winslake."

She replaced the bottle and stood with a hand grasping the top of the sideboard.

"It made me very uneasy," she admitted in a voice that shook, "because I don't like going against the law But I wasn't strong-willed enough. More than once I asked Douglas where it came from, but he wouldn't tell me. He just smiled." She bit her lip. "I shall never see him smile again . ... Please go."

★ ★ ★

As Emerson opened the front gate Charlton said:

"Sometimes I loathe myself, Emerson."

They were just going to get into the Wolseley when a voice hailed them. They turned and saw approaching the dapper little figure of Major Alexander Wildgoose. They waited on the pavement until the Major came up to them.

"Well, Inspector," he said, "how goes the case?"

"Very well, thank you," was the polite and utterly untruthful reply.

"Just been calling on the mother?"

"Yes."

"About to do the same myself," said the Major jovially. His manner was far more human than it had been at their last meeting. "Little woman needs looking after. Can't leave her by herself too much, can we? How's the son this morning? Bad headache and a guilty conscience, eh? Y'know, Inspector, never was keen on eating my own words—once a thing's said it's said—but I'm beginning to regret being a bit outspoken last night. I mean about young Winslake. Truth is, the boy'd annoyed me. Never had much patience with a man who couldn't hold his drink like a gentleman. Matter of fact, there's more in it than that. Got to consider the mother. Splendid little woman, that. Thousand pities. Not easy to keep up appearances. Damn nice little woman. May be all for the best, though. Last night's affair. Teach the boy a lesson. Dismissed with a caution, I take it?"

"Major, I'd better tell you now that Douglas Winslake is dead."

"Good God!"

"He died from the effects of cyanide poisoning."

"Does his mother know?"

"Yes."

"Must go to her. Good God!"

He swung round on the heel of his beautifully polished brown shoe, pushed open the gate and marched purposefully up the path. Charlton watched him for a moment, then opened the door of the car.

"Mr. Pickwick is apparently not alone in the field, Emerson," he remarked.

"Quite so, sir," agreed that burly young man, wondering what the devil the Skip was talking about.

XI.

The Uninvited Guest

WHEN Inspector Charlton left Highfield Road with Emerson by his side, he drove westward. They went the whole length of the High Street, turned to the right at the Centre and proceeded up Beastmarket Hill. As Charlton turned the Wolseley into Vanbrugh Road and pulled up outside Capri, he gave Emerson some brief instructions. There was no sign of D.C. Hartley at the top window of Colstonfields, the house opposite, but Charlton was confident that his man was on the alert.

They had to ring twice before the front door of Capri was opened by Mrs. Quentin. In a previous encounter with this pair of sharks Sergeant Martin had said of her "She looks like one of those females we used to call 'vamps' in the old silent days. Tall, dark and swognay, with a long cigarette-holder. Sort of woman 'oo'd seduce the 'ole Russian army before breakfast and make a regular thing of going round with the plans of the fortifications stuffed down the front of 'er dress—if it had one."

Time had gone by since the good sergeant had painted that word-picture, yet it was still substantially accurate, except, perhaps, that the exquisitely "permed" hair was not still so effortlessly black. She was wearing a long house-coat of red velvet and between her fingers—not in a holder—was a cigarette marked by lipstick.

Charlton raised his hat and said with a courteous smile: "Good morning, Mrs. Quentin. I expect you'll remember me?"

She looked him up and down with studied disdain. "Yes, I suppose I do," she drawled. "You're a policeman, aren't you? I saw you on point duty once."

Emerson was disappointed when his chief refused to rise to this bait.

"I wonder," said Charlton, "whether you and your husband can spare us a few minutes?"

"Well, it's very inconvenient. You people should fix an appointment instead of bursting in like this."

"I'm sorry, madam. As a matter of fact," he lied blandly, "I did try to ring you, but the line was out of order."

"Yes, and the wretched engineers haven't put it right yet. Nobody seems to care *what* happens these days. Why must our telephone go suddenly dead? Can you tell me that?"

He could have done, but the explanation would not have pleased her, so he said:

"I'm afraid I don't know, Mrs. Quentin. I expect it will be put right in a day or two. Is your husband in? I'd very much like to have a word with you both."

"If you must, I can't stop you. You'd better come in." They followed her across the wide parquet-floored hall into a lounge expensively furnished beyond the point where luxury ended and flashiness began. There she left them, without inviting them to sit down, while she went in search of her husband. Ten minutes went by before she returned with him.

Oliver Quentin had left the forties a year or two behind. His black hair showed signs of approaching baldness on top, but the back and sides were thick and curly. His complexion was pale and all the shaving in the world would not have rid his cleft and chubby chin of its "five o'clock shadow." He was putting on weight, and his brown eyes were large and lush. His short figure was encased in striped trousers and a black jacket, with a starched white collar and an unobtrusive tie. He looked a typical business man, with all the outward signs of success and financial stability.

Belle Quentin was first into the room, but her husband came round from behind her, like a squat tug fussily passing some taller, more slender vessel, and bore down upon the Inspector with a wide smile and outstretched hand.

"Why, Inspector! How are you? You're quite a stranger. Glad to see you again!"

Charlton had no cause to think that he was. It had been in this same room that his fist had sent Quentin reeling backwards on to the finely upholstered settee to which, having shaken hands, Quentin now directed his visitors.

"Do sit down, both of you." He swung round to his wife. "Cigarettes, my dear? Are there any left? So difficult to get, aren't they?"

This last remark was addressed to Charlton. As if she were demonstrating a new creation from Paris, Belle Quentin made her way across to an inlaid table by the window and brought back a massive silver box in which there were at least two hundred cigarettes. As Emerson followed Charlton's example and helped himself from the proffered box, he felt anything less than a handful was an insult to such hospitality.

"Now," said Quentin when the four cigarettes had been lighted and he and his wife were also seated, he in a deep easy chair and she on the arm of it, "what can we do for you?" He smiled genially. "You and I have had our little differences in the past, Inspector, but it's no use bearing malice, is it? Not these days. Too many other things to worry about. So let's have it."

"You've very likely heard that a man was poisoned in the Blue Boar Hotel last night?"

"A nasty business. Man called Hooker, wasn't it? Knew the chap by sight. He used to come here hawking, didn't he, my dear?"

"Yes," she drawled. "I always sent him packing. He didn't look honest."

"Oh, he was straight enough," said Quentin with an airy righteousness that made Charlton repress a smile. "It's darned bad luck on the fellow. What was it, Inspector—an accident? Swallowed something meant for the rats?"

"It was far more serious than that. Mr. Quentin, you and

Mrs. Quentin were in the Blue Boar last evening, weren't you?"

"Perfectly correct. We popped in for a quick one at about— when was it, my dear? Somewhere round half-past eight, wasn't it?"

"More or less. I never remember these things."

"I've been given to understand that you were in the Shades about a quarter of an hour and that Mrs. Quentin left five minutes before you did. Was that so?"

The suave man considered this question.

"Yes, I imagine you're right. You've been busy, Inspector!"

"Can you tell me why you did not leave together?"

"Now, that's one straight from the shoulder! You've touched on a rather tender point. As a matter of fact, my wife and I had a—well, a little tiff. Just a small difference of opinion. No need to go into details—an entirely personal matter. We both got slightly heated and the wife went off. A storm in a teacup, you know. All over before the evening was out."

"I see." Charlton turned to Mrs. Quentin. "What did you do when you left the Shades, madam?"

"I—er ..."

"She went—" Quentin began.

"Please let your wife answer."

"I went—home."

"Did you meet anyone you knew?"

"No, there weren't many people about, it was raining so."

"And you, Mr. Quentin? Did you come back too?"

"Well, yes and no. I was cross when the wife left me like that, and sat there in the Shades meditating upon the incomprehensible ways of women." His laugh did not ring true. "Then I decided that it wasn't doing much good hanging around, so I started off for home."

"And that was at approximately quarter to nine?"

"As near as makes no matter."

"You came straight back here?"

"Oh, yes; it wasn't the kind of evening for hanging about

in the streets."

"A witness has told us, Mr. Quentin," Charlton said coldly, "that at a quarter to nine he saw you hurrying along the High Street, but not in the direction of Vanbrugh Road."

Quentin opened his mouth as if to deny this statement, then slapped his knee with the palm of his hand.

"That's right!" he said. "That's absolutely right! I was forgetting. Yes, I remember now. When I left the Shades I was still feeling too hot under the collar to face the wife, so I decided to cool down a bit by going for a walk. I went past the Public Library and round as far as Highfield Road, then came back again along the High Street and up Beastmarket Hill. By the time I got home I was more like my old self, and I was glad to find that the wife was inclined to forgive and forget."

She drew at her cigarette and blew a cloud down her thin nostrils.

"More than you deserved," she said.

"True enough, maybe."

"What did you do then, Mr. Quentin?"

The other man laughed again.

"Persistent fellow, aren't you? It was an occasion for a celebration, so we had a loving cup."

"Where?"

"Don't tell me you don't know!" Quentin's tone was roguish. "I can't imagine that you've failed to have a chat with that sharp-tongued little vixen, Olive. Not that we've anything to hide. Far from it. Yes, I took the wife back to the Blue Boar and bought her a Scotch. Had one myself as well. We both needed it by then."

"Which brand was it, Mr. Quentin?"

"That's a curious question, if ever there was one! I haven't the least idea. One just asks for Scotch these days and considers oneself damned lucky to get any at all. What's the point exactly?"

"Just idle curiosity. I thought it might have been Mackinnon's

'Highland Velvet'."

It was an arrow at a venture and he could not be sure whether it had reached its mark, save that neither of them moved or spoke until he put his next question.

"What time did you get back to the Blue Boar, Mr. Quentin?"

"Well, I don't know what Olive's told you, and I don't want you to hold it against us afterwards, because I didn't spend the evening walking round with a stopwatch in my hand. Now, let me see. ... It's a good ten minutes' walk from here to the Blue Boar—a trifle longer in the other direction, which is an uphill climb part of the way. We left here at five-and-twenty past nine. I can vouch for that; I remember looking at my watch to see whether it was worth while going out again. I'd say we were back in the Blue Boar by five-and-twenty to ten. Now you'll want to know what time we left, I suppose?"

"Yes, please," said Charlton sweetly.

It was Belle who answered in her habitual "couldn't-care-less" tone:

"Quarter to. You looked at your watch."

"So I did. Lucky you thought of that, my dear. Yes, I looked at my watch again, and it was quarter to ten precisely. And that was the end of another day. We went straight home and got to bed."

"Did you see Hooker at all during the evening?"

Quentin shook his head.

"Never set eyes on the fellow."

"Do you know a man named Douglas Winslake?"

After an almost imperceptible pause, Quentin said: "Just a casual acquaintance. I've seen him in the Blue Boar and other pubs and usually pass the time of day with him. Photographer, isn't he?"

"Did you meet him last night?"

"Not to speak to. We saw him in the hotel bar in the Blue Boar. We didn't go into that bar, you understand. We stayed by the snack counter. Caught sight of Winslake through the door. He was sitting on a stool up against the bar and was well under the weather by all appearances. Let's hope he managed to find his way home!"

"You say you didn't see Hooker at all?"

"No."

"That's curious. I wonder you didn't notice him when you caught sight of Mr. Winslake. They were both in there at the time."

Quentin turned to look up at his wife.

"What do you say, my dear?"

"If this man wants us to say we saw him," she answered with lazy contempt, "we'd better say we did. Otherwise he'll never go."

"No," decided her husband. "I'm not saying anything that's not true. I didn't see Hooker in the hotel bar, and I'm not going to say that I did. Not for anybody."

Charlton stroked his chin.

"I'm rather surprised to hear that your acquaintance with Mr. Winslake was so slight, Mr. Quentin. I was under the impression that you were on fairly intimate terms."

"Far from it. Yet perhaps I misled you by what I said just now. One gets to know a lot of people socially in a little place like Lulverton; and it could be said, I suppose, that Winslake was more than a mere pub chum. He's been with us once or twice to Goodwood and Sandown Park. Not that any of us have more than a shilling or two on, just to give us an interest in the race."

"Did he ever come to this house?"

"A cocktail party now and then. Just a few friends, you know, and a rubber of bridge. Winslake was never a regular visitor."

"Do you know that he is dead, Mr. Quentin?"

He was watching them both closely. Quentin's face showed no more than shocked surprise, and the dismay in his voice was not overdone as he answered:

"Good heavens, is that so? I *am* sorry. A nice young fellow like that. How did it happen?"

"He was poisoned early this morning."

"What, in the police station?"

"You knew he was there?"

"It's common knowledge, isn't it? There won't be many Lulvertonians who don't know by this time that he was pinched last night for being drunk and disorderly."

"A few minutes ago," Charlton said smoothly, "you expressed the hope, Mr. Quentin, that Mr. Winslake managed to find his way home. I gather from this that you were unaware of what took place in the Blue Boar last night. Or was that just the impression you wished me to receive?"

Quentin waved two ringed hands in refutation.

"My dear fellow, please don't start leaping to wrong conclusions. You police would make the Archbishop of Canterbury contradict himself. When I said that, I meant ..."

"Yes? What *did* you mean?"

"Well, I can't really say I meant anything much. It was just the usually silly joke most people make about drunks. 'Hope he got home all right.'" Another two-handed gesture. "Nothing to it."

Charlton did not press the point further.

"I need hardly tell you, Mr. Quentin, that the police take an extremely serious view not only of what has already happened, but also of what may happen in the immediate future."

"I can well imagine that," Quentin agreed heartily, clearly relieved at this change in the conversation.

"We've little doubt that these two deaths are but the beginning—that they will be followed by more attacks. I don't want to frighten you—or you either, Mrs. Quentin—but it's quite on the cards that they'll start on *you* next."

"*Us?*" protested Quentin. "Nonsense! Why the devil should

130

they do that? And who are *they*, anyway?"

"I'm merely warning you both. I'm not empowered to tell you all that the police have discovered, but we've found out enough to make it necessary to put a man on to make sure that nothing unpleasant happens to you or Mrs. Quentin."

"Put a man on? I don't follow you."

"This is Detective-constable Emerson. He's had his instructions."

This was strictly true. Emerson had certainly had his instructions, but they varied in some respects from those that Charlton now proceeded to outline to the bewildered Quentins.

"Emerson will be your watch-dog. He'll act as your guard and will be responsible to me for your safety."

"But—"

"I've made arrangements for a camp-bed to be sent along here. Emerson can sleep in the hall and if you're the least worried or suspicious during the night, all you'll have to do will be to call out and—"

"Surely this isn't—"

"It's no trouble at all, I assure you. Emerson is a light sleeper" (Emerson slept like a log) "and he'll come at once to your help. If you want to go out, Emerson will come with you, won't you, Emerson?"

"Only too pleased, sir."

"Yes, Emerson will come with you and protect you if the need arises."

"Look here, Inspector—"

"No, Mr. Quentin—I know you think it's straining our manpower and you don't want to put us to any inconvenience, but that's our worry, not yours. I'm putting another man on outside the house, so that if Mrs. Quentin needs to go shopping or anything, she'll be looked after as well, so you won't be taken by surprise in that way."

He looked from Mr. Quentin to his wife with a disarming smile.

"That covers more or less every eventuality, doesn't it?" he said. "Oh, and one other thing, Emerson. You must keep a watchful eye on people coming into the house. Don't let them out of your sight. Make a point of being present during any conversation they may have with Mr. or Mrs. Quentin. I'm sure that Mr. and Mrs. Quentin won't mind, because it is only being done for their own benefit. In case of difficulty or danger, get to the nearest window and call out. Help will come at once."

Quentin said: "I don't like this at all, Charlton. It's completely unnecessary. We can't have the house full of detectives. What about feeding them and so forth?"

"That will all be attended to. Emerson won't want any of your rations; his meals will be brought in for him. And that reminds me. Be very careful what you eat. Examine all food that comes into the house and if you notice the smell of bitter almonds, let Emerson know at once."

Belle Quentin put in a languid word or two.

"All this sounds rather infantile, Inspector. I agree with my husband that we can't turn the house into a policemen's dormitory. What do you think the neighbours are going to say?"

"We can't worry about them, Mrs. Quentin. I'm sorry, but I can see no alternative. It'll only be for a day or two, I hope."

Quentin jumped to his feet, nearly dislodging Belle from the arm of the chair.

"I'm not standing for it!" he blustered. "You're acting without authority. I'll phone your superintendent at once."

"Didn't Mrs. Quentin say the line was out of order?"

"Then I'll go straight round and see him."

"By all means, Mr. Quentin. Emerson will be pleased to accompany you."

Quentin glared at him, but made no move towards the door.

"A lot of damned nonsense," he said.

"Look, sir," Charlton answered as if reasoning with a child. "I'm doing this for your protection and I can see no reason why either you or your wife should be unduly annoyed about it. I don't think you would like the police to get the idea that all these protests spring from a guilty conscience, would you?"

Quentin stood for a moment, then plumped down again in the chair.

"Have it your own way," he grunted.

★ ★ ★

Charlton drove back alone to police headquarters. There was a gentle smile on his handsome face. Yesterday evening he had said that he did not want to scare the Quentins, but he had since changed his views. A delightful little plan was beginning to take shape in his mind.

XII.

Family Conference in the Blue Boar

MEANWHILE Detective-sergeant Peter Bradfield was not idle. Having arranged for Stanley Dilks's bicycle to be collected and brought to police headquarters, he prepared to get busy on the telephone. His first call was to the police station at Southmouth.

Southmouth—or Southmouth-by-the-Sea as it had been renamed when part of it had been developed into a seaside resort of great popularity with holiday-makers—was some three miles to the south of Lulverton, with which, if building work ever got well under way again, it might one day merge in what has been described in another place as "a single uncomely and enormous blot on the fair countryside of Downshire." In the district known as Old Town were the harbour and docks.

This first call put through by Bradfield bore fruit. They were able to tell him that during the night a Ford V8 had been stolen from outside a house in Stoneleigh, a residential area on the northern outskirts of Southmouth. The car was the property of a Dr. Hope Smith, who had been called out by a sick patient in Stoneleigh. While he was in the house, the car had been quietly driven away. It was not a saloon, but the hooded model known as "club cabriolet." The Southmouth inspector—his name was Dixon—told Bradfield its number and also the colour of it, which was green. Scotland Yard, he said, had already been informed of the theft.

Bradfield considered it a reasonable assumption that this was the car that had knocked down Stanley Dilks. He therefore suggested to the inspector that the Yard might be told that the car in question had a damaged headlamp—probably on the off side. After a few more minutes' conversation, he rang off, well pleased with results so far.

He put on his hat and, with his hands in the pockets of his raincoat, went down the stairs and out into the High Street. In his inquiries concerning a green Ford V8 that might have been in Lulverton around seven o'clock that morning, he met with no success until he happened to fall in with Tom Fitch, the potman at the Blue Boar. In a bibbed apron and with his cap on the back of his head and a cigarette hanging from his mouth, this tall, robust young man was emerging from the passage-way between the hotel and the Shades just as Bradfield, as if he had no more to do than kill time, came strolling along the High Street.

When he saw Fitch, Bradfield paused in his saunter.

"Well, Tom," he said carelessly, "how are things here this morning after last night's excitement?"

"Quiet enough, considerin'," was the reply. "Miss Betty's taken it worst, but then she was struck on young Winslake. 'Tisn't no laughing matter, far as she's concerned. 'As 'e bin up afore the beak yet?"

Bradfield avoided an answer by asking:

"Tell me, Tom, were you here at seven o'clock this morning?"

Fitch nodded.

"I was rubbin' up the front brasswork. The guv'nor must 'ave it lookin' like a new penny. Very fussy, the guv'nor is. Sometimes I'd rather be back in the Raf. I'd got the porch light on, so as to see what I was doin'."

"I'm trying to find out something about a large car— probably green—that was in these parts between seven and seven fifteen. Did you see anything of it, Tom?"

"Ford V8, was it?"

Bradfield's hopes rose; his luck seemed to be in that morning. Fitch went on:

"There was a Ford V8 come along 'bout seven. I won't say it was green, 'cause it wasn't daylight then, but I'd know the lines of a V8 anywhere. It was runnin' with only one 'eadlight."

"Do you remember which one?"

"The near-side."

"Which way was it going?"

"It was coming away from the Centre."

Fitch jerked his thumb westward. Beyond the Centre, on the main road to the west, lay Mickleham village.

"Did it stop anywhere, or carry straight on?"

"It didn't go right down the High Street. It turned into Wrythe Street and that's the last I seen of it."

Bradfield gave himself time to ponder on this by pulling out his cigarette packet. It has already been mentioned that Wrythe Street was a turning out of the High Street on the same side as the Blue Boar and approximately half-way between that hostelry and the police station, which was on the other side of the road. The Grand Theatre was on the farther—that is, the eastern—corner of Wrythe Street. It seemed to Bradfield that it would have been quite simple for the V8 to have been brought to a stop as soon as it had turned into Wrythe Street; for the young man in Stanley Dilks's peaked cap to have slipped out of it with the breakfast tray without attracting attention; and for the car then to have continued along Wrythe Street, taken the first turning to the right into Horwell Street, then again to the right into Friar Lane, and so back to the High Street, not fifty yards east of the police station. The tray-carrier, his task accomplished, could have run up the road from the police station to the waiting car and been off and away in a matter of seconds.

"Did you see anyone come out of Wrythe Street just afterwards, Tom? A fellow with a tray of grub—one of Toni's boys?"

The potman shook his head.

"I only seen the car—and I wouldn't 'ave took much notice of that if 'e 'adn't been drivin' with only one 'ead-light. 'Why only one 'eadlight?' I says to meself, 'and if it comes to that, why any 'eadlights at all?' Just the sidelights would 'ave been enough for goin' through the town."

"Did you notice who was in the car?"

"No. The light was a bit of a dazzler and by the time I'd stopped blinkin', the car'd swung into Wrythe Street."

Which seemed, thought Bradfield, to be the answer to Fitch's question. The glaring headlight would distract attention from the car and its occupants.

"You didn't see anything at all of a boy in one of Toni's caps, either with or without a tray?"

"Not a thing."

"Did you notice anybody come out of the police station and run off down the road?"

Tom Fitch grinned broadly.

"You got some funny questions this mornin', ain't you? Somebody poisoned old Cart'orse?"

Bradfield smiled and was just going to say that Superintendent Kingsley was still in the best of health, when there was an interruption.

A voice said: "Ah!"

They both glanced round, to see Mr. Zephaniah Plumstead breathlessly bearing down upon them from the other side of the High Street. There was an expression that was a mixture of horror and incredulity on his red and chubby face.

"I cannot believe it, Sergeant!" he exclaimed before he had come to a stop. "I simply cannot believe it! I was just on my way to the police station to obtain an official denial. *You* can doubtless set my mind at rest. Tell me, I beg of you: was poor young Douglas Winslake poisoned in his cell this morning?"

"Where did you hear that, sir?" Bradfield asked.

The little man stamped his spatted foot.

"No matter where I heard it. Is this terrible report correct or is it a monstrous—ah—fabrication?"

Bradfield did not quite know how to deal with this. They were by no means alone in the High Street, for the business and shopping tasks were well under way, and Mr. Plumstead's loud, excited questions were attracting attention. A couple of men, three women and half a dozen boys began to form an embarrassing crowd.

"I suggest, sir," he said calmly, as if Mr. Plumstead had inquired about a lost umbrella, "that you ask at the police station. Perhaps they can help you."

He nodded to Fitch, stuck his hands in his raincoat pockets and wandered off towards the Grand Theatre. Mr. Plumstead watched him go, then turned back to Fitch.

"What an extremely off-hand young man!" he complained. "You were talking with him. What did he say?"

Fitch looked down at his questioner.

"'E was just tellin' me that 'e fancied Ocean Queen for the 2.30," he said. "Any ideas on the subject yourself, sir?"

This raised a laugh among the loiterers. Then one of them—a seedy, rat-faced little man with a miserable mongrel on a lead, and a string-bag full of vegetables in the other hand—said importantly:

"Winslake's been done in all right. Don't you worry about that. Put cyanide in his porridge, someone did, and before they could get the doctor round, Winslake had had it."

A woman said: "The p'lice was in Toni's first thing asking questions. I always said 'e was a Fascist."

"Let's go'n break 'is windows," one of the boys suggested eagerly.

"None er that, Elbert," replied the woman, "or I'll tell yer dad."

Mr. Plumstead said to nobody in particular:

"I cannot find words to express myself."

"Makes a nice change," grunted Tom Fitch, as he turned abruptly and left them to it.

★ ★ ★

During the enactment of this scene outside the Blue Boar on that miserable January morning, another discussion was in progress in the sitting-room at the rear of the building. As with all the other licensed premises in Lulverton, the Blue Boar opened its doors to the public at 11 a.m., and it still wanted ten minutes of that time. Those taking part in this discussion were Pop Collins, his stout, sunny-tempered helpmate, their two children, Bob and Betty, and Bob's wife, Mary. The contestants—for it was more of an altercation than a friendly family chat—were unequally matched. Ranged on one side were Pop, his son and his daughter-in-law; on the other, Mrs. Collins and Betty. The debate had been going on for some time and the subject was Douglas Winslake.

"But he's always so polite and nicely spoken," said Mrs. Collins, who was sitting in the high wooden armchair that she preferred to the low settee and easy-chairs in the cosy room.

"That cuts no ice with me, Mother," retorted her spouse, who was standing with his back to the fire with his hands tucked under his jacket and clasped together at the back, revealing an abundant expanse of pocketed, pearl-buttoned cardigan, and a handsome double-albert watch-chain with a crop of little medals and other knick-knacks pendant from it. "It doesn't make him a better husband for our girl. Fine words" his roving glances defied any of his family to contradict him—"butter no parsnips."

"But I love him!" whimpered poor Betty, who was crouched at one end of the settee, as far as she could get from her sister-in-law, who shared it with her.

Her father jerked the mouthpiece of his pipe in her direction.

"Now look here, Betty," he said. "You're—what? Just turned twenty. All you know about love, you've got from films and rubbishy books. And what happens? The first good-looking young chap who comes in for a pint, you start getting sentimental about. Calf-love—that's all it is. Young people of your age—boys and girls alike—always have half a dozen affairs before they get married. It's not natural otherwise."

"Dad," said his wife reproachfully, "you never told me. You always said I was the first and only girl in your life, didn't you?"

Mr. Collins relighted his pipe and puffed out a defensive cloud.

"We won't go into that now," he announced. "Let's stick to the point. Trouble with you women is, you can't see the wood for the trees. It's Betty's job to serve customers with drinks, not give 'em sheep's eyes."

"I didn't want to," said Betty in a tearful little voice. "You know I didn't want to go behind the bar. You know I wanted to take up music and you wouldn't let me!"

"Music!" scoffed Pop. "Teaching kids their five-finger exercises. No life for any girl of mine. You've got good hours, good food and a roof over your head. What more do you want?"

Young Bob had been standing at the window, looking out into the yard. Now he turned to say:

"Winslake's a wrong 'un. What could he give you if you married him? Would you both live on his mother? He hasn't got a penny to bless himself with."

"He takes lovely photos," said Mrs. Collins.

"Maybe," answered her son, "but how many does he sell? There's too many photographers in Lulverton already—Mackeast's, Thakerson's, Bellpark Studios—"

"All right Bob," said Mr. Collins. "That's enough to go on with. My point is that whether or not Winslake'll make a success of it, he's not the man I want for Betty. Let her wait a bit. There's better fish in the sea"—again the challenging glance— "than ever came out of it."

"I think you're all being horrible!" wailed Betty.

"Not all of us, dear," her mother assured her. "I think that once Douglas can settle down—"

"Settle *down?*" said Bob from the window. "He can't even settle *up*. He's been chucked out of Toni's for having meals on the slate and then trying to dodge paying. He's lost money to

Jimmy Hooker on the nags and can't pay that either. And now he goes and gets himself in jug for smashing up our pub."

"Bob," warned his mother, "you know Dad doesn't like it called a pub. It's the Blue Boar Hotel and it's got a history, dear."

"Nothing to the history it'll get now there's been a murder in it," said Bob, and turned back to look out of me window again.

Mary Collins had taken little part in the conversation. Now she said, as if apropos of nothing:

"That Mr. Goodwin's ever so nice, isn't he?"

"He's a pig!" said Betty with decision.

"That's enough of that, young lady," her father reproved her sharply. "Mr. Goodwin's a real gentleman and I'll not stand you calling him names. If it hadn't been for him and the likes of him, we shouldn't be here now."

"What have you got against him?" Mary asked from the other end of the settee. "Why don't you like him?"

"Because I don't. That's why."

Her brother said without taking his eyes off the yard:

"She doesn't like him because he doesn't like Winslake. And it's easy to see why he doesn't: Bill Goodwin's a man and Winslake's a worm."

In one swift movement Betty was on her feet.

"You horrid beast! I'm not going to listen to any more!"

She turned and made for the door. Just as her hand was on the knob, Bob said:

"Before you go, d'you mind if I ask you a question? ... Have you ever heard of Phyllis Wildgoose?"

"Why?"

"I can tell you something interesting about her."

"Well, I don't want to hear it."

In spite of which statement she released the door-knob and took a step back into the room.

"Last year," Bob told her coolly, "Winslake was engaged to Phyllis Wildgoose."

"That's not true!"

"It *is*, you know. It was broken off in September—and do you know why?"

"Whatever you say, I shan't believe it. You're trying to turn me against Douglas."

"They both belonged to the Wilmshurst Tennis Club. There was a flannel dance there one Saturday evening. Winslake got there two hours late and as tight as an owl. The girl tried to get him to go home, but he wouldn't. He insisted on dancing with her and finished up flat on the deck, too sloshed to do anything but be sick."

"You've been drunk at dances!" said Betty with spirit.

"He never has," retorted Mary in her man's defence.

"We won't argue about that," Bob said without heat. "You haven't had the whole story yet. Winslake never had a sou. When he got engaged to Phyllis Wildgoose he couldn't afford to buy the ring. Phyllis gave him the money."

"What about it? Even if you're telling the truth, she's not the first girl——"

"Wait a minute, Bets. The engagement was going to be formally announced at the dance. Phyllis chose the ring on the Friday, and on the Saturday morning she drew the money out of her savings bank account and gave it to Winslake, so he could go and buy the ring. D'you know what he did?"

Betty did not move. Her hands were clenched at her sides.

"Then I'll tell you," Bob went on. "He ran through the lot. In twelve hours or less it was gone—every penny. Part of it went on booze——"

"Bob," said his mother, "dad doesn't like that word."

"Strong drink, then. And the rest of it he parted with to creditors who saw he was flush and prised it out of him while they'd got the chance. That's your Douglas Winslake. A really nice fellow."

"I don't believe it," said Betty in a very small voice.

"Ask any member of the Wilmshurst. They'll all tell you the same thing. Phyllis never explained why she broke off the engagement and she didn't say a word in public afterwards about the ring, but the story got round. Winslake helped by telling everybody, without being asked, that he had his pocket picked before he could get to the jewellers." Bob looked rather troubled as he added: "I wouldn't have said anything about this, Bets, but I don't want you to get mixed up with that fellow. None of us do."

Betty stood biting her lip. Then she began to cry.

Mrs. Collins rose from her chair.

"There, there," she said as Betty ran to her for comfort.

Pop pulled his gold watch from the pocket of his cardigan.

"Two minutes to," he said briskly, as if nothing had happened. "Bob and Mary, you take the Shades. Betty, you take the hotel bar."

"But, Dad," protested Mrs. Collins, "Betty's not—"

"Oh, yes, she is. If she stops snivelling, she'll be all right. It's time she learnt that this is a hotel, not a ..."

He sought in his mind for an appropriate establishment, failed to find one, and said instead: "Where's Fitch?"

Bob was still at the window.

"He's just come round into the yard," he said.

"Then tell him to get ready to open up."

Mrs. Collins shepherded Betty out of the room. Mary followed them. Bob unlatched the casement, pushed open the window and called out to Fitch:

"Tom, it's just on opening time."

"Very good, Mister Bob." He came to the window and asked in an undertone: "'Ave you 'eard the latest?"

Bob listened to what he had to say, then turned back towards his father.

"Dad, Winslake's dead. Tom's heard that he's been poisoned."

Mr. Collins took this news with composure.

"That'll keep *him* out of the family," was all he said, and his fingers strayed to the ring on his other hand.

XIII.

A Pair of White Rabbits

THE box office of the Grand Theatre was open, but before he went in Bradfield made a reconnaissance of the immediate neighborhood. The entrance to the theatre was across the corner, with curved stone steps leading up into the *foyer*. The only ground-floor opening in the wall of the building facing Wrythe Street was the stage door, which was near the back of the theatre. The other side of Wrythe Street was flanked by the wall of a butcher's shop. This had no break in it between the High Street and the wooden gates leading into the back yard. Wrythe Street was narrow and there was no pavement on either side, but there was enough room for the door of even a large car to be opened for a passenger to alight. The chance of this being observed, especially during the dark hours, was reduced to a minimum by the high walls on either side.

Trying not to behave too conspicuously, Bradfield examined the roadway. He saw nothing of interest there and, with the thought that the malefactors might have had the decency to leave a broken saucer or a piece of fried liver by way of a clue for a hard-working C.I.D. man, he went on down Wrythe Street, along Horwell Street and into Friar Lane. On the High Street corner of Friar Lane, with its entrance in the side street, was a newsagent's shop.

When he pushed open the door it rang a bell which brought out of the back parlour a long tobacco-stained moustache with a tall, stooping bald-headed man bringing up the rear.

"Good morning," smiled Bradfield. "A *Telegraph*, please."

The moustache looked astonished at this temerity.

"No morning papers left."

"Yes, I suppose it's rather late for them. Have you twenty Gold Flake, please?"

"Not a cigarette in the place," said the moustache with immense relish. "No cigarettes of any kind. And it's going to get worse."

Bradfield refrained from making the obvious remark and said in the place of it:

"What time do you open in the mornings?"

"No good coming. Only regulars served—and not always them. Ices every third Tuesday."

"Thanks. I'll remember that. Nothing like an ice every third Tuesday. Were you open at seven o'clock this morning?"

"Half-past six."

"Do you get much traffic coming past here into the High Street?"

The moustache looked baffled. Bradfield decided that it would be better to let it into his confidence.

"I'm a police officer," he explained. "We're trying to trace a car—a large green Ford V8. It was seen in Lulverton soon after seven o'clock this morning—perhaps a minute or two before the hour—and I believe it came along Friar Lane and turned into the High Street. Did you notice it at all?"

"No. I was in the shop getting the papers ready for the boy to deliver, but it was dark outside and I didn't see anything."

Bradfield was just going to murmur his thanks and leave the shop when the moustache went on:

"Tell you what, though. A customer came in soon after seven. Very angry he was. He said he'd nearly got run over."

"That's interesting. Did he give you any details?"

"He'd come along the High Street and as he stepped off the pavement to walk across to my shop a car came out of Friar Lane and just missed knocking him down."

"Was this customer known to you?"

"He's the commissionaire at the Grand. Can't call his name to mind. Newman or something."

"Did he describe the car?"

The moustache permitted itself a quiver of amusement.

"Yes, very fluently—and the driver as well. But it wouldn't be much help to you. Wait a minute. He did say one thing—that there was only one headlamp working. He said he thought the driver must have been finding his way home after an all-night drinking party."

"Good. That's very helpful."

It looked as if his theory had been correct. The car had not continued along Wrythe Street on some lawful mission in the northern part of the town, but had been driven back into the High Street by the quickest route. He now added:

"I'll slip along to the Grand and have a word or two with the commissionaire. Many thanks."

He smiled and moved towards the door.

"Just a minute."

With the deftness that comes of long practice, a packet of Gold Flake was produced from under the counter.

"Twenty enough?" asked the moustache.

When he left the shop Bradfield glanced at the fascia and gave an approving grunt. Perkins seemed a very nice name for a moustache.

★ ★ ★

He inquired for the manager at the box office of the Grand Theatre and in a few moments was shown into Goodwin's little office off the *foyer.*

"Well, Peter," smiled Goodwin after he had supplied his visitor with a chair and a cigarette, "how goes the case?"

"No official statement yet," Bradfield smiled back.

"Plenty of unofficial ones, though! Have you heard the fantastic story going round that Douglas Winslake was poisoned in the hoosegow this morning? The yarns that get started!"

"This one's true enough, Bill."

Goodwin looked incredulous.

146

"No! You're joking!"

"I wish I was. Keep it to yourself, but somebody sent breakfast in to him. There was cyanide in the porridge and it killed him. Things have been pretty hectic since. Hooker wasn't our fault, but Winslake ..."

He shrugged his shoulders instead of finishing the sentence. Goodwin played with his handlebar moustache. He said at length:

"Not too jolly. Are the two affairs linked, do you imagine?"

"They must be, Bill. Hooker and Winslake were together last night. Our view is—this is off the record, Bill—our own view is that Winslake was mixed up in something shady and, after he'd had the odd tongue loosener, was b.f. enough to tell Hooker all about it. Then Winslake's buddies got to hear of this and wasted no time in shutting Hooker's mouth; and did the same this morning to Winslake, so that he shouldn't turn King's evidence to save his skin over the Hooker murder. What time do your staff get here in the mornings, Bill?"

"Depends who they are. The first to come are the women cleaners. They turn up at about eight."

"Who's the caretaker?"

"In the plural: old Charley Newmarch and his missis. Been here for years, ever since Marie Lloyd and Chevalier used to play here. Charley was in the Boer War the last really serious scrap there was, according to him. He acts as commissionaire and shouts the odds in the *foyer*. What's this leading up to, Peter? You intrigue me."

"Can you have the Newmarches fetched, Bill? I'd like to shoot a few questions at them."

Goodwin got up and left the room. When he came back he said:

"I've sent for them. Is this to do with Hooker and Winslake? Maybe I'm dull, but I can't see the connection."

"You will soon," Bradfield promised him.

Within a few minutes there was a knock on the door and, at Goodwin's invitation, an old couple came into the office. Charley Newmarch, for all his sixty-eight years, still carried himself like the sergeant-major he had once been. He was tall, with a large head thinly thatched with hair, and a grey moustache twisted into two fierce points that must, in their black prime, have put terror into the hearts of many besides the Queen's enemies. Mrs. Newmarch was a shy little grey wisp by the side of her burly husband.

Bill Goodwin said with an encouraging smile:

"Sorry to bring you all the way down, but there's a little matter that's cropped up." He waved his artificial hand towards Bradfield. "This is a police officer, and he wants to ask you a few questions." He had risen to his feet. "Mrs. Newmarch, please have this chair."

"There are two points," Bradfield explained. "The first one concerns *you,* Mr. Newmarch. I've been given to understand by. Mr. Perkins, the tobacconist on the corner of Friar Lane, that you called in there this morning. That was so, wasn't it?"

"Yessir," said old Charley smartly. "Ounce of Nosegay Special."

"And when you were about to cross Friar Lane to go into the shop you narrowly escaped being run over by a car?"

"Quite right, sir."

"I'm glad it didn't hit you, Mr. Newmarch. Now, can you tell me anything about this car?"

"It was a big one. Took up most of the lane. And one of the 'eadlights wasn't on parade."

"Did you notice the make or number?"

"'Fraid not, sir. I was too confused, as you might say. It only missed me by inches."

"Who was driving it—a man or a woman?"

"A man, sir."

"Can you describe him?"

"No, sir—only that 'e was wearing a cloth cap with the peak pulled well down, and the collar of 'is overcoat was turned up."

"Would you recognize him again?"

"I didn't catch sight of 'is face, sir. It all 'appened too quick to notice much."

"Did he shout at you?"

"No, sir, but I might've said a thing or two myself if 'e'd stopped long enough."

"Which way did the car turn, Mr. Newmarch?"

"Towards the Centre."

"Did it stop farther up the High Street or did it go straight on?"

"I couldn't say, sir. I didn't wait to see."

"And when you came out of Mr. Perkins's shop you returned here?"

Charley nodded.

"Was there any sign of the car in the High Street?"

"None, sir. There wasn't any cars at all, far as I can remember."

"How long were you in the shop?"

"Five or six minutes. Me and Mr. Perkins usually 'ave a little chinwag when I go in, and this morning was no exception."

"Thank you, Mr. Newmarch. Now perhaps your wife can help us with my next question. We believe that this car came into Lulverton from the direction of Mickleham, and when it reached the corner of Wrythe Street it turned down it and stopped alongside this building for somebody to get out. Did either of you see anything of this?"

The inquiry drew a blank.

"Was there anyone else in the theatre at that time who might help us? It was just about seven o'clock."

Mrs. Newmarch answered timidly: "There was Mr. Roberts, sir."

"The Great Desro, eh? What on earth was he doing here at that hour in the morning?"

"'E came to feed the rabbits, sir."

Goodwin put in: "Roberts uses a couple of white rabbits for one of his tricks."

"Mr. Roberts won't let anyone else see to them, except 'is daughter," explained Charley. "We offered to give them their food while they was 'ere this week, but Mr. Roberts wouldn't 'ear of it. 'E mixes the food 'imself and warms it up over a gas-ring backstage."

Bradfield said casually: "It's not of any great importance, but what time did Mr. Roberts get here this morning?"

"'Bout quarter to seven, sir," replied Charley. "I let 'im in myself through the stage door. 'E 'ad the middlings and cabbage leaves and stuff in a dixie."

"Did you watch him preparing it?"

"No, sir. I went back upstairs."

"And what time did he leave?"

"Just turned quarter-past seven, at a rough guess, sir. 'E was coming out of the stage door with the empty dixie—or I s'pose it was empty, though I didn't see in because the lid was on. 'E was just off back to 'is hotel to get 'is own breakfast. I remember 'im passing the remark that all good soldiers feed their animals first. I popped in to 'ave a look at the rabbits, sir, and they was tucking in with a will."

Bradfield said with a smile: "Thank you, both of you. I think that's the lot for the moment."

At a word from Goodwin, Charley and his wife left the room. When the door had closed behind them Bradfield said:

"Bill—in confidence—what do you know about this Roberts fellow?"

"We engaged him for a week. As conjurors go, he's not in the top class. He does the sort of stuff that goes down well at children's Christmas parties. The only really clever trick he does is with those two rabbits. I must confess that I can't see how it's done. At the end of his turn he gives an exhibition of clairvoyance, which, of course, is a fiddle."

"Newmarch spoke of a daughter."

"Yes. Joy Roberts. Attractive kid of seventeen or so. She helps him with the clairvoyant stuff. You know the sort of thing? She goes down into the audience and collects things from them on a tray. Roberts is blindfolded, and he guesses what the articles are and describes the people they belong to. Joy's very smart at it. They must have rehearsed it for weeks. She gives Roberts the tip by the way in which she phrases her questions. For instance, 'What have I got in my hand? ' tells him that it's a man's wrist-watch; and 'What am I now holding up?' means that it's an elephant."

It was the first incongruous thing that came into Bill Goodwin's head, yet subsequent events were to make his choice of an elephant almost prophetic.

"Where are they staying?" Bradfield asked.

"At the Bunch of Grapes. It's a popular place with pros and commercials. Not so expensive as the Blue Boar."

He took a cigarette from the yellow packet that Bradfield held out to him. When they had lighted up, he said:

"I suppose you know that Roberts is Mrs. Hooker's brother?"

★ ★ ★

With clenched hands pressed dramatically to his temples, Peter Bradfield demanded:

"Why doesn't somebody tell us these things?"

"Good Lord! Didn't you know? I thought no secret was hidden from you professional hawkshaws."

"Why the devil didn't the idiot mention it when we questioned him last night?"

"Probably because you didn't take the precaution of asking him. I didn't know myself then. He told me after we'd been dismissed from the Blue Boar. He didn't make any bones about it, but I imagine he's not very proud of that branch of the family. Not that he's a snob. Roberts senior was a navvy.

He worked on the Grand Union Canal. The children were brought up in Islington. Roberts improved himself, but the sister—Clarice he called her—got busy with the gin bottle almost before she'd gone into long frocks, and finally ran off with Jimmy Hooker, who she'd met in a pub. Hooker had Romany blood in him, but he was a Londoner by birth."

"But," said Bradfield, "Hooker and Roberts were in the Blue Boar at the same time, shoulder to shoulder almost. Didn't they recognize each other?"

"Oh, yes, but they're not on speaking terms. I realized afterwards that it was Roberts that Hooker was getting at in his remarks about some people becoming too big for their boots. When he opened his heart to me, Roberts said that if he'd known Hooker was in there, wild horses wouldn't have dragged him in."

"Hooker was standing at the bar when you and Roberts came in. Didn't Roberts see him?"

"Apparently not. Hooker was the first to do any identifying. He started making funny remarks. At the time I thought they were against me for refusing to take wine with him."

"Was it you or Roberts who suggested you should pop along to the Blue Boar for a quick one?"

"Roberts. Frankly, I'm not particularly struck on the fellow, but he seemed so damned lonely that the big, generous heart of William Frederick Goodwin, bachelor of this parish, took pity on him. I'm sorry it did—otherwise I might have kept out of this frolic."

Bradfield stood up and buttoned his raincoat.

Thanks, Bill. I think the Skip will want a little chat with the Great Desro."

"Feel in the mood for a pint, Peter? When you called, I was just thinking of turning my steps in the direction of the Blue Boar. I like the beer there."

"Is that the only attraction?" Bradfield asked innocently.

Bill Goodwin took his overcoat down from a peg.

"How very observant you are," he said, as Bradfield helped him into it.

★ ★ ★

There were no other customers in the hotel bar when they went in, and Olive Dove was not yet on duty in the front lounge. Betty Collins, still unaware of Douglas; Winslake's death, was sitting behind the counter listlessly obeying her father's request of half an hour before to "get that thing polished up," the thing in question being the brass elephant that young Bob had brought home from India. She laid aside the cloth when she saw them walking across the lounge.

"Nothing about what I've just told you, Bill," warned Bradfield as they neared the door into the bar.

"What do you take me for?" muttered Goodwin in reply, then went on in his normal hearty voice as they stepped up to the counter: "Morning, Betty. Two pints of rough, please."

The colour had risen in her cheeks.

"We don't sell rough," she said distantly. "If you want draught beer, there's bitter, mild ale or Burton." Goodwin took the rebuke in good part. After asking Bradfield what he would like to drink, he ordered two pints of mild and bitter. She drew them without a word and pushed the tankards across the counter, one towards Bradfield with a sweet smile, and the other towards Goodwin with the smile switched off. Then she took up the polishing cloth again and resumed work on Jumbo.

Bradfield and Goodwin stood drinking their beer and talking about anything except Winslake and Hooker. The tankards had been refilled and Bradfield had just said that he must knock this one back quickly because there was work to be done, when the vestibule door leading in from the street was pushed open with unecessary violence. All three looked to see who was coming in so noisily.

153

To Betty and Goodwin it was a stranger, but Bradfield recognized Mrs. Hooker. She was still dressed in her leopard-skin coat and scarlet bandeau. From her appearance and from the top-heavy fashion in which she made her approach, he surmised that she had wasted no time in spending a substantial part of her ten-pound windfall on gin.

She came through the doorway into the hotel bar and took up a position against the counter just where her late husband had stood before he fell to the floor. Not anxious to get involved with her, Bradfield had edged Bill Goodwin nearer to the fireplace.

"Give us a large gin, love," said Mrs. Hooker with a slur in her shrill voice.

Betty complied with this request, her every movement eloquent of disapproval.

"Nasty, dull day agine," Mrs. Hooker went on chattily.

Without expressing any opinion about the weather, Betty put the gin glass on the counter, placed a jug of water beside it, reinstated the Indian elephant in its position on the shelf above the till, and picked up a book. Clarice Hooker disregarded the water-jug and took a sip at the neat gin. Betty was apparently absorbed in her book and her manner had not been encouraging, but the woman had reached the stage when she had to talk to somebody.

"What's the book, dearie?" she asked. "A nice love tile?"

Betty glanced up from the page and said "No" very clearly.

A dreamy look came into Mrs. Hooker's pale damp eyes.

"I like a nice love tile. Kisses and weddin' bells and 'appy ever after." She fumbled in her bag and produced a pocket handkerchief that had been clean when it was bought. With this she dabbed her eyes as she added: "It's all so lovely." This emotion did not last long. She put the handkerchief away and said: "Was it in this bar that my ole man copped it?"

By Bradfield's side, Bill Goodwin drew a sharp breath. Betty looked up again from her book, interested in spite of herself.

"Who do you mean?" she asked.

"Mr. James 'Ooker, my beloved 'usband and may 'is soul rest in peace."

The effect of this pious sentiment was marred by the alcoholic cackle of laughter with which the bereaved widow followed it. Betty looked apprehensive as she answered:

"Yes, it was in here. He was standing just where you are now."

"Was 'e though? Well, a bar's as good a place as any for snuffin' it in."

She looked around her with eyes that had long been in need of spectacles, and noticed Bradfield for the first time.

"Well!" she said with jarring good fellowship. "If it isn't Pugnose 'isself! What'll yer drink—and yer pal? I've still got some er that ten quid left."

"Not for me, thank you," Bradfield replied with a polite smile. "I've got to be off."

Mrs. Hooker tossed her head.

"'Ave it yer own way," she said in a tone that was intended to convey ladylike indifference. "All the sime ter me, *I'm* sure. Anyone'd think yer was frightened er bein' poisoned."

Bradfield drained his tankard and stepped across to place it on the counter.

"To be perfectly frank with you, madam," he said, "I am."

Her eyes narrowed and with hands on her hips she stuck out her head towards him.

"Meanin' what? That I'm a—Crippen? You keep a civil tongue in yer 'ead, Pugnose, or I'll 'ave the lore on yer!"

"Please don't get so excited, Mrs. Hooker," he said easily. "I'm not suggesting anything like that. All I meant was that poisoning can become a habit and that none of us will be easy in our minds until we've found out who gave cyanide to your husband."

She was not to be mollified.

"Smooth talk—that's all that is."

"Any of us may be next. It might be me or you; it might even be your brother."

Mrs. Hooker was taken off her guard.

"You keep my brother out er this! 'E don't know nothink about the murder, see? So don't try and pin anythink on 'im."

"I'm not. I was only suggesting—"

"Then you keep yer suggestions ter yerself, Pugnose!"

She drew her leopard-skin coat around her and, with a ridiculous assumption of offended dignity, left the hotel bar with her high heels wobbling dangerously. They waited in silence until the lobby door had slammed behind her, then Bill Goodwin gave a deep sigh of relief.

"'She was a phantom of delight,'" he murmured, "'when first she gleamed upon my sight ...'"

"'A lovely apparition sent,' capped Bradfield, "'to be a moment's ornament.'"

Goodwin looked at him with a frown of disapproval.

"Only amateur sleuths are allowed to quote the classics. You should remember that."

"I'll try not to let it occur again, sir," replied Bradfield humbly. "I must now double away smartly, as our Army P.T. instructor used to say."

He raised his hat to Betty, made a courtly bow, and left them alone together. There was silence in the hotel bar for a full minute. Bill sipped the remains of his pint, while Betty sat engrossed, one might have thought, in her book.

"Betty," said Bill at last.

No answer.

"Betty, I'm talking to you."

She looked up and asked whether he needed any more beer.

"No, Betty. I want to ask you a question. Why have you got so confoundedly stand-offish with me?"

"I treat you the same as all the other customers."

"Oh, no, you don't! You turn up that little nose of yours, as if I was something you'd trodden in."

"I don't. It must be your imagination."

"What have I done—or not done? You used not to behave like this. I don't think I deserve it, you know. I've never made passes, or got squiffy and tried to wreck the joint."

"Don't say that!" she flared at him. "I know who you're talking about and you can stop it!"

"That was a slip, Betty. I'm sorry. I only meant it in general terms, just to show that I'm always the perfect little gent. You're so darned cold and unfriendly. Tell me where I've gone off the rails, won't you?"

She sat looking down at her book and playing with a page with restless fingers.

"Won't you tell me, Betty?" he said after a while.

She stayed silent.

"Is it the old moustachio? It'll be a shocking sacrifice, but I'll prune it just to please you."

She shook her head.

"Is it the scars of battle?" He slightly raised the hand with the leather glove on it. "Don't mind saying if it is."

Betty shot him a glance of distress.

"No, no! That would be beastly. You mustn't think—"

"Then what is it, Betty?"

She dropped her head again and avoided his eyes as she said: "Phyllis Wildgoose."

He looked puzzled. "Phyllis Wildgoose? What's she got to do with it?"

"She's a friend of yours, isn't she?"

"Well, she belongs to the Wilmshurst. I've played a few sets with her, but that's as far as it goes. I'm not much of a partner, with only one arm. You're not trying to say that she and I— why, that's just damned silly! Where did you get hold of this yarn?"

"Somebody told me."

"Who was it? ... Come on, let's have it! Was it Winslake?"

"He said you were running after her."

"Of all the infernal liars! And you believed him. That's the worst part of it. Why didn't you give me a chance to deny it?"

Betty did not reply.

"Dammit!" he exploded. "I don't like to speak ill of the dead, but that young—"

He bit on the words. Betty drew a frightened breath. "What do you mean?" she asked quickly. "Has anything happened to him?"

Bill Goodwin looked down at her. There was something like pity in his eyes.

"I'm afraid it has," he told her quietly. "If you want a friend, my dear, you know where to come."

He turned and left her without looking back.

XIV.

Bull In a China Shop

SERGEANT PETERS, the finger-print expert, bad been summoned from the headquarters of the Downshire County Constabulary at Whitchester, and had carried out a detailed examination of the tray and breakfast things. He was now closeted with Inspector Charlton in the Inspector's room.

"There are ten articles, sir," Peters explained. "The tray, two plates, two covers, a knife and fork, a cup without a saucer, and two spoons—one for the porridge and the other for the coffee. I've taken the dabs of Constable Marryat and Winslake, the only two people in the station who handled the stuff. It was Marryat who took the tray into the cell. His prints were on it, but not Winslake's. Sergeant Harrison says the boy who delivered the tray was wearing gloves. There were no prints on the covers. Harrison handled them, but only by the little wooden knobs, which didn't yield anything clear enough to be of much use. Winslake's prints were on both plates. Marryat says Winslake took the porridge plate off the tray, but after a couple of spoonfuls of the stuff, told Marryat he didn't like the taste of it and pushed it away. He reached for the other plate and it was just as he was getting busy with his knife and fork on the liver that the poison—"

Charlton gave an impatient gesture.

"I know all this, Peters. I've already heard Marryat's story. What I'm anxious to know is whether you found any prints that may help us."

Sergeant Peters was young and enthusiastic. He now looked pained.

"I was trying to muster the facts in their right sequence, sir," he said in an injured tone.

Charlton smiled an apology.

"Sorry, Peters. Don't take it to heart. I've had rather a worrying time this morning."

Thus soothed, Sergeant Peters said:

"O.K., sir. I'd say that all the stuff was wiped with a cloth before it was brought in here, but there was one little bit they missed. It was under the edge of the porridge plate—prints of two different fingers about three inches apart. From their position, I'd say they were the first and second fingers of a right hand. The thumbprint, which would have come somewhere between them on the top of the plate as it was lifted up, wasn't there. Wiped off, I suppose."

The Inspector was looking pleased.

"Now we're getting somewhere, Peters! Have you taken the usual steps?"

"Yes, sir. I've photographed them and sent the prints up to the Yard for identification. A man's already on the train with them. With any luck the report from the C.R.O.* will be back today."

"Nice work. Anything else?"

"No, sir."

"Then back to your lair in darkest Whitchester. How's the wife?"

"Next Wednesday."

"Don't forget to call him Harry, after me."

"Can't do that, sir. The wife's mother says it's going to be a girl."

★ ★ ★

A few minutes after Sergeant Peters had left Charlton's room, Bradfield strolled in. With a deft flick of his wrist, he sent his hat flying through the air on to a peg of the stand in the corner, and dropped into the chair on the other side of the desk at

---

* Criminal Record Office.

which sat his chief deep in thought, doodling with a pencil on his blotting-pad. Though there was a considerable disparity in their ages and Charlton was the senior officer, there was little formality between these two, who had not only worked on so many cases together, but were also very good friends.

Charlton put the finishing touches to a cubist design and looked up.

"Well, Peter. What news?"

Bradfield gave him a concise report on his activities since they had parted company earlier in the morning. Charlton listened without interruption until the end. Then he said:

"Did old Plumstead follow your suggestion and come along here to ask about Winslake?"

"Apparently not. I spoke to Harrison about it just now. He said Mr. Zephaniah P. had not been in. He probably learnt all he wanted from the crowd that gathered. The Winslake poisoning seems to be common knowledge already."

"You can't keep anything dark in Lulverton."

He went into another brown study and it was nearly a minute before he shifted restlessly in his chair and murmured more to himself than to his companion.

"No, it's impossible."

In a brisker tone he went on:

"Let's think about the Great Desro, Peter. First, he's the brother of Mrs. Hooker—or is according to Goodwin."

"I don't think there's much doubt about it. In the Blue Boar just now I managed to provoke her. She didn't actually admit the relationship, but when I made an oblique reference to her brother, she was up in arms at once. She protested violently that he knew nothing about the murder—I hadn't suggested he did know anything—and warned us to keep him out of it. She was much more touchy than she need have been—unless she'd a guilty conscience. If I had to choose from Goodwin, Wildgoose and Roberts for the murderer, I'd lay my money on Roberts."

"We'll take it that he's Mrs. Hooker's brother, then. When it comes to conjuring—again according to Goodwin—he's a second-rater. If he's a failure at his job, he's probably hard up. His sister was no better off than he while Hooker was alive, because Hooker kept her short of money and, by carrying them about with him, made certain she didn't lay hands on his savings. There was no love lost between the Hookers, and she's obviously glad he's dead. In fact, she makes so little attempt to seem sorry that it's a point in her favour. We'll assume that Roberts—no. You give me your version, Peter."

"Well, as you say, they both needed cash, and Jimmy Hooker had it in large lumps. For some reason of his own, Jimmy got a supply of cyanide from Winslake—that's if Zeph is to be believed."

"I've seen Mrs. Winslake. She confirms that Winslake told her it was for Hooker, who was going to use it as an insecticide. That sounds highly unlikely. I may be wrong, but I think its only uses in that sphere are for wasps' nests and the killing-bottles used by entomologists. This country is mercifully free from wasps in January, and I can't see Hooker as a bug-hunter. Winslake was probably lying. For the moment, let's take it that he wasn't."

"Mrs. Hooker finds out that Jimmy has a supply of the stuff. Maybe he was going to use it on her. She decides to use it on him. Her brother Des is playing at the Grand this week—"

"A very lucky coincidence."

"She gets in touch with Des, tells him about the money she'll share with him once Jimmy's out of the way and passes him over the bottle of cyanide that Jimmy's left hidden—so he thinks—in a safe place at home. She also tells her brother that Jimmy's favourite haunt is the Blue Boar, and that he's always to be found there between half-past nine and ten."

"Betty Collins told us," Charlton reminded him, "that Hooker was more often in the Shades than in the hotel. But carry on..."

162

"Desro comes off the stage of the Grand after his session of parlour magic—not forgetting the white rabbits. Just in passing, Bill Goodwin says that Desro's trick with the bunnies is the only clever thing he does. Do you think," he added tentatively, "that we should see the show?"

Charlton gravely considered this.

"Yes," he said at last, "it's our duty to go. We could come out before the Eight Lawson Lovelies do their dancing act."

"I shouldn't like to miss that."

"I'll leave it to you, Peter, to get a couple of tickets. Make it the second house tomorrow night. You and I are likely to have important business on hand this evening."

His assistant raised his eyebrows inquiringly, but Charlton did not choose to be more explicit just then. He invited Bradfield to continue.

"Desro," said Bradfield, "invites Bill Goodwin up to the Blue Boar for a drink. The rest is child's play. Des gets as close as he can to Jimmy and takes the first opportunity to put over his last conjuring trick of the day."

"Quite convincing, Peter. And the murder of Winslake?"

"There's one little incident that tends to connect Desro with that. I mean the feeding of the rabbits."

"Yes, an interesting point. I was imagining that Mr. X— or Messrs. X—got the food ready well beforehand—the food for Winslake, that is—and kept it hot in a vacuum container, but it's not impossible that Desro warmed up breakfast for Winslake and his precious rabbits at the same time."

"Have you thought about the breakfast things? It might help a lot if we could find out where they came from."

"They're definitely not from Toni's; and Quentin wouldn't be fool enough to use articles out of his own kitchen. Where's Desro staying?"

"The Bunch of Grapes."

"You'd better go along there and make a check. It doesn't look like hotel stuff to me. Besides, it's all new, not a chip or a scratch or a dent. If the shops hadn't been shut I'd say it was specially bought for the occasion. The missing saucer's a significant detail; saucers are in short supply in the shops. I wonder..."

He reached out his hand for the telephone, which was connected to the internal switchboard downstairs.

"Marryat," he said when the duty man answered, "find out for me, will you, whether there were any reports of housebreaking in the district last night. ... Yes, Whitchester, Paulsfield, Littleworth, Southmouth—anywhere within, say, twenty miles. ... Thanks, Marryat."

He replaced the hand-microphone and said to Bradfield:

"Was old Charley Newmarch around while Desro was getting the rabbits' food ready?"

"No. Charley let Desro in through the stage door at about six forty-five. Desro must be fond of his rabbits to get up at that time in the morning to feed them. Then Charley went back upstairs to his flat, leaving Desro to get on with it. Around seven o'clock Charley went along to buy some tobacco from Mr. Perkins, on the corner of Friar Lane. Charley told me that it was just turned quarter-past seven when he got back. At the stage door he met Desro, who was just off. Charley went to inspect the rabbits and found them enjoying their breakfast."

"So your theory is...?"

Bradfield looked thoughtful.

"The times make it awkward. It looks as if Desro couldn't have been the driver of the V8. But he might have had accomplices. During the night they sneaked Dr. Hope Smith's car. Then they knocked down Stanley Dilks and took his cap, having hired another boy who was prepared to take a bit of risk for a couple of quid. He might not have known that the food was poisoned. They could have told him some yarn to explain the reason for what they wanted him to do. While the accomplice stayed with the boy in the car, Desro was busy getting the breakfast warmed up in the Grand. At seven o'clock or thereabouts the car slipped into Lulverton and pulled up outside the stage door of the Grand. Desro had the tray ready and handed it out to the boy, who took it along to police headquarters. Desro went back into the Grand, and the driver of the car brought it back into the High Street, nearly knocking down Charley Newmarch in the process."

"This is all very ingenious, Peter, but tell me this: why did Desro have to murder Winslake?"

"It wouldn't be difficult to evolve a few theories. Perhaps Winslake saw him slip the cyanide into Jimmy's tankard. Or perhaps he thought that, as the poison had come from Winslake, Winslake would report the matter to us and we'd work back to Desro via Mrs. Hooker. Or perhaps——"

Charlton held up his hand.

"Your imagination's too vivid for a policeman, Peter. You ought to be writing copy for Fiddler's Wonderworking Pick-me-up."

"Send half a crown for a dozen sample capsules," Bradfield added with a smile. "But, you know, I still think Desro's concerned in this. Mrs. Hooker went up in the air like a jet-propelled rocket when I mentioned him casually to see what her reactions would be."

"I'm afraid I can't agree with you over Desro, Peter. Admitted that Mrs. Hooker—and possibly Desro as well will profit out of Hooker's death. In spite of that, I still hold to the opinion that I expressed last night: that Hooker was killed because he'd got hold of some information that would make it uncomfortable for somebody if Hooker passed it on to us. There doesn't seem much doubt that Hooker got this information from Winslake, which gives us a perfect motive for this morning's affair. It was no good silencing Hooker if Winslake lived to tell the tale—as he undoubtedly would have told it, if only to save his own skin."

He lighted a cigarette.

"Coming back to the cyanide," he continued, "I told you just now that Mrs. Winslake agrees that she caught her son transferring some of it to a bottle that had been used for aspirin tablets. I say 'caught' because his manner showed that he was up to something; and I think we can take it that he was lying when he told his mother that Hooker wanted it for killing insects. If Hooker was troubled with fleas or the common simex, he'd be far more likely to buy a shilling packet of D.D.T. from the chemist."

"That doesn't mean that Winslake didn't supply Hooker with cyanide."

"Granted. Hooker may have had some other purpose in mind. Mrs. Hooker fired some rather odd questions at us this morning about the taste and effects of cyanide." He sat thinking for a moment or two. "No, it isn't at all probable. When people are poisoned with cyanide they don't have much opportunity afterwards to discuss their symptoms. Mrs. Hooker must have been imagining things. In any case, Hooker hadn't the makings of a poisoner. He might have cracked her skull with a hatchet when he was in drink, but I can't see him playing the other sly game. My own view is that Winslake didn't tell his mother the truth."

"Maybe not. But why?"

"I can think of two reasons: the first, that he was proposing to commit murder; the second, that he was going to supply the means for somebody else to commit murder. The first fits in very neatly with what happened in the Blue Boar yesterday evening, but doesn't explain this morning's episode. We can dispose entirely of any idea that Winslake smuggled poison into the cell *per anum* or otherwise—and committed suicide. The cyanide was unquestionably in the porridge and Marryat was there as Winslake ate some of it. Besides, if Winslake took his own life, there is no rhyme or reason in the other events this morning. Winslake's breakfast wasn't arranged by anonymous well-wishers. If it was, they went about it in a very peculiar way. The theory we cannot entirely dismiss is that Winslake murdered Hooker. I don't believe he did, but there is plenty of evidence to support it. He was in possession of a supply of cyanide. Hooker was becoming a serious nuisance. Winslake was the only person in the bar last night who was seen by witnesses to put anything into Hooker's tankard of beer. There's not a shred of direct evidence against anybody else. If he'd been charged with the murder, his counsel would have had a hard struggle to convince the jury he didn't do it."

"And the second reason?"

"Taking everything into account, that is the more probable of the two. There are some interesting points about it. If Winslake didn't murder Hooker, we come back once again to my original assumption that they were both killed by one or more other persons to shut their mouths. The need for this was sudden. Winslake was overheard spilling the beans to Hooker, and Hooker had to be put out of the way *pronto*. But surely such an emergency was not foreseen by our naughty friends? They could have had no idea in advance that cyanide would be in sudden demand—not for Hooker, anyway. Yet on the evidence of Mrs. Winslake her surprise visit to her son's studio took place as long ago as last Monday morning. If Winslake was going to hand the poison over to somebody else, that somebody else must have had another purpose for it than the murders of Hooker and Winslake. We can take it that the purpose was criminal and that Winslake knew it. Nothing else would explain his guilty air when his mother walked in. What do you think they needed it for?"

"Not necessarily as a poison, perhaps?" suggested Bradfield.

"I wonder." He took a slip of paper out of his pocket, unfolded it and read out: "Extraction of gold and silver from ores. Electro plating. Heat treatment of steel. Reagent in analytical chemistry. Paper manufacture. Pharmaceutical preparations. Fumigant. Insecticides. Fixative in photography. Process engraving and lithography." He glanced up at Bradfield.

"Take your pick, Peter."

"After you, sir," was the polite reply.

The telephone bell rang. P.C. Marryat was on the line. Charlton listened to him until he finished speaking, then said:

"Good. Get Southmouth again, please, Marryat. I'll hold on." He turned to Bradfield. "There was a shop broken into in Southmouth early this morning. They hullo! Put me through to Inspector Dixon, please... Inspector Dixon?... This is Charlton. ... Fine, thanks. They tell me you had a housebreaking job last night. Can you give me details?... What did they take?... Yes, it does sound rather curious. ... I'm coming in to Southmouth this afternoon. I'll be able to explain why they took those particular things. . . Yes, we had a murder case here last night, and I think the two affairs are linked. Have you got a line on it? ... That's interesting. Was it a saloon?... Thanks very much, Dixon. I'll see you this afternoon. Till then."

He rang off and said to Bradfield with a note of quiet satisfaction in his deep voice:

"You probably got the gist of that, Peter. It means you can cancel your call at the Bunch of Grapes. It was a lock-up hardware shop in the Stoneleigh district. They got in without doing any damage by slipping the catch of a back window. The shopkeeper would probably not have noticed that he'd had visitors if they'd left the place in a tidier condition. The stock was all higgledy-piggledy, as if someone had groped round more or less in the dark. The shopkeeper had left the window-blind pulled down, but they couldn't afford to take the risk and must have worked with a small flash-lamp—and in a hurry. The shopkeeper's made a rough check of his stock and reports the loss of a knife, a fork and a spoon from a cutlery display case in the window. Dixon didn't mention anything else, and I left the question of the plates, etc., because the cutlery's enough for us to go on. The job was obviously done by the fellows we're after."

"Did Inspector Dixon say something about a car?"

"It was seen by a constable in that neighbourhood at two o'clock this morning. He didn't get much chance to see it properly and didn't take the number, but he's quite certain, from the shape of the bonnet, that it was a Ford V8, and that it wasn't a saloon, but a touring model with the hood up. Dixon says they've been in touch with Dr. Hope Smith, who confirms the description. He left it outside his patient's house at a quarter to two. When he came out again at ten past, the car had gone, so when the constable saw it it was being driven by one of the thieves—a man who was also in the plot that gave rise to the killing of Hooker and Winslake."

He stubbed out his cigarette.

"There's one thing sticks out a mile, Peter, and that is that there's some busy little brain behind the whole business. I've a notion that it belongs to Mr. Oliver Quentin: and if the trap that I am now preparing for him is well enough laid—and if luck is on our side—I think we shall catch him tonight."

XV.

Lunch at Toni's

SOME while before the stage in the conversation between
Charlton and his first assistant that was reached at the end
of the previous chapter, another discussion was in progress
in Capri, where Mr. and Mrs. Oliver Quentin were having
a heart-to-heart talk in the upstairs sitting-room which, in
more spacious times, would have been known as the lady's
boudoir—or, if the French is to be translated literally, sulking-
place. Downstairs in the hall Detective-constable Emerson
was eating the lunch that had been brought in for him—a
packet of sandwiches and a vacuum flask of tea.

Although Emerson would not have heard a word of their
conversation, the two upstairs were speaking in undertones.
Mr. Quentin's usually suave manner was markedly absent
and he was inclined to be irritable—a state of mind that was
not improved by the commendable, if somewhat disdainful,
composure of his wife, whose line of argument was, "You got
us into this jam, so now you can get us out of it."

"But what the hell can I do, Belle?" he demanded, stopping
short in his uneasy pacing and waving his cigar at her. "I told
Kochowski yesterday that if he didn't hear any more from me
before six o'clock this evening they were to go through with
it. How the devil can I get in touch with him?"

His wife, who was seated with languid grace on the settee,
blew out a cloud of cigarette smoke and said in the supercilious
tone that always annoyed him:

"You shouldn't have started it. You've got ideas that are too
big for you—that's *your* trouble, Olly. Why don't you stick to
the easy stuff, where there's not much risk? You haven't enough
brains to be more than a small-time crook. Even that whisky
job was outside your class and nearly got us all pinched."

170

"You can cut that kind of talk out," he answered roughly. "It doesn't help. How are we going to contact Kochowski? Charlton didn't put that man in the house for our benefit."

"You don't say?" she drawled. "I *am* surprised." Quentin took no notice of this sarcasm, but went on:

"He's there to keep an eye on us. If I leave the house he'll stick to me like glue. And I can't lead him off while you get a message to Kochowski, because there's another man outside. Charlton said so."

"He may have been bluffing."

He shook his head.

"I doubt it. He's probably got the house surrounded. We daren't take a chance. That Charlton's suspicious enough already. He must be, or he wouldn't have put the man in here. If we start any funny stuff, sneaking out over the back fence—"

"And damn silly you'd look doing it, Olly."

"We might land ourselves in big trouble. It would be the same if we tried to give the fellow downstairs the slip. I don't think Charlton *knows* anything, however much he suspects."

"Meaning the Molhapur hold-up or those two—"

"Careful, Belle!"

"A pity about Doug. He was a good-looking boy. I'm rather cross over that, Olly. Don't you think you could have—"

"Shut your—mouth!"

"Oooh! Losing his little temper, is he? Getting rattled."

"Of course I'm rattled! So would you be if you had any sense. Anyway, Hooker was your idea."

"We had to do something quick, didn't we?"

"Too damned dangerous. It shook me badly when Charlton suddenly turned up this morning. I don't mind admitting it. How did he get on to us so soon?"

"Because we were fools enough to go back to the place. We should have stopped away. Charlton's got a long memory and he's been waiting for you to do precisely what you have done—play right into his hands. Why do you want to see

Kochowski—to call off the holdup?"

"To warn him. We can't tell whether the police got anything out of Winslake. Besides, Charlton's no fool. He can put two and two together as quick as the next man. Kochowski and the boys may walk right into trouble tonight."

"Would they squeak on us?"

"It's only Kochowski I'm worried about. The rest of them take their orders from him. They don't know I'm concerned in it."

"Can you trust Kochowski?"

"He might take his medicine and look to me for a sweetener when he came out. I'd say we can depend on him, but only so long as he doesn't think he's being double-crossed. He's a bit that way. If he and the others get caught tonight, Kochowski may get the idea that I'm to blame—that I've shopped him to save myself. Then the balloon would go up, believe me! That's why I want to talk to him, Belle. If I can warn him in advance he'll only have himself to blame if he goes through with it and gets pinched."

With the cigar between his fingers he threw out his hands in a gesture of helplessness.

"That's how we're placed, Belle."

"Does Kochowski know about Hooker and Doug?"

"No. I gave those jobs to—well, you know who. It cost me three hundred—a hundred for the first and two hundred for the other—cash in advance."

"Where did he get the boy from?"

"I don't know. I left it entirely to him."

"And the hold-up? Has he heard about that?"

"Not a word from me."

"What happens if they catch the boy and he blabs?"

"Let's hope they don't."

Belle Quentin flicked the ash from her cigarette.

"You know, Olly," she said without visible emotion, "I think we've had it this time."

"Oh, no, we haven't, not while there's still a chance. Charlton can suspect all he likes, but he'll never get us for murder. It's only the other fellow's word against ours, and the Indian police have probably got his record. I've a clean sheet. As for Kochowski ..."

He tossed his cigar butt into the fireplace and, without further words, left the room.

Down in the hall he put on his overcoat under the suspicious eyes of Emerson, who was just finishing his last sandwich.

"Shan't be more than half an hour, officer," Quentin said affably. "Just going to slip out for a quick lunch. The wife's a bit off colour and doesn't want anything to eat, so she'll stay behind. Your inspector warned us that we were in some danger, and I think I'd prefer you to stay here with her than bother about me. I can look after myself."

Emerson carefully folded up the paper in which his lunch had been wrapped, brushed some imaginary crumbs off his knees and relieved the chair of the weight of his massive young body.

"I'll come with you, sir," he said.

"But you've had your meal, officer. Please don't bother."

"That's all right, sir. I could do with a chance to stretch my legs."

Quentin managed to produce a jovial laugh.

"My dear fellow, this is all too damned silly for words! I'm certain your inspector didn't intend you to take your instructions too literally. Nothing unpleasant will happen to me—I can promise you that! Unless it's a result of Toni's cooking. You're being too conscientious, old chap. Get yourself a drink while I'm out. There's whisky and beer in the lounge, and as many cigarettes as you want in the box on the table."

"Very kind of you, sir, but we'd better be on the safe side. I'll step along with you."

He reached for his hat and raincoat. Quentin had no alternative but to accept his company. As they emerged into the road Detective-constable Hartley in the house opposite saw them and increased his vigilance.

Quentin and Emerson walked side by side down Beastmarket Hill. When they reached Mr. Barucci's catering establishment Quentin walked in ahead of his escort and found an empty table for two. They sat down opposite each other and Quentin picked up the menu.

★ ★ ★

"The eminent Monsieur Lecoq," Charlton was saying almost at the same moment, "has laid it down that the investigator should regard probabilities with suspicion and should always begin by believing anything that seems incredible. A very attractive system, Peter, and Monsieur Lecoq rose to fame by it, but I'm not always prepared to take the risk."

Bradfield said: "They order things differently in France."

"In this instance, I'm readier to believe the most likely thing, which is that Hooker and Winslake were both done away with to prevent a plot from miscarrying. I don't imagine they were killed because of something that has already happened, but to stop them from warning us in advance of something that's *going* to happen. Do you remember our conversation in the Blue Boar last night? We were pulling Bert Martin's leg about the present of an elephant from the Maharajah of Molhapur?"

"Yes, I remember. The exhibition in London."

"As you know, we had advance information about it some weeks ago. This morning I've been making a few more enquiries. The collection—jewellery, gold and silver ornaments, ivory, silk and so on—is being brought to this country in a British cruiser. She is due to dock at Southmouth this afternoon."

Bradfield gave a low whistle of comprehension.

"The exhibits," Charlton went on, "are to be transferred from the cruiser to a special van, in which they'll be taken up to London for the exhibition, which opens tomorrow week. The van is scheduled to leave Southmouth at nine o'clock this evening. Within a quarter of an hour it will be climbing Cowhanger."

Northward of Lulverton were the South Downs. When the main road from Southmouth to London had left Lulverton behind, it wormed its way between Dog Down to the west and High Down to the east. In spite of this wriggling, there was a steep gradient on both the southern and northern approaches. This was Cowhanger Hill, in the old days quite a test, but a mere trifle to the modern motor-car.

"It would be worth somebody's while," Charlton went on, "to intercept the van just there, persuade the occupants that it would be safer not to argue too much, and either drive the van away, or transfer the treasures of the East to some other vehicle. What do you think of that, Peter?"

"A very pretty notion. Do you imagine it's occurred to friend Quentin?"

"If not to him, certainly to somebody else. Cast your mind back to last night, to the conversation in the Shades between Hooker and Winslake. Young Bob Collins didn't hear much of it, but one word he caught was 'Cowhanger.' Just before that, Collins heard Winslake say something to the effect that he knew a surer way of making money than betting on horses. We can only guess at the part Winslake was due to play in tonight's highway robbery. Perhaps they needed photographs of some of the exhibits as a preliminary to selling them back to their lawful owners. But we can be fairly certain that he was going to be involved in it, because he promised to pay off his debt to Hooker on Saturday—that is tomorrow—morning."

He tapped the ash off his cigarette.

"This is no petty theft, Peter. If it succeeds, it will go down to history as one of the biggest robberies of the century. Those exhibits, which are being lent for the occasion by the Maharajah and all the richest men in Molhapur State, are

175

beyond price. They're irreplaceable. I gather that their value in cash today, sold, through the fences and the black market, is upwards of half a million pounds. High stakes, you know—and worth committing a couple of murders for. Our job now is to see that the plot doesn't succeed."

"How do we set about it?"

"These are the official arrangements as they stand at the moment. The collection is under the supervision of a Mr. Vijaykar, a trusted Hindu representative of the Maharajah. The cruiser will be met at Southmouth by an official of the Anglo-Molhapur Society. I understand that his name is Jackson. Vijaykar and Jackson will travel to London with the collection—not in the van, but in a car, which will follow it. They will have a chauffeur, with a plain-clothes man sitting alongside him. The van is the property of the Invincible Safe Deposit Company, who are to be responsible for the collection while it is in transit. The van will be locked and sealed, and will be in charge of two employees of the Safe Deposit Company, one of them at the wheel. The two vehicles will have a mobile escort—one police motor-cyclist going on in front and the other bringing up the rear."

"I suppose Quentin and his merry men will know all this?"

"Perhaps not in detail, but enough to make their plans in advance. This exhibition is not a military secret. By asking a few casual questions in the Lord Nelson and other pubs in Old Town, they could have got enough information to work on—when the cruiser is due to arrive, how the stuff is being taken to London, what time of the day the van will leave Southmouth—and so forth. We'll pop into Southmouth this afternoon, Peter, and have a chat with the port authorities and dock police. I think we can persuade them to modify their arrangements."

Bradfield glanced furtively at his watch. His quickeyed chief noticed the action.

"Is it lunch-time?" he asked.

"No," said Bradfield, "but it was."

★ ★ ★

Detective-constable Emerson had his moments of mental brightness; he sometimes acted on his own initiative.

When the constable whose duty it was to collect the empty vacuum flask from Capri arrived there in the afternoon, Emerson handed him at the same time the paper in which his sandwiches had been wrapped. It was now folded round one of Toni's menu cards and a report from Emerson to his chief. The packet was handed to Charlton shortly after he and Bradfield had returned from their snack.

"At 12.50 p.m.," Emerson's report ran, "Q came downstairs and informed me that he was going out to lunch. He expressed the wish that he should go alone, but I accompanied him, leaving Mrs. Q in the house. We went to Toni's Resteraunt"— Emerson's spelling was not one of his strongest points— "where Q ordered lunch and I had a coffee. I had my back to the street door. I went through the actions of examining his food for poison before allowing him to eat it."

"That must have been worth watching, Peter," Charlton commented after he had read it out. "The good Emerson's a thundering bad actor."

"There were other customers in Toni's," the report continued, "but Q did not attempt to speak or signal to them. When he had finished his food he had coffee. While he was drinking it he suddenly put down his cup and said, 'Somebody has just gone by outside. I did not see him properly, but I think it was Insp. Charlton. He was in a great hurry. I wonder whether he was on the way up to my house to speak to you about something important.' I was not decieved by this manoever, but decided to act as he wished. There was nobody near enough for him to hand them a note without leaving his seat so I took a chance that he would not signal to anyone while my back was turned and left my chair.

"I walked as far as the shop door and went through the actions of looking out. When I turned round, Q was sitting just as I had left him, but he had a pencil in his hand. He probably thought that I was going to go out into the street. I went back to the table and sat down again. Q took out a note-book and scribbled in it with the words, 'I am just sending myself a note about something I have remembered that I ought to do. I am very forgetful.' I answered, 'Everybody seems to be suffering from loss of memory these days. It must be the rations.' I do not think he guessed that I suspected him of a trick.

"We talked for a little while longer, then he asked the waitress for the bill. As she wrote it out she said, 'Is there any message for your friend? ' Q replied, 'I don't understand you. You must be confusing me with somebody else.' The waitress did not say any more. I made sure that he did not slip a message into her hand as he took the bill. He left a half-crown tip under his coffee-cup. As he walked up to the cash-desk to pay the bill which included coffee for self I picked up the menu, which was the only thing he could have left a message on. I am sending it sir with this report and you will see that there are some words written on the back of it. I put it in my pocket and followed Q to the door. Just before we left the Resteraunt, Q called back to the waitress, 'I've left something on the table.' Then he said to me, 'I always believe in tipping well.' We came back here to Capri and I am sending you this report without delay in case you want to put a watch on Toni's."

After Emerson's signature there was this postscript:

"The waitress was the small dark one with the turned-up nose and the engagement ring. She may be a confederate. Q called her Hilda. He seems to be well known there."

Before Charlton read this report aloud to Bradfield, they had examined the menu card. On the back of it were scribbled the words: "Cancel tonight's arrangements. Suspect complications."

When Charlton finished reading and laid the sheets aside, Bradfield said:

"Reynard is breaking cover. Do we question the girl?"

His chief considered this point for some time before he said:

"I'm not quite sure. She may be in the plot. Toni Barucci may be in it as well, for all we know, except that this morning's business with Winslake's breakfast strongly suggests that he isn't. They would have thought of another way. This girl, though ..."

"She's O.K. I'm in and out of Toni's for the odd cup of tea more often than I'd care to admit to my superior officer in the presence of witnesses, and Hilda and I are old friends. She and I have had many a session of badinage and exchange of abuse—she's nearly as hot at it as Olive Dove at the Blue Boar—and I'm willing to bet any money that she's straight."

"Then it's a risk worth taking. Go along to Toni's now, Peter, and see if you can get any information out of her. You can charge the tea up to expenses. And try not to be more than a couple of hours."

★ ★ ★

Bradfield was back within twenty minutes and had not wasted his time. Hilda's story had soon been told.

"Quentin and his wife are regular customers there," Bradfield explained to Charlton, "and so is another gentleman whose name Hilda can't remember. She only heard it mentioned once and says there was something foreign about it."

"Was it Kochowski?"

"I asked her that. She said it might have been, but she didn't seem at all certain. According to her, Quentin and this other fellow play a sort of Box and Cox act in Toni's. She says they're never there together, but they've fallen into the habit of exchanging messages, with Hilda acting as go-between."

"What sort of messages?"

"Always verbal and innocent enough on the face of it.

'Tell my friend I'll see him at the usual place at eight o'clock on Saturday evening,' or 'If my friend comes in, please say everything went off all right.' This has been going on for some time and Hilda has got so used to it that when she gave Quentin his bill today, she asked him whether there was any message for his friend. The poor girl was quite startled when he told her that she must be muddling him up with somebody else, because he didn't know what she was talking about. Then he gave her a wink. She guessed what was expected of her and said no more about it. She admits that she's not over-fond of Mr. Quentin or his friend, but the sizeable tips they produce between them do a lot to lessen her dislike. Emerson says in his note that Quentin called back to her that he'd left something on the table. Obviously he was drawing her attention to the menu card, but all Hilda found there was half a dollar, so when the friend comes in later, there'll be no message for him."

"Does Hilda expect him at any particular time?"

"I asked her that. She said he varies, but very often comes in at six o'clock for a coffee and a sandwich."

"Did she describe him?"

"She did. There doesn't seem much doubt that it's the same man as Bill Goodwin told us about—the fellow called Kochowski. Hilda also compared him to a vulture—a long, scraggy neck and a beak of a nose. She says he's between thirty and thirty-five, tall and haggard with a lean and hungry look, like our old school pal, Cassius. He wears a shabby mackintosh and a wide-brimmed black hat. Hilda is rather frightened of him."

"The looks like another job for you, Peter. Go back to Hilda now and tell her to give this message to Kochowski— we'll call him that—when he comes in." He thought out the wording. "Yes, tell her to say, 'All is well. Go right ahead.' Be in the neighbourhood of Toni's well before six o'clock. When Kochowski has conferred with Hilda and come out again, get on his tail and stick there. If you lose him, come back here and wait for further instructions from me. What I imagine he'll do is to assemble his forces at some point on Cowhanger Hill ready to intercept the van. There's no telling exactly what part of the hill they'll choose for this—probably somewhere where there are bushes or trees to get behind on both sides of the road. I shall be with the convoy. If you're lucky enough to spot these fellows taking up their positions, come back as far as you can towards Lulverton and signal to the driver of the van. Then you'll be able to tell us exactly where to expect the attack. Is that all clear?"

"Perfectly, sir."

"You'd better arrange with Hilda to give you a signal from the window of Toni's, indicating that she's passed on the message to Kochowski."

"I'll do that."

"Oh, and one other thing, Peter..."

He told him what it was.

XVI

Woodcock Near the Gin

AT eight o'clock that Friday evening, and for the second time that day, Inspector Charlton called at Capri. He brought with him Nurse Bentall, a large, competent woman, who remained outside in the car while he went into the house. Emerson, who was still on duty, opened the front door to him. Before he went to inform his reluctant hosts of the arrival of a visitor, he murmured into his superior's ear:

"Did you get my report, sir?"

"Yes, thanks. Very useful. Good work, Emerson. Anything else?"

"Nothing much, sir. As soon as we got back from lunch, he went upstairs. He's been down once or twice. I've only seen Mrs. Q once since lunch. She came down and went along into the kitchen. She made a crack as she sailed past, 'What!' she said. 'Are you still here, you ridiculous man? Why don't you go back to the police station and find some useful work to do—sweep out the cells or something.' I'll give her cells if I get the chance, the meadow lady!"

"Was her manner cheerful or depressed?"

"She's not the cheerful sort, sir. She's the narky type all claws! But I'd say she was happy enough just then. That bit about cleaning out the cells was her idea of a joke. When she came out of the kitchen, it was with a cup of tea for me. I'm still alive, so she must have been in a good temper."

"For all that, you shouldn't have drunk it, Emerson. It might have been doped."

"I was badly in need of a cup of tea, sir," explained Emerson with an earnest expression on his open, healthy young face.

"What about Quentin? How's he behaving?"

"Scary, sir. Wanders about like a fellow outside a maternity ward. Kidding himself everything's going to be all right, but still worried as hell."

"Has anyone called?"

"Only the laundry, sir, at four o'clock. Quentin took it in and said there wasn't anything to go back, because they weren't expecting them and it wasn't ready."

"All above board, do you think?"

"No doubt of it, sir. I was watching the whole time. It was a Nonpareil Laundry van and I recognized the driver. Quentin just took the box from him, said what I've just told you, and that was that."

"Right. Now please find Quentin and say I'd like a few words with him."

★ ★ ★

Quentin was upstairs, telling his wife for the twenty-third time that Kochowski must have got the message by now and all would be well, when Emerson knocked on the door. Quentin jumped like a startled cat, and it was the less panicky Belle who called out:

"What is it?"

Emerson did not open the door, but said through the panel:

"Inspector Charlton presents his compliments, ma'am, and could Mr. Quentin give him a minute or two downstairs?"

"Tell the Inspector that my husband will follow you down."

"Very good, ma'am."

Inside the room they heard his heavy footsteps as he went away. They gave him time to get out of earshot before they spoke. Quentin's thumb-nail was between his teeth. Belle said:

"That Charlton man's getting a pest."

"I can't stand much more, Belle. My nerve's going, I've bitten off more than I can chew this time."

"Try the other thumb," she suggested viciously.

"What does he want?"

"Better go down and ask him. He must be aching to tell you."

Mechanically Quentin turned towards the mirror over the fireplace and smoothed back his brilliantined hair. Then he brushed the lapels of his black jacket with his hand, squared his shoulders and made for the door.

When he joined Charlton in the hall, his smile of welcome was not a very convincing performance. He did not extend his hand—and Quentin was an enthusiastic shaker of hands, usually with his left hand on the other fellow's shoulder—because the trembling of it might have given his feelings away. He took Charlton into the lounge, directed him to a chair and produced the big cigarette-box again. This time Charlton refused there were certain niceties in these affairs.

"Mr. Quentin," he said, "I'm here to ask for your co-operation."

"By all the means in my power," Quentin gushed. "How can I assist you?"

"I have my car outside and I want you to be good enough to take a short ride with me. I shall be able to explain my purpose better when we reach our destination."

"But this is a very extraordinary request!"

"Not at all, Mr. Quentin. It's quite straightforward. No law-abiding man should be in the least alarmed."

"Alarmed?" protested Quentin, trying to stop quivering. "I'm not in the least alarmed. I am merely curious. Has anything serious transpired over these—er—deplorable murders?"

"I'm not in a position to tell you any more, sir. All I ask is that you come with me now, to help me to ensure that justice is done. You have my word that I have no other end in view."

With no small satisfaction he watched Oliver Quentin grappling with this new dilemma. Eventually the other man said with an attempt at righteous vexation over the inconvenience of it:

"If you insist, I suppose I have no alternative. How long

shall we be gone?"

"I don't think our business should take more than an hour."

"My wife—"

"I have made the necessary arrangements, Mr. Quentin. I have brought along with me a Nurse Bentall—a very reliable person. She is waiting in the car outside. While we are away, she'll be glad to come in and sit with Mrs. Quentin. My assistant, Emerson, will come with us. In his place I shall leave another of my men, who will look after the house until we return. So if you'll please inform Mrs. Quentin accordingly, we'll get ready to leave."

★ ★ ★

Belle's beautifully made-up face showed no more than bored interest when her husband came back into the room.

"Well," she said calmly, "what was it this time?"

"I don't like it, Belle," he almost whispered. "I don't like it at all. He's too damned polite. He's going to take me off somewhere in his car."

"Where?"

"He wouldn't tell me, except that I'm going to help him to see justice is done."

Her scarlet lip twisted in a sneer.

"And that's the last thing you want, isn't it? He's got you in a lovely velvet-lined trap, Olly, and you won't be able to wriggle out of it unless you use your poor little brains as you've never used them before."

"What's his game?" Quentin demanded.

"Don't shout, you fool! I'd say his game is to make you give yourself away. He's not sure yet, or he'd have come out into the open and you'd have been in the bracelets by now."

"Belle, *please!*"

"You've got to face it, Olly. Do you think I'm enjoying

myself? We're both in this up to the neck together. Stop behaving like an old woman, for God's sake!"

Her voice had risen. She, too, was losing some of her self-control. He dropped into a chair and sank his head in his hands.

"I can't go through with it," he muttered thickly. "I shall crack up, Belle."

"Then what'll happen to me?"

He raised his head to look at her.

"You'll be all right. You'd get away with anything. It's me I'm worried about." He got slowly to his feet. "I suppose I shall have to go now. Charlton's brought a Nurse Someone with him. She's probably a police nark, so watch out. If I don't come back tonight, you'll know the worst has happened."

They stood facing each other. She was a head taller than he. She put her thin hands on his shoulders and said with almost affection in her voice:

"Listen to me, Olly. Stand up to Charlton. It's our only chance. Deny everything. Tell him to prove it. Where's his evidence? He's trying to frighten you. Don't let him do it. You're a man, Olly. Act like one and we'll get away with it."

"We shan't. I know we shan't. It's all over, Belle."

Her hands fell away from his shoulders. She looked down at him for a time and, even in his misery, he noticed how old she looked and remembered that he had loved her once. Then her lips curled back from her teeth and she said:

"You rat!"

Her arm swung in an upward curve and the flat of her hand caught him a blow on the side of the face that sent him reeling.

He regained his balance and she thought he was going to attack her, but he stood rubbing his cheek and there was no anger in his voice as he said:

"You shouldn't have done that, Belle. You're all I've got left."

Her glance was contemptuous.

"Get out!"

He stood uncertainly, then turned and walked to the door. Before he left the room he said:

"If I don't come back tonight, you can take it I'm in custody. You'll have to make your own arrangements, Belle, but if they arrest me, they'll be coming after you as well. Good-bye, old girl."

She did not answer him or look in his direction. When the door had closed behind him, she turned the key in the lock and went across to the fireplace. The room was heated by means of a gas fire controlled by a tap to the side of the fireplace. The linoleum had been cut to fit round it. She went down on one knee and pulled back the linoleum. From a small cavity in the floorboards underneath she extracted a bottle labelled to the effect that it contained aspirin tablets. She unscrewed the cap and tipped the contents of the bottle into the palm of her hand. Yes, she thought, there were two left. One would be enough. She scooped them back into the bottle and replaced the cap. After a moment's indecision, when she glanced round at her handbag on the settee, she returned the bottle to its hiding-place and re-adjusted the linoleum over it.

XVII.

Kochowski Smiles

THE night was dark and cold. The sky was overcast, but there was as yet no rain. Emerson took the wheel of the Wolseley, while Inspector Charlton and Oliver Quentin rode in the back.

Whether or not she had anticipated such an effect, Mrs. Quentin's assault upon her husband had restored some of his courage; it had made him ready not to give up without a struggle. Consequently, his manner during the first part of their drive showed a confidence that Charlton found slightly puzzling. He knew Quentin for a tricky customer and began to wonder whether the smooth little man was going to put over what is known as a fast one. But, thought Charlton, it would have to be unusually fast to interfere with his own plans.

Emerson drove southward through Lulverton and on some miles until they turned off the road through a gateway flanked by high stone pillars. Quentin asked breezily: "Where are we? I must confess that I've lost myself."

"Southmouth docks," Charlton told him and then went on quite casually as if Quentin knew all about it: "The *Beaconsfield* berthed this afternoon."

Quentin drew a sharp breath.

"The *Beaconsfield?* What is that—a ship? I'm afraid I don't follow all this, Inspector."

The car came to a stop. Emerson switched on the inside light.

Charlton chuckled.

"I wonder you've not heard of the *Beaconsfield,* Mr. Quentin. She's been much in the news recently. She's the cruiser that has brought the Molhapur collection from India for the exhibition in London,"

188

"Oh, yes. I do remember seeing something about it. At Lanchester House, isn't it?"

"Quite so. A very valuable collection. My colleagues. and I will heave a sigh of relief when it arrives safely at its destination."

"I'm sure you will. It's undoubtedly a great responsibility. But tell me this, Inspector: what has it to do with me?" He laughed. "Am I to be given a special preview of the Rajah's treasures?"

"No, that's not quite the idea. I think it's time I took you into my confidence, Mr. Quentin."

Even Emerson, who was somewhat slow on the uptake, saw the funny side of this. He turned a laugh into a cough. Charlton continued:

"We've received a report from an extremely trustworthy source that an attempt is to be made by certain persons to steal this collection while it's on its way up to London."

"But—"

"Just a moment, Mr. Quentin. We've been making exhaustive enquiries and we have reason to believe that we have identified the man who is behind this ambitious scheme." He paused before he went on. "I think you know Toni's Restaurant?"

Quentin was hunched—almost crouched—in his comer. "Of course I know it. My wife and I often take meals there. What is the—"

"Good. The man we're interested in is, like yourself, a regular customer. I can give you a brief description of him. His name's Kochowski. He's a tall, thin foreigner and has a hooked nose. He usually wears a black felt hat with a generous brim to it. His hair is long and untidy. Do you remember ever having seen him in Toni's?" Quentin had a quick answer to this.

"No, I can't say that I have. I'll go so far as to say that I definitely haven't. He must be a striking man and I should certainly have noticed him if I'd seen him. If you have brought me here to identify him, I shall be of no use to you at all."

Charlton clicked his tongue.

"That's a nuisance. I was hoping you could help. Still, it's worth trying. This fellow was seen in Toni's earlier this evening."

The other man tried to seem unconcerned.

"Really?"

"Yes. He was there a few minutes before six o'clock. We've questioned the waitresses and found the girl who served him."

"Oh, yes?"

He was tensed to snapping-point.

"It was the rather attractive little brunette. Hilda, I think they call her. I expect you know her. Unfortunately, she had very little to tell us. Our quarry had a hurried snack and went on his way. He was a little bit too quick for us."

It was a struggle for Quentin not to display relief. The girl had kept her mouth shut. The money on tips had not been wasted. Perhaps it would be better not to deny knowledge of Kochowski too strenuously.

"I'm very sorry to hear it, Inspector. As a matter of fact, now I come to think about it, I believe I know the man you mean. I've seen him in Lulverton once or twice. A very shifty-looking gentleman!"

"You're right. And as slippery as he's shifty. But I think we may catch him tonight." He smiled brightly at Quentin. "And that's where you come in."

"Naturally, you can count on me. I'm only too anxious to assist."

"Fine! Let's go inside."

He opened the door of the car and got out. Quentin followed him into a bulding. In an office on the ground floor half a dozen men were assembled. Charlton introduced Quentin to them. One was Mr. Jackson, the elderly, bearded secretary of the Anglo-Molhapur Society. A second was Mr. Vijaykar, a small wiry Hindu gentleman of indeterminate age, whose most noticeable feature was his wide and perpetual smile.

A third was a representative of the Invincible Safe Deposit Company. The others were dock officials. When Quentin had shaken hands with them all, Charlton said:

"I've asked Mr. Quentin to come along this evening because he's one of the few people who can identify Kochowski."

"Not so fast, Inspector," protested Quentin with an awkward smile. "I'm not acquainted with this fellow. You say his name's Kochowski, but it was news to me. I've seen him around Lulverton a few times, but that's as far as my knowledge of him goes."

"I quite appreciate that," Charlton assured him. "Now, let me give you an idea of the position. The Molhapur collection is being taken to London in a closed van. The exhibits are worth a great deal of money. Mr. Vijaykar will agree, I think?"

Mr. Vijaykar did not nod. He jerked his head sideways and backwards, as is the way of his kind when a sign of acquiescence is called for.

"Indeed I do," he smiled. "One cannot talk in terms of hard cash when considering the collection. Some of the articles are beyond price. The theft of them would be as the theft of the sun from the sky. There are Persian manuscripts as precious as radium. There are necklaces of pearls." He ran his hands down the front of his body. "Great necklaces of many pearls, set with sapphires and covering the chest of the wearer. There are the armbands of the women. There are horses' saddles studded with diamonds. Swords with their hilts as rich with diamonds as the saddles. Brassware inlaid with the famous peacock design—work on which a man might have spent fifteen years of his life. Hookahs, jade ornaments of matchless beauty and craftsmanship, Persian carpets, rare spices and perfumes ..."

He gave a little gesture.

"It will be an exhibition worth going to see. The jewels alone could be sold for many lacs of rupees in the capitals of the world. If they were stolen, Molhapur would meet with the greatest disaster in its history."

From the happy expression on his face, it would have seemed that Mr. Vijaykar viewed the prospect of such a catastrophe with delight. Yet this could hardly have been so, for Molhapur's plight would not have been more serious than his own.

"So you see, Mr. Quentin," said Charlton, "that we are taking every precaution to ensure the safety of the collection. We've discovered that this man Kochowski intends to commit highway robbery by holding up the van when it reaches Cowhanger Hill. What we are proposing to do is to take them in the act, and I want you to come with us, so that when we have caught Kochowski and his accomplices you can identify the ringleader as the man you have seen in Lulverton."

The whole thing was so transparent that he wondered whether Quentin would see through it. Not that it really mattered if he did. He would not dare to refuse. Nevertheless, he was relieved when Quentin immediately replied:

"Why, of course!"

Quentin was feeling more confident now. Why should he worry too much? Maybe this smiling, grey-haired inspector of the C.I.D. was endeavouring to trap him, but did that matter? Kochowski had got the message, and he and the boys would keep well away from Cowhanger that night. If he, Quentin, could only make Charlton believe that he knew nothing about the hold-up, he might allay any suspicions the police might have on the subject of those two murders. Why the devil had he consented? Belle was always too impetuous. Why had he consented? Because half a million was a lot of money. Those pearls and sapphires. ... A great pity...Yes, but perhaps it was all for the best. Belle might be sorry she had slapped his face. No, she wouldn't. Belle was hard—as hard and cutting as one of the Rajah's diamonds. So:

"Why, of course!" he said effusively, then added with a roguish grin: "I hope there'll be no danger!"

"That remains to be seen," the Inspector answered, with a grimness that Mr. Quentin did not fully appreciate.

* * *

A couple of hours or so before Charlton had called at Capri to collect the reluctant Quentin, Sergeant Bradfield took up an unobtrusive position in the shadowy arcade of a drapery store opposite Toni's Restaurant. He had already had a quiet word or two with Hilda, so that when the hook-nosed man arrived he would receive from her the reassuring message: "All is well. Go right ahead." Hilda had also promised that, when this had been done, she would give Bradfield a signal from the window.

The Centre was well lighted and Bradfield had little difficulty in noting all those who went in or came out of Toni's. As the first of the town clocks was striking six and the others, having politely given place to it, were preparing to follow its example, Bradfield observed a tall, hunched-shouldered figure, with hands pushed into the pockets of his soiled mackintosh, walking with rapid, bouncing steps down Beastmarket Hill. The man paused outside Toni's and—an almost unconscious gesture, it seemed to the watching detective—pulled his wide hat-brim still further down over his brows before he entered the restaurant.

The man could not have stayed for more than the quickest of snacks, for within five minutes he was out again. As he made his way back up Beastmarket Hill, Hilda came to the window and waved gaily to an imaginary passer-by. Her lynx-eyed employer saw this little performance from the back of the shop and called her over to him.

She said: "Yes, Mr. Barucci?"

But he changed his mind and sent her away again with an imperious wave of his jewelled hand. This was a disappointment to Hilda. Her successful deception of Mr. Quentin's friend—for he had accepted without question the message she had given him—had persuaded her that she had in her the makings of a Secret Service agent. She would have liked to tell Mr. Barucci of her love affair with a distinguished foreign ambassador.

★ ★ ★

Joseph Kochowski was a European. If one had to be more precise, one would have had some excuse for calling him a Pole, for he had been born in Brest-Litovsk. As a soldier, he had come across the Straits of Dover in a trawler during the evacuation of Dunkirk and, on arrival in England, had taken the first opportunity to dispose of his uniform and change into more comfortable civilian attire. In the character of a Polish refugee, he had taken up residence in a lodging-house near the docks—an establishment where they did not ask too many awkward questions—and had made a modest living for himself by discreet transgressions of the laws of the country that had given him sanctuary. It had been in the course of one of these little enterprises—the theft of a lorry-load of Mackinnon's "Highland Velvet" whisky—that he had come into business contact with Mr. Oliver Quentin. The acquaintance had ripened, not into friendship, but into a sincere respect for each other's abilities, particularly in the difficult art—difficult because, although easy to execute, it is not always so simple to evade subsequent vengeance—of the double cross. It had been Mr. Kochowski who had first seen the possibilities lying in the Anglo-Molhapur exhibition. He had confided in Mr. Quentin, who had approved of the scheme, but only on the distinct understanding that he himself would not be expected to take an active part in the brigandage, but would merely supply financial backing and afterwards assist in the dispersal of the Indian treasures.

As he walked up Beastmarket Hill, Mr. Kochowski had every cause to be confident in the success of the evening's undertaking.

The plan was well laid. The van containing the exhibits would be leaving Southmouth docks at nine o'clock. Behind it would follow a private car, in which would be travelling the two representatives—the Indian from Molhapur and the man from the Society in London. There would be some kind of police escort, but Mr. Kochowski's informant had been uncertain of the details. Nevertheless, Mr. Kochowski felt reasonably sure that he and the boys would be able to deal with them. There would be eleven with him, including young Winslake. Which reminded Mr. Kochowski that he had not heard from Winslake since Tuesday. Still, Winslake knew the details and would doubtless arrive at the rendezvous at the appointed time.

At the bottom of Cowhanger Hill, on the landward side, the London road took a sharp turn to the right and ran for some distance along the northern foot of High Down before it turned again to the left. Mr. Kochowski proposed to divide his forces into two parties. The first party would be hidden at the side of the road a short way from the bottom of the hill; the second would be similarly concealed round the corner, fifty or sixty yards on. As soon as the van turned the corner, the first party would intercept the car behind, thus leaving the second party, under the personal direction of Mr. Kochowski, to deal with the occupants of the van.

The van, Mr. Kochowski's informant had said, was being supplied by a London safe-deposit company. It was chocolate brown in colour and was entirely enclosed, its only opening, apart from a ventilator, being a door in the near side, just behind the driver's cab. Generally, the informant had continued, nobody travelled inside the van. After the valuables had been stowed away the door was locked and sealed, and the key retained by a representative of the safe-deposit company, who did not travel with the van, but made his own way to the destination. The driver of the van and his companion, although both employed by the safe-deposit company, had no means of opening the van once it was locked.

It was Mr. Kochowski's intention to overpower the two men in the van and then, with one of his own assistants at the wheel—for he himself could not drive—take it away to a secluded spot not far distant, where Adams, an expert burglar, would be waiting with his tools, which included an oxy-acetylene blow-pipe. When Adams had got the van open, all the smaller articles of high value would be removed to another vehicle and transported to a safe place for eventual disposal through channels with which Mr. Kochowski's association with Oliver Quentin had made him familiar. He would get young Winslake to drive the van. If Winslake failed to arrive, some other man must do it. Dipper Hicks seemed the best choice. In fact Dipper might be more suitable than Winslake, who easily lost his head and lacked Dipper's experience in such criminal affairs.

But that was a detail. The main plan itself was well laid. Mr. Joseph Kochowski allowed himself the luxury of a smile.

XVIII.

When Greek Meets Greek

AT fourteen minutes past nine Sergeant Peter Bradfield
stepped out into the London road at a point between
Cowhanger Hill and Lulverton, and, facing the vehicle that
approached him from the south, raised his hands above his
head and brought them down in wide sweeps to his sides. It
was the prearranged signal and the man sitting next to the
driver said:

"Pull up. That's one of the C.I.D. chaps."

The driver obeyed, and Emerson, at the wheel of the
Wolseley, brought it to a stop behind the van. In the back seat
Inspector Charlton politely requested Quentin to stay where
he was, then got out of the car to walk ahead and speak to
Bradfield.

"Keep your voice down, Peter," he warned as they stood
together by the driving cab of the van. "I've got Quentin in
the car and I don't want to frighten him too soon. What's the
position?"

"Hilda passed on your message to the foreign type. I've
been following him about ever since like a faithful dog. He's
collected his covey of toughs—a dozen or so of them, as far
as I could estimate—and they're now all poised to pounce.
It wasn't easy in the dark to find out exactly what was going
on, but I've made certain of one or two things. Spring-heeled
Jack has prepared his little ambush just where the road bears
to the right on the other side of Cowhanger. He's split his
henchmen into two. One lot is tucked away out of sight at
the bottom of the hill, and the rest of them are lurking behind
the bushes round the corner—about forty yards along, at a
rough guess."

"Have they a car?"

"Yes. It's been driven across the grass into a dip, so that it can't be seen from the road."

"Hope Smith's V8?"

"I think not. It looked more like a big saloon."

"Are they armed?"

"Sure to be, though I couldn't get close enough to be certain. The strategy seems to be that the fellows this side of the corner will let the van go past and then hold up the car, leaving the van to their chums round the corner. What's happened to the mobile escort? I thought there were to be a couple of motor-cyclists?"

"I've taken them off. They might have complicated things. I want to make it as simple as possible for Kochowski."

Charlton turned his head to speak to the two men in the cab of the van. They were both past their prime and were now looking somewhat ill at ease.

"There's a certain amount of risk," he told them, "but if you do exactly as I say you, should be all right."

"I don't like the smell of it," said the driver.

"No," agreed his companion, "this looks a bit more than we bargained for. What do you want us to do?"

"Drive on till you're stopped. Don't resist. Just behave as if you've been taken completely by surprise. If they want to tie you up, let them. They're not interested in you fellows; all they want to get hold of is the collection."

"You say they've got guns?" asked the driver.

"Yes, we believe so, but they won't use them unless they're forced to."

The driver shook his head.

"No. You'd better leave me out. I've got a wife and two kids to keep."

"Me, too," said the other, "only it's five nippers."

Bradfield said to the chief: "I'll drive it if you like, sir.

"Good. Emerson had better come with you. All right, you two. Please get out."

They wasted no time in doing as he asked. Bradfield took the driver's place, and Emerson was brought along to occupy the seat beside him.

"It's the same advice for you, Peter," Charlton said through the window. "Don't put up a fight if you can avoid it. Leave that part to me. This is what I propose to do. . .

In a few terse sentences he outlined his plan to Bradfield and Emerson, after which he walked back to the Wolseley.

Bradfield started the engine. When the van moved forward the Wolseley did not follow. Charlton had reseated himself by Quentin's side, while the two other men took the front seats.

Quentin asked: "What's happening exactly?"

"We're going to wait here a minute or two to let the van get ahead."

"I don't see any point in that, Inspector."

"It's just a precaution. We don't know how many men we're going to come up against. I don't want to run you into any more danger than I can help."

"Don't worry about me. If you take my advice you'll drive straight on and get this business over. My wife will soon be wondering what's happened to me."

Charlton pulled a packet of cigarettes from his pocket.

"I think we'll wait," he said. "Care for a smoke?"

★ ★ ★

The van climbed Cowhanger Hill and went down the other side. Bradfield and Emerson were on the alert, but the headlights picked out nothing save the grass and bushes on either side of the road, even when they drew near to the corner.

"They're well hidden," said Bradfield.

He gave a warning hoot on the horn and swung the big vehicle round the corner. In the beam of the headlights forty yards ahead of them they saw the figure of a man—a tall, thin man with a wide-brimmed hat, who walked with bouncing steps in the same direction as they. He looked round, then stopped and turned to face the approaching van. As they got closer he gave the hitch-hiker's conventional thumb-sign over his shoulder.

Bradfield said: "The poor fellow must be tired out. He's had an exhausting day. Let's give him a lift, shall we?"

"Under the lug if I get half a chance," growled Emerson.

"Oh, no," Bradfield disagreed firmly. "The Skip says we must let the nice gentleman tie us up with the pretty rope."

He brought the van to a stop. Joseph Kochowski stepped up to the open window on Emerson's side.

"Are you going my way?" he asked in an accent that betrayed his foreign origin.

"Which way's that?" Bradfield asked.

"Guildford."

"O.K. Jump in."

Kochowski opened the door with his left hand, but did not accept the invitation to jump in. Instead he snatched his other hand from his mackintosh pocket, with his thin fingers gripped round the butt of a Luger. Simultaneously the door on Bradfield's side was pulled open and another gun appeared.

"What's this?" asked Bradfield in a tone of mild surprise. "A stick-up?"

"Get out quickly!" ordered Kochowski, "and do not attempt any tricks. If you do it will be the worse for you."

"I'm afraid you're in for a disappointment. We're going back empty to London. There's not even a rasher of bacon or a tin of bully."

"Get out!"

"All right, if you're really set on it."

Emerson climbed out first and was followed by Bradfield. The man who had opened the off-side door came round the front of the van with his gun at the ready. As he came into the beam from the headlamps Bradfield recognized him.

"Well, well!" he said. "If it isn't Dipper Hicks!"

I don't like to see you in this company, Dipper. They're not honest."

Kochowski said to Hicks, a wizened little rogue of fifty, with almost the same number of convictions:

"Keep them covered. I search them for guns."

While this was being done Hicks said uneasily:

"These are a couple of kipper-feet from Lulverton. We was told the van'd be driven by the safe-deposit people's men. I don't fancy it, Kochowski."

"No names, you fool!"

"Then 'ow about me? The s'll be after me fer this. If I'd known I'd be coming up against the local cops I shouldn't've touched the job."

"That is a risk you have taken."

"But what's these two doin' in the van? We'd best watch out. It may be a trap."

Kochowski's upper lip twisted.

"If it is a trap, it is they who fall into it. Get in the van and do not talk so much."

"Do yer want me to drive?"

"Yes; I have not the knowledge."

Other men, all with weapons in their hands, had collected round them. As Dipper Hicks climbed into the driver's cab Kochowski said to the rest:

"Guard closely these men. Bring them in the auto to the place arranged. If they give trouble, shoot. We have many things to lose if you fail."

He got in beside Hicks, who started the engine and drove the van away.

Bradfield and Emerson, with self-loaders uncomfortably close to the small of their backs, were taken across the grass and down the slope to the car, a big saloon, for the legal possession of which Kochowski would have been hard put to produce a convincing explanation. One of the captors opened the door and instructed the two detectives to get in. Others piled in after them and, with a couple standing on the running-boards, the car was driven back onto the highway.

Dipper Hicks, guided by Kochowski, did not turn to the left when the main road bore northward, but continued straight on along a narrow lane—scarcely more than a cart-track—which eventually brought them to an extensive clump of beech trees and undergrowth. In the centre of this was a clearing, where Hicks brought the van to a stop.

Their arrival was expected. As they descended from the cab two men came out from among the trees.

"O.K.?" said one.

"Yes," answered Kochowski, "but there is great need for speed, Adams. Get that door open and do it quickly. Hicks, keep watch."

Shortly afterwards the saloon car drew up some yards behind the van. One of the men on the running-boards called out to Kochowski:

"What do you want done with these two?"

The Pole was more interested in the Molhapur treasure than his prisoners.

"One man remain to guard them," he answered. "The rest of you will help us when the van has been opened."

★ ★ ★

Inspector Charlton pulled back his sleeve and looked at his watch.

"It's time we went," he decided.

He and Quentin were now sitting in the front seats. The two employees of the safe-deposit company were in the back, having consented, after Charlton had assured them that they were now unlikely to get involved in a gun battle, to see the thing through.

As the Wolseley began to move forward, Quentin, who was now quite convinced that Kochowski had received his message and would act upon it, said in an amiable tone:

"You know, Inspector, I'm beginning to find this all rather exciting. Your job must be very interesting. Really, I'm quite looking forward to being called upon to identify this sinister alien for you. Let's hope it's the same man as I have seen in Toni's."

Charlton changed gear.

"I don't think you've mentioned having seen him in there," he said.

Quentin passed it off with a wave of his hand.

"Once or twice," he admitted airily.

"Yes," said Charlton, "if it isn't the same man it will be a disappointment for both of us. My ambition is to get everybody concerned in this robbery a nice long term of imprisonment."

"I can appreciate that. I wish you every success."

"Thank you, Mr. Quentin."

The Wolseley climbed Cowhanger, breasted the summit and went slowly down the other side with headlights off. They had not gone far before the side-lamps picked out a figure standing by the side of the road. It was a lance-corporal in battledress, and he was giving the same signal as Bradfield had done a short while before.

Charlton stopped the car and got out to speak to him. After they had exchanged a few murmured words, Charlton climbed back into the car and moved forward again with the soldier on the running-board.

Quentin was beginning to feel that something had gone wrong.

"Has anything happened?" he asked.

Charlton answered: "As this looked like being something more than we could tackle with the police personnel available, I called in the military. We've been given the services of a couple of detachments of the Downshire Light Infantry— men fully trained in fieldcraft and commando tactics. Kochowski's split his men into two groups. The corporal has just told me that the first group has been rounded up, and they're now waiting for transport to take them to Lulverton police station."

Quentin was biting his nails.

"And Kochowski?" he mumbled.

"He is with the second group, which is now being similarly dealt with."

He drove for a while before he added:

"Your wish for my success looks like being fulfilled, Mr. Quentin. In a minute or two I shall be asking you to identify him."

Quentin was shaking with fright.

"Inspector," he said, "I'm not feeling very well. I get these little turns. The old ticker is not what it was. I wonder if I might be taken home?"

"Certainly, Mr. Quentin, but I'll just get you to identify Kochowski first. It would be a pity for you to miss that, wouldn't it?"

As others had done before him, Oliver Quentin had much the same feelings as a mouse at the mercy of a charmingly courteous cat.

★ ★ ★

It was not necessary for Adams to bring his portable oxy-acetylene blow-pipe into use. In fact it was not necessary for him to go to work on the door at all, for almost before his jemmy had been inserted near the lock the door swung open, pushed from within, and instantly there was a burst of tommy-gun fire from the van's interior.

A moment later, somewhere in the undergrowth, a whistle was blown, and from several points around the clearing powerful beams of light shot out and centred on the van.

The man with Bradfield and Emerson was taken completely by surprise. Bradfield jumped at him, knocked the gun from his hand with a swift downward blow on the forearm, then sent him staggering backwards with a straight left to the chin.

"Look after him," he told Emerson. "If he gets awkward tap him on the crust with the gun."

He disappeared into the darkness in the direction from which they had come.

The young sergeant behind the tommy-gun in the van had aimed deliberately high, but it had been enough to send Kochowski and his men down on their faces. He now spoke from the darkness inside the vehicle.

"Chuck those guns away," he said, "or I'll give you another burst."

Kochowski snarled something in his mother tongue and raised himself to take aim. The sergeant squeezed the trigger again, still aiming into the air.

"That's the last chance," he called. "Next time I'll do you."

There was more than a hint in his voice that he meant this. Kochowski threw his Luger from him, and the others were wise enough to copy his example. The sergeant jumped down from the van and was followed by six other ranks, all armed with rifles. On an order from the sergeant one of the soldiers collected the pistols, unloaded them and put them away in the van.

The sergeant told Kochowski and his henchmen to stand up. As they were scrambling to their feet, other armed men in battledress emerged into the lighted clearing from numerous directions. Two of them had Kochowski's scout, Dipper Hicks, safely in their care.

★ ★ ★

Bradfield met the Wolseley just before it reached the corner and was able to direct Charlton to the scene of all the recent excitement. Charlton brought his car to a stop on the edge of the clearing and politely requested Quentin to alight. With

Charlton on one side of him and Bradfield on the other, Quentin walked forward.

Kochowski had his back turned to them and was standing looking at the ground.

As the trio drew near to the group by the van Charlton said in a voice loud enough for all to hear:

"It'll certainly be a weight off my mind, sir, if you can identify Kochowski."

The Pole raised his head with a jerk and spun round with a suddenness that brought half a dozen weapons to bear on him. The sergeant gave a sharp order and two soldiers caught hold of Kochowski's arms. He fixed his fierce eyes on the three men coming out of the surrounding darkness. When he saw who it was who walked between the other two, he said with clenched teeth:

"Quentin! Filthy traitor!"

His English deserted him and he continued his abuse in Polish. Quentin threw out his hands towards Charlton in dramatic disclaimer.

"The man's crazy, Inspector! I don't know what he's talking about. I've never seen him before."

Charlton raised his eyebrows in surprise.

"Not in Toni's?"

"Well, yes. Perhaps I've caught sight of him occasionally in there."

Kochowski shouted:

"Squeaking rat! You give me the instructions and then you bring the police! For that you—"

He struggled to get away from the men who held him, but they were young and strong.

"Really, Inspector," expostulated Quentin, "this is entirely beyond me. What is this about my giving orders?"

With his chin stuck forward, Kochowski sneered:

"You do not know? You have forgotten? But you did not forget to bring the police!"

Quentin turned again to Charlton.

"I recommend you to take no notice of all this nonsense, Inspector. If you question some of the other men they'll confirm that I'm in no way concerned with this disgraceful affair. As for issuing orders..."

He shrugged his shoulders and left the sentence unfinished.

Kochowski was spluttering with rage.

"The girl gives to me the message. You have told her that all is well and I am to carry on. Now I have fallen in the trap and it is you—"

Quentin's mouth had fallen open.

"All is well?" he repeated dully. "But that wasn't the message I left with—"

His body stiffened and his mouth clapped shut.

Charlton said quietly: "Then what message *did* you leave with her, Mr. Quentin?"

XIX

A Tragic Discovery

THE five-day week is a most agreeable arrangement, but until the criminal population of these islands can be persuaded not to practise their calling on Saturdays and Sundays the police stations will have to keep open for business over the week-end.

Consequently, Inspector Charlton and Sergeant Bradfield both arrived early at headquarters on the Saturday morning following the skirmish under the shadow of High Down. Nor were they the only toilers. They had not been ten minutes in Charlton's first-floor office before they were joined by Superintendent Kingsley, who, as a concession to the week-end custom, had discarded his uniform in favour of a sports coat and flannel trousers. As he came into the room the two C.I.D. men were examining a report from the analyst on the glasses and other articles removed from the Blue Boar on the Thursday evening.

"Now, Harry," said the Super, having plumped his great body down with a suddenness that startled the chair into a loud creak of distress, "tell Uncle Tiny all that happened last night."

"An extremely successful expedition. Quentin, Kochowski, our old friend Dipper Hicks and nine others are under lock and key until they come up before the magistrates. I'm asking for all of them to be remanded in custody."

"Who's the second fellow you mentioned?"

"Kcchowski? He's a foreigner—possibly a Pole. This is the first time we've come up against him. I'm having his record looked into. I'll give you a brief outline of events, Tiny. I had every reason to suspect that an attempt was going to be made on the Molhapur collection while it was on its way to

London, and that the egregious Quentin was mixed up in the conspiracy. It was no good catching the rest of the gang unless we could catch Quentin at the same time—and in such a way that he couldn't wriggle out of it afterwards. We found that he had been exchanging messages with this Kochowski through the agency of one of the waitresses at Toni's."

"Which one?" asked the Super, who was always interested in little details like that.

"Hilda. The dark one with the turned-up nose."

"Don't be unkind," remonstrated the Super. "She's a pretty little filly. Tip-tilted has a better sound."

"Call it what you like, Tiny," smiled Charlton. "The messages were verbal. At lunch-time yesterday Quentin called in at Toni's. Emerson was with him, just to keep an eye on him, but Quentin took a chance and scribbled a note for Kochowski on the menu card, in the hope that Hilda would pass it on to Kochowski. It was an urgent warning for Kochowski not to proceed with a matter already decided upon. Bradfield took a hand, and by using his sex appeal on Hilda induced—"

"Funny creatures, women," observed the Super.

"He induced the girl to tell Kochowski, when he presented himself later in the day, that all was well and he was to go right ahead. I sought out Quentin and gave him to understand that his original message had been passed on to Kochowski. This took a great load off his mind—so much so that, when I suggested he might be able to identify Kochowski, he leapt at the invitation. I said we were hoping to catch Kochowski on Cowhanger Hill, and Quentin, in the comforting belief that Kochowski wouldn't be there, gladly agreed to go along with us."

"What was the point of that?" asked the Super.

"I'll come to it in a minute. The van was due to leave Southmouth docks at nine o'clock last night—and it did, but not with the Molhapur collection. Those valuables are still in a safe place in Southmouth and will be taken up to

209

London under police escort later on today. No, when the van started on its journey it carried a party of the Downshires armed with tommy-guns and rifles. By arrangement with the C.O., another detachment of men was detailed to assist. Vijaykar, the Maharajah's envoy, and Jackson, the secretary of the Anglo-Molhapur Society, were prevailed upon—without much difficulty—to stay behind in Southmouth. The van was followed by my car, with Emerson driving and Quentin and myself in the back. Bradfield, who was working on his own, put in some good tracking work and was able to report that Kochowski and Co. were waiting for us near the corner at the bottom of the other side of Cowhanger. I won't go into all the details, Tiny. It's enough to say that Kochowski fell into the trap and we caught them all red-handed in the act of forcing open the van."

"And Quentin?"

"I must confess," Charlton said with a grin, "that I duped him cruelly. While Kochowski and his merry men were being accounted for by Bradfield and the Downshire Light Infantry, we in my car held back."

He looked over to Bradfield, who had taken up his favourite position with his elbow on the filing cabinet.

"I'm sorry about that, Peter—letting you do all the dangerous work."

"That's as it should be, sir," Bradfield answered. "I'm the younger man."

"Remind me to hobble round on sticks in future."

He turned back to the Super.

"When Kochowski had been made prisoner I strolled up to him with Quentin. As I had gambled he would, Kochowski immediately jumped to the conclusion that Quentin had double-crossed him. He called him by a lot of offensive names in two languages. Quentin—I almost felt sorry for the fellow!—Quentin spluttered that he didn't know what Kochowski was talking about, because he'd never seen the man before. I said,

'What? Not in Toni's?' He replied that maybe he'd seen him once or twice in there. Then Kochowski raised his voice again and accused Quentin of sending him orders to proceed with the hold-up and then squeaking to the police. Quentin said, 'I sent you orders? I certainly did no such thing!' Kochowski said, 'The waitress gave me the message that all was well and I was to carry on.' Quentin was dumbfounded. He said, 'But that wasn't the message I left with her.'"

The Super's broad shoulders shook with his deep laughter. "What a fool!"

"Yes, he was so eager to justify himself to Kochowski that he forgot I was listening as well. I asked him to repeat the message he'd given Hilda, and then gave him the usual warning. He refused to answer, so we bundled them all into the van and brought them back here. We questioned Kochowski and Quentin separately. Kochowski, who's a man with a very vindictive nature, is still convinced that Quentin betrayed him. He told us enough to put Quentin in the dock.

"When Bradfield and I interrogated Quentin he began by denying everything. He said that I'd misunderstood his last remark; that what he had intended to say was that he'd left no such message with the waitress as Kochowski had suggested. I produced the menu-card and asked him whether the words on the back were in his handwriting. He denied it. I supplied him with a sheet of paper and asked him to write 'Cancel tonight's arrangements. Suspect complications.' He refused, insisting on being legally represented. I left it at that, but added that the waitress had made a statement. I imagine friend Quentin has passed a very restless night."

With his long, thick legs stretched out and his hands thrust into his trouser pockets, the Super sat in deep thought for a full minute. Then he said:

"And the poisonings?"

"At the moment Kochowski's charged with attempted robbery and Quentin with being an accessory before the fact. I think we're all agreed that Hooker and Winslake were killed to prevent the plot from miscarrying. I'm not sure about Kochowski. There's no direct evidence to connect him with either of the murders. Nobody saw him in the Blue Boar on Thursday night. As for the poisoned breakfast, the only description of the driver of the V8 is that he was wearing a cap and an overcoat with the collar turned up. There was nothing to stop Kochowski from leaving his noticeable hat at home, of course, but—"

"I can help a bit here, sir," Bradfield interrupted. "Kochowski can't drive a car. I heard him tell Dipper Hicks so last night and there was no reason for him to lie about it."

The Super asked Charlton: "Have you questioned Kochowski about the murders?"

"Not yet. I want to be on firmer ground before I do that. I didn't mention it to Quentin either."

"What's the next step, then?"

"Peters found some fingerprints on the plate used for the poisoned porridge. We've sent photos up to the C.R.O., but there's no report come back yet. The Ford V8 is still missing. It belongs to a Dr. Hope Smith of Southmouth, and was stolen from outside the house of a patient he was visiting in the early hours of yesterday. It was probably abandoned after it had served its turn. We shall find it eventually, but it won't be much help to us. I'd like to get hold of the boy who delivered the breakfast tray here."

"So should I," agreed the Super dourly, then turned from a subject that was distasteful to him by asking:

"The woman—Mrs. Quentin. How about her?"

"She's as deep in it as her husband—perhaps deeper as far as the murders are concerned. Do you remember what Mrs. Collins junior told us about the Quentins when they were in the Shades on Thursday evening? After Mrs. Quentin had eavesdropped on Hooker and Winslake, who were talking just on the other side of the partition, she leant across and told Quentin about it—or we can reasonably suppose that she did. A short discussion followed, from which it was evident that Mrs. Quentin was trying to get her husband to agree to something. It's not unlikely that she was suggesting the murder of Hooker. Quentin must have been persuaded. His wife was the first to leave the Shades. When I questioned them Quentin said that they had had a squabble over something and that his wife got up and deserted him. I asked her what she did next and she said she went home. According to Quentin he followed her shortly afterwards. When he reached Capri there was a reconciliation between them and they came back to the Blue Boar for a final drink. Quentin wanted me to believe that he went straight back to Capri after the tiff in the Shades, but a witness—Goodwin, the manager of the Grand—says that at a quarter to nine, when Quentin should have been on his way home, he saw him hurrying along the High Street in the opposite direction. Where he was off to we can only conjecture at the moment, but there's no doubt in my mind that Mrs. Quentin went home to fetch a dose of cyanide for Hooker."

"Which of the two put it in his tankard?" asked the Super with a show of innocent curiosity.

"Neither of them, Tiny. You know that as well as I do. One or the other of them passed the cyanide over to an accomplice."

"And the first name that occurs to me, Harry, is Winslake."

"No, it wasn't Winslake. We've had the report from the analyst. The only article that had contained cyanide was the tankard used by Hooker. The goblet glass from which Winslake tipped the gin into Hooker's beer showed not the slightest traces of the poison."

"We've had all this out before," said the Super, "and I'm not going to press the point, but don't forget that Winslake could have had the cyanide in a tube in the palm of his hand and shot it into the tankard at the same time as the gin."

"I don't deny it, Tiny. Bradfield and I discussed this at some length yesterday and we agreed that if Winslake had had to face a charge of murder, counsel for the defence wouldn't have had an easy time. Winslake had the motive, the means and the opportunity. We must keep him on our list of suspects for the first poisoning, but not for the second. I refuse to believe that he committed suicide."

The Super rubbed his chin.

"I wonder whether Winslake murdered Hooker on the instructions of Quentin or this fellow Kochowski, and was then murdered himself to stop him from blabbing? It must have been a shock to somebody when Winslake was taken into custody. What do you say to that, Harry?"

"There again I'm not contradicting you. There's no evidence to show that Quentin had any sort of contact with Winslake after Winslake's talk with Hooker in the Shades. The only person the Quentins spoke to in the hotel was Olive Dove, the snack-bar attendant."

"And Pop Collins," Bradfield reminded him.

"Yes, that's quite correct. Olive refused to serve Quentin with double Scotches and Quentin demanded to see Collins. But although Quentin was not noticed talking to Winslake, he might easily have done so. He could have got Winslake into a quiet corner—perhaps in the back yard of the Blue Boar— and said to him, 'Look here, Doug, I heard you telling Hooker all about tomorrow night's affair. I suppose you realize that he's a police nark?' Winslake wouldn't have been too drunk to see the force of this and might have been quite ready to atone for his little indiscretion by seeing to it that the information he had given Hooker would go no further."

He lit another cigarette.

"But if Winslake murdered Hooker," he said, "I'm the Maharajah, of Molhapur."

★ ★ ★

John Harvey, an ancient shepherd, left the village of Barns Bottom behind and made his slow way between the thick, high hedges along the narrow winding lane a mile to the north of the downs, until he reached the gate of the field that was his objective.

It was only after he had opened the gate and gone into the field that he noticed the big green car drawn up close to the hedge.

Old Harvey's brain worked slowly, yet, as he stood and looked at it, the thought came into his mind that it was a very curious place to park a car in the depth of winter. He stepped towards it and peered through the window. The front seats were empty, but in the back, as if it had been lumped in like a sack of potatoes, lay the body of a young man with his fair curly hair matted with dried blood.

★ ★ ★

In the Inspector's room in Lulverton police headquarters the discussion continued.

"On Thursday evening in the Blue Boar," Charlton was saying, "we made a list of everybody who had any chance at all of doctoring Hooker's beer. Apart from Winslake, they were Goodwin, the Great Desro, Betty Collins and Major Wildgoose."

Superintendent Kingsley chuckled.

"I can't somehow see old Wildgoose mixing himself up in things like that. Too much of a *bar a sahib*. He belongs to my golf club. They say he was a bit of a rip in his younger days and went out to India to dodge the duns, but that was some time back."

"How's he placed financially?" asked Charlton.

"Living on his army pension. A widower, you know. Two daughters, both fine girls. One's married to a man called Marlow. He's a research chemist with Wallingtons, the pharmaceutical manufacturers at Southmouth. A clever young fellow, but he walks round in a dream with his hair all over the place, a smear on his nose, holes burnt in his clothes, and bottles of chemicals in all his pockets. Quite a trial for his unfortunate wife. They have a small boy of three. The younger daughter I don't know much about, except that she lives with them—and so does the Major. They all share a house in Birch Grove, a turning out of Highfield Road."

"Not usually a very successful arrangement," commented Charlton. "I gather that the Major is thinking of marrying again."

"Really?" said the Super in a slightly aggrieved tone. He prided himself on knowing everything about everybody in Lulverton, and this was news to him. "Who's the lady?"

"Mrs. Winslake, the mother of Douglas."

"No! Well, that *is* a surprise. I knew that drunken young hound was playing around with Phyllis Wildgoose—the unmarried one—a while back and that there was some trouble, but I've not heard about the other affair. Maybe the Major's not too sorry about the turn of events."

"You're right. Winslake would have made a difficult stepson. I'm not going to say, though, that that was sufficient reason for the Major to murder him, even though there might have been an opportunity to pick his son-in-law's pocket for the cyanide. My conviction is that the person who administered the poison was in league with Quentin and received his instructions from that unwholesome individual soon after a quarter to nine on Thursday evening. I'm willing to wager that when Goodwin saw Quentin going past the theatre, Quentin was on his way to find his accomplice, in order to give him those instructions."

"And how did this accomplice come into possession of the cyanide?"

"In one of several ways. He might have gone to the Quentin's house and collected it; or the Quentins might have brought it back with them and passed it over to him."

"You're assuming that the poison was supplied by the Quentins. That may not have been so, Harry. Winslake,

Wildgoose or any of the others might have had it in his pocket. The Quentins were in the snack-bar for a time. They might have got a message through, perhaps by giving a pre-arranged signal for the poisoning to be put in hand."

"Far fetched, I'm afraid, Tiny. It would have had to be a very complicated system of signalling to let the other person know that Winslake had just spilled the beans to Hooker, who was to be liquidated forthwith. Quentin would have needed flags or a semaphore for that. Another important consideration is opportunity. Take Major Wildgoose. If he did it, how did he do it? Goodwin and Desro were standing between him and Hooker and he couldn't have reached Hooker's tankard without attracting attention."

"He might have done it before they came in."

"Then the time factor comes into it, If Wildgoose had poisoned the drink before those two arrived, Hooker would have died much sooner than he did. So we're left with Goodwin, Desro and Betty."

"I'd count the girl out," advised the Super; "and Goodwin's not the type. I knew his father. Grand chap. The boy's a chip of the old block. You're looking for a man who can drive a car, aren't you? Don't forget Goodwin has only one arm."

"I know that, Tiny. I'm not suggesting he was involved. He's merely on my list of those who could have got at Hooker's tankard. Not that inability to drive a car proves him innocent. Hooker's murderer wasn't necessarily at the wheel of the Ford V8 yesterday morning."

Bradfield broke a long silence.

"So we come back," he said, "to the Great Desro."

"Yes," the Super took him up. "What do we know about him?"

"He's Mrs. Hooker's brother," Charlton told him, "and might benefit by Hooker's death, particularly if it had been agreed between him and his sister that it would be to his advantage financially if Hooker were put out of the way. That's the first point. Second, it was he who suggested that Goodwin and he should go along to the Blue Boar for a drink. Third, he's a conjuror—perhaps not a very clever one, but good enough to palm a phial of cyanide. Fourth, he handled the last drink Hooker was supplied with. He passed it along the counter to him, reaching across Goodwin. Fifth, he arrived early at the Grand Theatre this morning with a dixie. This apparently contained food for the white rabbits he uses for his act, but it might have also contained Winslake's breakfast, brought along to heat up over the gas-ring in the theatre. The caretaker wasn't there to watch what he did. Desro was in the theatre until just after quarterpast seven."

"Where did he go after that?"

"I haven't gone into it yet. If his only purpose was to feed his rabbits, he probably went back to the Bunch of Grapes, where he's staying with his daughter, who helps him with his act."

"Better ask him to produce an alibi. If any of the Bunch of Grapes staff can say that he went straight back there, he couldn't have had a hand in the Winslake poisoning—or, at any rate, couldn't have driven the boy away in the car."

"That wouldn't get us far. We're up against not one man, but an organized gang. Even if Desro can prove that he was in the hotel or the Grand Theatre when the car was being driven round the district; even if he can prove that he was not concerned in the collision with Stanley Dilks, the boy from Toni's—a vile trick that was; even if he can prove those things, that's not to say he didn't prepare the poisoned porridge. The biggest thing in Desro's favour is that he's a bird of passage. He's doing his act in Penzance one week and in the Orkneys the next. He couldn't be a regular member of Quentin's mob of wide kids, and it isn't likely that they co-opted him at the last minute to take part in the Molhapur robbery. If there had been no Molhapur exhibition, and Hooker had nevertheless been murdered in the circumstances in which he was murdered, I would have put Desro high up on my list of suspects—as high as, if not higher than, Winslake—but as things were, I prefer to look elsewhere for my quarry."

"Well," said the Super, settling himself more comfortably in his chair, "if we're going to rule out Wildgoose, Goodwin, Desro and the Collins girl, there's no one left on the list, is there?"

Charlton sat drawing squares on his blotting-pad. Then he said:

"There can't possibly be anyone else. It *must* be one of—"

He suddenly broke off and looked at Bradfield.

"Good heavens, Peter! What fools we've been! Why didn't we see it before?"

"See what, sir?"

"You remember the evidence of Betty Collins? Hooker never let his tankard go dry. He started the evening with a pint, then had it refilled from time to time with half pints. That's part of the answer."

"And the rest?" asked his perplexed assistant.

Charlton's lips twitched in a mischievous smile.

"Fiddler's Wonder-working Pick-me-up," he said.

XX.

Complimentary Tickets

THERE was no immediate opportunity for Charlton to explain his last cryptic remark, for at that moment the telephone bell rang. The caller was Detective-constable Hartley, speaking from the house called Capri. By one of those coincidences that are never explained, full service had become available on the line to that residence very soon after the arrest of Mr. Quentin. Hartley's tone was urgent as he asked Charlton to come round to Capri as soon as possible.

Charlton started out forthwith in the Wolseley, leaving Bradfield behind to deal with any matters that might arise at police headquarters. Hartley, a dark, thin, earnest man of thirty-five, with more brains and less brawn than his colleague Emerson, opened the front door of Capri to his chief.

"What's happened, Hartley?" asked Charlton.

"It's Mrs. Quentin, sir. Nurse Bentall and I have had a bit of a time with her. She went to bed last night quietly enough, with Nurse Bentall keeping her company in a chair. This morning, when she found that her husband hadn't come home—they sleep in separate rooms, you know—she got very excited. I heard her leading off and went upstairs in case Nurse Bentall wanted help, but Nurse managed to pacify her. By that time they were both in Mrs. Quentin's sitting-room. There's a gas fire in there, sir, and after half-an-hour or so, Mrs. Quentin said it was on too high. Nurse went to turn it down, but Mrs. Quentin said she'd do it. Nurse couldn't see much harm in letting her. Mrs. Quentin didn't touch the tap. She pulled back the lino round it, crouched down to stop Nurse from seeing what she was up to. But Nurse noticed there was something fishy going on and tried to stop her. Mrs. Quentin struggled like a wildcat and Nurse had to call me in from the landing, where I'd been hanging round for fear of more trouble. I'd say, sir, that she's got something hidden under the lino. I didn't touch it, thinking it better to leave it to you. We tried getting Mrs. Quentin out of the room, but couldn't manage it without using force. I rang you at once, sir."

"Quite right, Hartley. You'd better come up with me."

Hartley followed him up the staircase and along the passage to the door of Mrs. Quentin's sulking-place. When Charlton knocked, Nurse Bentall invited them to come in.

Belle Quentin was crouched on the settee with her long, slim legs drawn up under her. The expression on her face was not pleasant to see and she looked ten years older than when Charlton had met her on the previous day. Nurse Bentall was sitting upright in a chair near the gas fire, knitting a blue jumper as if nothing out of the way had happened to disturb her composure. It was she who greeted Charlton with:

"Good morning, Inspector. I'm glad you have arrived."

"I came immediately, Nurse."

The woman on the settee looked up at him and said in a voice devoid of emotion:

"What have you done with him?"

He answered in the same level tone:

"Your husband has been arrested, Mrs. Quentin, on a charge of having been concerned in an attempted robbery. I am investigating the murder of James Hooker and Douglas Winslake, and it is my duty to warn you that anything you say—"

"You can't make me give evidence against my husband."

"That is not my intention, madam. I'm not forcing you to answer any questions, but if you do so, your answers will be written down and may be used later in evidence."

Hartley got out his note-book.

"Have you any cyanide of potassium in your possession, Mrs. Quentin?" Charlton asked.

"Why should I? It's deadly poison."

"Have you any of it in the house?"

"No, of course not. Well, I suppose we haven't. I don't know what it looks like."

"The late Douglas Winslake had a quantity of cyanide in his photographic studio. We understand that he passed over some of it to some other person. Was that other person yourself, Mrs. Quentin?"

"I've told you—no."

"Did you ever see Mr. Winslake hand a small bottle of grey powder to anyone else?"

"Cyanide isn't a grey—"

"You were going to say...?"

"Oh, nothing."

She uncurled herself and reached out for the cigarette box and book of matches on the small table by the settee. As she lighted a Sobranie and drew hard on it, Charlton asked:

"When you left Mr. Quentin in the Blue Boar Shades on Thursday evening, you came back alone to this house, didn't you?"

"Yes. I told you so yesterday."

"After some little time, your husband arrived, I believe?"

"Yes. I said I was sorry for losing my temper with him, and we went back together to the Blue Boar for a last drink before they closed."

"That was your only purpose in leaving this house?"

"Why else should we have gone?"

"I'm going to suggest to you, Mrs. Quentin, that you returned here, not because you'd had a quarrel with your husband, but to fetch the cyanide that had been supplied to you by Douglas Winslake. I am suggesting that you or your husband passed the cyanide over to a third party with instructions to poison James Hooker. I am suggesting that the remainder of the poison that you obtained from Douglas Winslake is now in this house. Do you deny any of these statements?"

Belle Quentin jumped up from the settee. She said savagely:

"Haven't I got enough to put up with without you worrying me to death with your blasted questions? Get out of my house, all of you!"

"By all means, madam," Charlton answered smoothly, "but first I should like to have a look round this room."

Half an hour later, having called in at police headquarters, he was on his way to see Messrs. Wallington Ltd., the manufacturing chemists at Southmouth, taking with him a bottle that had once contained aspirin tablets.

★ ★ ★

Old John Harvey had never used a telephone in his long life, so it was Mr. Etheridge, the proprietor of the only shop in Barns Bottom village, who put through a call to Lulverton police headquarters. Bradfield answered it and, in the absence of his superior, assumed responsibility. He immediately telephoned Dr. Lorimer and then, with a constable at the wheel and the police photographer in the back seat with his apparatus, set off in a car for Barns Bottom. Later in the morning, when Charlton came back from Southmouth, Bradfield delivered his report.

"Lorimer said the poor kid had been dead about twenty-four hours. His skull was fractured and pieces of bone were driven into the brain. We found the weapon on the floor of the back of the car—a heavy adjustable spanner with a wooden handle."

"Any fingerprints?"

"Peters has got it now. He's going to let us know. I'm not very hopeful. Nobody but a crazy fool would have held it with his bare hand. On the back seat was a peaked cap with a 'Toni's Restaurant' band. The cap was marked 'S. Dilks' inside."

"Have you found out who the boy was?"

"Not yet. When we got the body back in the ambulance, Sergeant Harrison and Marryat had a look at him. They both identified him as the one who delivered the breakfast-tray yesterday morning."

"Write out a description, Peter, and see that it's circulated. Anything else that might help us?"

"Nothing much, I'm afraid. It was Dr. Hope Smith's car all right and the off-side lamp was damaged—glass and bulb smashed. There were scratches on the bonnet, where the handlebar of young Dilks's bike must have caught it. I made general inquiries in Barns Bottom and the surrounding cottages, but nobody seems to have seen the car until old Harvey, the shepherd, found it."

Charlton grunted.

"We've a nice little collection of murders on our hands, haven't we?" he said. "It's about time we laid our man by the heels."

"We've got to find out first who he is."

"Oh, I know that already, Peter. It came to me while we were chatting with the Super this morning. The trouble is to prove it. I dropped in here just after you'd left for Barns Bottom. The report on the fingerprints on the porridge plate had just come in from the Yard. They had no record of them. A bit of a disappointment, but they may come in useful later. Our man may not have already been through the hands of the police."

"You've been to Southmouth, haven't you?"

"Yes, I've had a very interesting and profitable talk with one of the research chemists at Wallingtons. His name is Stewart Marlow."

"Old Wildgoose's son-in-law?"

"Yes. Under the seal of professional secrecy, he carried out an experiment for me. The result was extremely successful."

"What was he experimenting with?" asked Bradfield, who did not like being tantalized.

"Toffee."

Charlton rose from his chair.

"You'll be glad to know," he went on, "that Belle Quentin is now in custody. She made some damaging admissions this morning. Under the lino in that upstairs sitting-room, I found enough cyanide to justify arresting her on suspicion of having been concerned in the murders."

He shrugged his shoulders.

"How we're going to pin on a certain gentleman the responsibility for the actual administration of the poison is quite a problem."

He stepped towards the hat-stand.

"Let's seek inspiration in a beer," he suggested.

"The Bunch of Grapes?"

"No, the Blue Boar. I've a little question I want to ask Miss Betty."

★ ★ ★

As Charlton and Bradfield were putting on their overcoats in police headquarters, Bill Goodwin was talking to Betty Collins in the hotel bar of the Blue Boar. There were no other customers in just then and Goodwin was taking advantage of the opportunity thus afforded.

"Won't you try to forget Winslake?" he was saying earnestly across the counter. "It would be better if you did, Betty. I hate to say it about a fellow who's no longer here to speak up for himself, but he wasn't worth it. You didn't really love him, did you, dear?"

"Yes," she answered defensively.

"Are you sure?"

"Yes," she said again, then dropped her eyes and added, "I think so."

"Did he ever ask you to marry him?"

"He said he couldn't afford it."

"He did propose to you?"

"No, not exactly. He knew Dad was against it. Dad didn't like him. Mum did, though."

"Would you have been happy with him, Betty?"

"I was always happy with him. He was so—gay, so romantic, so different from the stuffy people that Lulverton's full of. People who can't think of anything but making money and living terribly respectable lives. Douglas wasn't like any of them. He loved danger and thrills—anything with some excitement in it. He was a born adventurer."

The description was not well chosen, but he took no cheap advantage of it. He said instead:

"I don't think you'd have been happy long. You know, Betty, I'm all for fun and games and the occasional slaughter of the fatted calf, but there's a lot in being respectable. It's a good cure for insomnia. You don't jump as if stung every time anyone knocks at the door."

He took a pull at his beer.

"Have you heard about the attempted hold-up on Cowhanger last night?"

"Yes. Why?"

"Everybody involved in it was pinched *in flagrante delicto* and will get a nice long stretch in the jail-house. Will you believe me when I tell you, dear, that if he hadn't died yesterday morning, Winslake would have been in that business and would now be waiting trial with the others?"

She bit her lip, but did not contradict him.

"That's why he was poisoned, Betty—because he knew too much and might have blabbed to the police when they questioned him about the Hooker affair. ... Claude Duval and Jerry Abershaw cut dashing figures as gentlemen of the road, but they must have been a great anxiety to their wives."

He leant towards her across the counter. She did not draw back.

"Betty, dear, it's too soon afterwards for me to start talking about something I'm desperately keen to mention. We won't go into it just yet. For the moment, take this word of advice. Put Winslake out of your mind. Everybody's sorry to see a healthy young bloke come to such an end, but if he'd lived and you'd gone on with him, he'd have made every moment of your life wretched."

He stood upright, felt in the pocket of his waistcoat and produced an envelope, which he laid on the counter.

"It's a bit of an anti-climax," he added with a wry grin, "but there's a couple of tickets for the second house tonight. Get one of the family to come along with you. It'll do you a power of good to have an hour or two's—"

He broke off short, for Charlton and Bradfield were coming in. They exchanged greetings and Bill Goodwin bought beer. The conversation that followed was carefully kept off the subject uppermost in the minds of all of them, and after five minutes of small-talk and some more beer at Charlton's expense, Goodwin said he must go. As he picked up his hat, he said:

"They tell me you're both coming to the show this evening. Is that so?"

"Yes," Charlton agreed, "we hope to get along to the second house."

"I'll see you then," smiled Goodwin and, with another smile for Betty, he left them.

Charlton wasted no time; other customers might arrive at any moment.

"Miss Collins," he said, "I've just one other question to ask you about Thursday night. Did you supply Hooker with a fresh tankard when he came in?"

She thought about this for some moments.

"No," she finally decided. "He brought it in with him from the Shades."

"Thank you. That's just what I wanted to know."

Soon after the two detectives had departed, Pop Collins came through the door behind the counter.

227

"What did those two want?" he asked.

"The Inspector asked me whether Jimmy brought his tankard in from the Shades on Thursday."

Her father was stroking his signet-ring with his thumb and forefinger.

"What did you tell 'em?"

"That he did."

He grunted, then picked up the envelope that Goodwin had left on the counter. He opened the flap and pulled out the two tickets.

"Whose are these?"

"Mr. Goodwin gave them to me. You'd better take Mum."

"It's likely Mr. Goodwin didn't have that idea in mind," said her father drily. "You ought to go. Mr. Goodwin's a very agreeable gentleman and a man of importance in Lulverton. It won't do to offend him."

"I've got nobody to go with."

"Oh, yes, you have. Tell your mother to look me out a starched collar."

XXI.

Spotlight on X

"FOR this performance, walk this way! Odd numbers on the right, even numbers on the left! For tickets for this performance, walk this way! Advance booking, left-hand window! Odd numbers on the right, even numbers on the left!"

One-time Regimental Sergeant-major Charles New-march had lost some of the terrifying power of his old parade-ground bellow, yet, as he stood by the paybox in the *foyer* of the Grand Theatre in all the splendour of his blue and gold-braided uniform and shiny-peaked cap, his voice was still robust enough to bring every ex-serviceman over a wide area involuntarily to attention. Though this automatic tautening of the muscles lasted but a split second, it was accompanied by a well-nigh overpowering urge to slink into some dark corner or down a side street, and was followed, when the moment of relief came, by the tremulous smile of one suddenly awakened from some ghastly nightmare.

"Advance booking, left-hand window! For this performance walk this way! Odd numbers on the right, even numbers on the left!..."

From Mondays to Fridays there was only one performance a night at the Grand Theatre, but on Saturdays there were two, one at 5.30 and the other at 8.15. At five minutes past eight on this particular Saturday evening, while old Charley continued to exercise his lungs, the audience for the second house were beginning to assemble. The queues for the pit and gallery had already been allowed to pass through the turnstiles into the theatre, and now the more affluent—the ones who could run to as much as four shillings and sixpence for a seat—were arriving.

The paybox was in the centre of the *foyer*, between two flights of stairs that led up to a wide, iron-balustraded balcony, on the left and right of which were double doors giving access to the passages leading to the auditorium. At each of these two entrances was stationed a smartly uniformed girl whose job it was to tear the tickets in two and call out from time to time, "Even numbers this way, please," or "Odd numbers this way, please," as the case might be. Charley, down below, assisted them in this, but people took little notice of him and went up whichever flight of stairs took their fancy, sorting themselves out when they reached the top. Consequently, the efforts of the management to avoid confusion were brought to naught.

Against the balustrade, a row of chairs had been placed for the convenience of patrons. At ten minutes past eight, when the *foyer*, staircases and balcony were crowded with persons all moving in different directions, a man leapt with surprising nimbleness on to one of these chairs and proceeded to address the gathering. He wore a dark overcoat, a black Homburg hat and a grey woollen muffler undone to reveal a winged collar and a blue bow with white spots. At first his voice was not heard in the general hubbub, but it was not long before the umbrella he waved to give point to his utterances attracted the attention of everyone, and even Charley Newmarch was reduced to. astonished silence. The man on the chair was Mr. Zephaniah Plumstead and he was in good form.

"...Hell is eternal! Repent before it is too late! Come not into this den of vice, this cesspit of iniquity, this noisome resort of the Evil One! Save your souls before the jaws of Hell open to receive you! Go back to your homes! This is no place for you. I speak to you all from the depths of my heart. There can be no salvation for a man or a woman who has eyes closed to the light and creeps in the fetid darkness of unrighteousness. Turn your thoughts from the tinsel and trumperies! Stay not a moment longer! Tarry not to witness the ungodly spectacle, the bedizened dancing harpies, the—"

"You'll 'ave to stop that, sir," Charley called up to him.

"I shall not stop. That is my mission, to lift my voice against the great forces of evil, the serried ranks of the wrongdoers, the spiritually unclean..."

Most of his audience had stopped moving, but there was one woman who came purposefully—if somewhat drunkenly—up the stairs. Her imitation leopard-skin coat was thrown open to display a low-cut evening gown of the most painful magenta and her hair had been twisted on top of her head into a hideous knot, in which was tucked an artificial rose of red velvet that clashed almost audibly with her gown. In one hand was an evening bag of tarnished brocade; in the other a fan. She looked like one of Cinderella's sisters off to the ball. It need not be added that this vision was Mrs. Clarice Hooker.

She paused by Mr. Plumstead, who was continuing to trumpet, and said in her harsh, slurred voice, waving her fan at him in solemn objurgation:

"Get off that chair, yer silly ole fool. Makin' a public exhibition er yerself. Come and 'ave a gin."

Mr. Plumstead had broken off and turned to look down at her.

"Woman!" he said in a loud voice. "Do not think that I do not know you—a painted Jezebel, whose husband is not yet in his grave!"

He gesticulated with both arms dramatically, just missing a light-fitting with his umbrella.

"Look upon her, all that are here present! Blush for her—weep for her, that her heart should be so hard that she can come to this place, this cesspit of iniquity—"

A hoarse male voice said:

"You've called it that once already."

"Bow down your heads before her shame. A widow but two days, and here she stands, clad not in the weeds of grief, but in the sorry finery of a daughter of darkness!"

"You rude old—," said Mrs. Hooker with great clarity, but in quite a friendly way. The first seven or eight double gins always sweetened her temper.

There can be no telling how this incident would have ended, had the principal participants been left to themselves. But they were not. Charley Newmarch deserted his post by the paybox window and stumped up the stairs with the two waxed points of his moustache signalling trouble for somebody. As he reached the balcony and was pushing his way through the delighted throng, Bill Goodwin—fetched in a hurry by one of the girl attendants came from the other side, and the two of them converged on Mrs. Hooker and Mr. Plumstead.

It was at this juncture that Inspector Charlton and Sergeant Bradfield came into the *foyer* from the street. Everyone else was turned towards the balcony. The two detectives followed their gaze.

"What's afoot?" asked Bradfield. "Another busman's holiday for us?"

On the balcony, Bill Goodwin was saying to Mr. Plumstead:

"I think you'd better get down off that chair, sir. You're causing a disturbance."

Mrs. Hooker swayed majestically.

"He called me a painted Jezebel," she announced in a pleased tone.

"And so you are!" proclaimed Mr. Plumstead. "Bold, brazen daughter of the Evil One, mend your ways ere it is too late. Hell is eternal."

"You said *that* before, too," the hoarse voice reminded him. "Learn up some new clack."

"Come along, please, sir," said Goodwin politely. "The curtain will be going up in a minute or two."

"I shall not descend until this shameful performance is cancelled. Give these misguided people back their money. Bond slave of Satan! Panderer to the worst instincts of human

232

nature! Close down your vile palace of glittering vice! Pestilent parasite!"

Bradfield murmured to Charlton:

"He shoots a pretty line of alliteration. Are we going to interfere in this?"

"Certainly we are," answered his chief.

As they elbowed their way up the stairs, an excited whisper ran through the assembly:

"The police!"

The crowd fell back and allowed the two detectives to reach the storm centre.

"What's the trouble here, Mr. Goodwin?" Charlton asked briskly.

"The way of the transgressor—" Mr. Plumstead began, but Charlton stopped him.

"Be good enough to keep quiet, sir. Now, Mr. Goodwin?"

"This gentleman insists on standing on a chair and making an inflammatory speech. He's made some slanderous allegations against this theatre and refuses to leave unless we call off the show. Can you use your influence with him, Inspector?" He murmured into Charlton's ear, "I don't think he means any harm. Just misguided that's all."

Mrs. Hooker looked round into Charlton's face, nearly losing her balance.

"'E called me a painted Jezebel," she told him with the pride of a child.

"Flaunting female!" said the unrepentant Mr. Plumstead.

She jerked her fan at him.

"Now, look 'ere! A joke's a joke, but you'd best not go too far with it, or I'll 'ave one or two things to say about *you*, yer ole 'umbug."

Charlton said: "Mr. Plumstead, please get down off that chair."

The little evangelist decided that it would be advisable to obey. There was a vaguely menacing note in the Inspector's quiet voice—a hint of harshness in the comforting depth of it. Accordingly he descended from his improvised rostrum.

Charlton asked him:

"Have you ever attended a performance at this theatre, Mr. Plumstead?"

"A thousand times no!"

"Then I fail to see how you can criticize the management. You've said some unfair things about Mr. Goodwin and you should give him an opportunity to prove that your charges are unfounded. I came here this evening in a private capacity and I don't want any unpleasantness to spoil my enjoyment. I speak for Sergeant Bradfield as well. As an alternative to taking official action, I am going to ask Mr. Goodwin here to supply you with a complimentary seat for the performance that is just going to begin. If, after you have seen it, you are still of the same mind, you will then be in a position to take the appropriate legal steps."

"That's fair enough," said the hoarse voice.

Mr. Plumstead looked doubtfully from one to the other of the group, then his eyes sought the floor. When he looked up, it was at Charlton.

"Never since my childhood," he said in a subdued tone with no trace of the earlier fervour, "have I entered a theatre or a music-hall. I go into public houses and to racecourses in search of lost sheep. Why should I not seek them out in such places as this?"

He turned to Goodwin.

"I did wrong to call you by cruel names. Please forgive me. I will indeed witness the performance, but only on one condition." He beamed around him. "And that is that I pay for the seat!"

There was a general laugh and the crowd began to break up and file through the entrance doors into the auditorium. Goodwin escorted Mr. Plumstead to the cloak-room, in order to deposit his overcoat, hat and umbrella, while Charlton and

234

Bradfield found their way to their seats in the front row of the dress circle. While Charlton, who was at the end of the row, was glancing through the programme, Bradfield leant over to look down at the stalls. In a minute or two, he turned to Charlton to say:

"Bill's put him in a centre gangway seat in the fifth row. There are one or two other old familiar faces down there."

Without looking up from the programme, Charlton said:

"Desro's number eight—the last turn before the interval. What did you say?"

"Pop Collins is in the front row with young Betty. It isn't often old Pop gives himself an evening off. And take a look at who's sitting just behind them."

Charlton bent forward, then relapsed into his seat with a non-committal grunt.

Bradfield asked:

"Who are those two on his right, do you know?"

"The son-in-law, Stewart Marlow. The girl's probably his wife, but it may be the sister, Phyllis Wildgoose."

The members of the orchestra had taken their places and now struck up the overture. The indicator at the side of the stage was switched on to read "1". Just as the house lights went down, Bradfield caught sight of Mrs. Hooker sitting alone in a stage box with the dignity of a tipsy empress.

The first turn was a couple of acrobats, When they had finished throwing each other about for the day and the curtain was going down, Bradfield looked round to speak to Charlton and was surprised to discover that he was no longer by his side.

★ ★ ★

As the duettists, Marie and Max—Two Voices and a Piano—who were number six on the bill, were taking their call in front of the curtain, Charlton slipped back into his seat. Bradfield glanced at him inquiringly, but Charlton did not enlighten him.

235

They sat through the next turn—Nikolai and his Marvellous Performing Dogs—then, as the bulbs of the indicator winked and transformed themselves from a "7" into an "8", Charlton rose again to his feet. He bent down to murmur to Bradfield:

"Stay where you are, Peter, and keep your fingers crossed. I'm going to try to out-Desro Desro."

Bradfield was full of curiosity, but he did no more than nod assent.

When the curtain rose again, the stage was empty except for the small tables, the chair and other accessories that are the stock-in-trade of the illusionist. Then, with a fanfare by the orchestra, the Great Desro came on from the wings—a tall, Mephistophelean figure in dress-overcoat and opera-hat. There was a round of applause as he came to the footlights and bowed. As the orchestra continued to play, he removed his hat and overcoat and placed them on the chair.

There followed a number of conventional conjuring tricks with a pack of cards, silk handkerchiefs, large-sized wooden dice, an egg in a black bag, beer-bottles that disappeared after being covered by cardboard cones, and lighted cigarettes that were plucked out of the empty air, to the noisy delight of the audience, who clapped and whistled at the end of every trick.

Desro used no patter for this part of his turn, but went through it with a musical accompaniment. No smile came to his long saturnine face.

When he had uncoupled four steel rings, bounced them on the stage to show that they were unbroken circles, and then re-linked them, there was another flourish on the trumpets and a piece more apparatus was wheeled on the stage by an attractive young person whose costume might have qualified her for the "bedizened dancing harpy" class against which Mr. Plumstead had inveighed so fiercely, but who was rapturously received by the younger males in the audience and those of their seniors who were not accompanied by their womenfolk.

This, thought Bradfield, would be Joy Roberts.

She pushed the contrivance to the middle of the stage and then stood back from it. The framework was of chromium-plated tubular steel and in general construction it resembled a tea-trolley. The four sides and top were filled in with metal lattice-work of a mesh sufficiently open for the audience to see right through—or to imagine they could, which was all that really mattered.

On the floor of this cage-on-wheels was a white rabbit, quite unconcerned by the publicity it was getting. Bradfield wondered where its companion was.

The Great Desro stepped up to the cage and, standing to one side of it, opened the top, which was hinged, took a grip on the rabbit's ears and lifted it out. Holding the creature at arm's length—it had gone through all this before and gave no more than a token wriggle—he came forward to the floats. Then he raised his other hand and transferred his grasp so that he now had one ear of the rabbit in each hand.

For a second he stood there with arms straight out in front of him. This was the cue for the drummer in the orchestra pit. He got busy with his sticks. As he reached the climax of the roll, Desro's hands were suddenly snatched apart.

Some of the women gave little whimpers at the thought of poor bunny's ears being wrenched from their roots, but they were swiftly reassured, for now Desro had both ears, uninjured, in his left hand. And in his right hand was another white rabbit.

For a moment there was a silence of disbelief, then the applause started. In the dress circle, Bradfield joined in. Bill Goodwin had said that this was Desro's only clever trick, and Bradfield now had cause to agree. With his arms on the red plush rail, he looked down at the stalls. Major Wildgoose was leaning across his daughter to speak to Stewart Marlow. Across the gangway, Mr. Zephaniah Plumstead—a seeming convert to iniquity—was clapping energetically. In the front row, Betty Collins was doing the same, while her father was putting his hands to the more practical purpose of relighting his pipe. Bradfield's glance travelled to the stage box. Mrs. Hooker was not easily discernible, but Bradfield received the impression that she was nodding her head as if in gracious acknowledgment of her brother's skill.

Bradfield relaxed physically, but not mentally. Perhaps this was Desro's finest trick, yet it was surely not to be the highlight of the evening. Bradfield felt certain that Inspector Charlton also had something up his sleeve, though it might not be so innocuous as a white rabbit.

The Great Desro turned from the footlights. Joy Roberts stepped forward and opened the top of the cage. The two tenants were put back into their portable home, which Joy then wheeled off through the wings. Desro, however, was not to remain alone. As his daughter passed out of view, Bill Goodwin strolled on from the other side and came to the centre of the stage. While Desro picked up three billiard balls and began moodily to juggle with them, Goodwin announced:

"Ladies and gentlemen, we come now to the most astounding part of the Great Desro's performance. He is not only a magician; he is also an amazing clairvoyant. He can see objects hidden from the sight of us ordinary human beings. This is not a conjuring trick. There is no quickness of the hand to deceive the eye, no palming, no mirrors. The Great Desro can look back into the past and gaze, perhaps, into the future."

This was the cue for the reappearance of Joy. She was holding a tray. Goodwin explained that in a few moments she would collect articles from various members of the audience, and that these articles and their owners would then be described by the Great Desro, he having first been blindfolded. Goodwin made the usual humorous reference to the possibility of the property not being returned to its owners, which was greeted by the equally usual laughter.

The house lights were switched on and, while Joy went down into the audience with her tray, Goodwin proceeded to bandage the eyes of Desro, who continued to juggle with his billiard balls.

Joy came back on the stage. A number of articles were now on the tray, which she carried to one of the tables. Goodwin led Desro to the floats and placed him so that he faced the audience, then moved several paces away from him. Joy took an enamelled compact off the tray and held it up so that all could see it.

"What do I hold in my hand?" she asked.

For the first time during his performance the Great Desro spoke.

"A flat powder-box from a lady's handbag."

"Is it enamelled?"

"Yes."

"What is its colour?"

"Blue."

"Is its owner sitting in the fourth row of the stalls?"

"No, she is in the sixth row."

"On which side of the house?"

Desro pointed to his left.

"Is the lady wearing a hat?"

"No, she is bareheaded."

"What is her age?"

The Great Desro's voice took on an even more sardonic note as he answered:

"That is a secret shared only by the lady and myself."

This raised a laugh.

"Is she married?"

"She wears a wedding-ring."

After a few more questions, all of which Desro answered, the catechism came to an end. Goodwin walked across to the table. Joy handed him the compact, which he carried to the footlights.

"Will the lady in the sixth row of the stalls please signify that this is her property and that the answers given by the Great Desro are correct?"

Heads were turned, necks were craned, and people at the

back were on their feet to catch sight of her, but the lady was shy and it was left to her escort to rise and say:

"Quite correct."

As the applause started, Goodwin went down the steps at the side of the stage and returned the compact to its blushing owner. Several more things—a silver pencil, a tobacco pouch, a cigarette case—were all accurately described by Desro.

A single article remained on the tray. Joy took it in her hand and Bradfield had a hunch that something momentous was about to happen.

"I am now holding up the last of the articles collected from the audience," said Joy. "What is it?"

Desro's answers to previous questions had come promptly. Now he seemed to hesitate and it was some seconds before he said:

"It is a charm—an emblem to avoid evil."

"Is it of some precious metal?"

"Yes, it is of silver."

"What is the shape of it?"

"It is in the form of an animal."

"Is the animal of which this is a model large or small?"

"Large."

"Very large?"

"Yes, very large indeed."

"Is it a European animal?"

"No, it comes from the East."

"Has it horns or has it tusks?"

"Elephants do not have horns."

The trinket was too small for most of the audience to identify it, but Bill Goodwin gave them a lead by clapping his artificial hand against the other. When the applause had died down, Joy put her next question.

"Does this charm belong to a lady or a gentleman?"

"To a gentleman."

"Does it usually hang from his watch-chain?"

"Yes."

"Is the gentleman wearing evening dress?"

"No."

"Is his collar starched or soft?"

"Starched."

"Is the gentleman young?"

"No, he is middle-aged."

"Can you tell us any more about him?"

This was a question Joy had not put when dealing with any of the other articles, nor had Desro touched them. Now, still facing the audience, he held out his hand.

"Give me the charm."

Joy stepped forward and placed it in his outstretched palm. He closed his fingers on it, then pressed his clenched hand against his bandaged brow.

There was a hushed pause. This was something different. The house lights were dimmed and the only illumination on the stage was a green lime on Desro that gave him a weird appearance. After a while he began to speak, and his voice was of one talking in a trance.

"I see a street upon which the glaring sun beats down. There are many people in the street. They are not white people. In the gutters, women in coloured *saris* sit on their heels. In front of them are baskets heaped with red chillis, which they offer for sale. ... I seem to be walking along the street. I pass a Hindu temple with its steeple over the shrine, and I come to a great palace. I move towards the mighty gateway. ... All around me are beggars who cry for alms. '*Bakhshish*, sahib! *Bakhshish*, sahib!' I do not heed them. ... To the sides of the gateway—each in its own enclosure—stand two elephants. Their tusks are richly ornamented. ... I pass through the gateway. I am in the courtyard of the palace of a great ruler—the palace of the Maharajah of Molhapur... The vision fades."

Desro stopped speaking. From the audience there was not a

sound. Desro brought his fist away from his brow, then pressed it back upon it.

"There are clouds. They eddy and whirl around me, so that I cannot see clearly. ... Now there is a lifting of the clouds, as if a light wind had swept them for a moment aside. I see—what is it I see? No, it is not the palace of the Maharajah of Molhapur. I am in another place and now there are no longer dark faces around me. ... I see other faces—the faces of white men. They do not wear the flimsy clothing of the tropics. They are more heavily and warmly clad, for now I am in a colder clime. ... These men whom I see are drinking. They hold glasses in their hands. ... I see one hand in which there is no glass. It is a left hand and on the little finger is a signet-ring of gold..."

Bradfield was gripping the brass rail over the plush. This was it—the greatest trick of the evening.

"...Yet, though there is no glass, there is something else in this hand. I try, but cannot see what it is. ... My glance travels a few feet and fixes upon a drinking vessel that stands alone on a surface of polished wood. This drinking vessel is not of glass, but of metal that shines and twinkles like the stars."

The voice took on a tenser note.

"What is this I see?... The hand... It moves towards the tankard... It passes over it. ... Do I see something fall from the hand into the liquid that the vessel contains? Yes, I saw it clearly. It was a sweetmeat such as children love—a toffee. ... Again the vision fades... No, it returns... I see another hand—a right hand, a hand rougher and more soiled than the first... It takes the tankard by the handle and bears it away from that place... The bright lights are dimmed and I walk forward as I did into the palace of that eastern town. ... But now there is no sky of unclouded blue. Instead there is rain, and the street is dark, save for the dim light from the gas-lamps. ... I walk but a few paces and come to the entrance of another building not far removed from that which I have just left... But there are no elephants on either side of this entrance. No, there is above it

242

the semblance of another animal. This, too, has tusks, yet it is not an elephant. It is a wild hog—a boar, and the colour of it is the colour of the sky in distant Molhapur."

The audience was no longer silent. All over the house there was excited whispering.

The Great Desro went on:

"In my vision I see this man who carries the tankard place it down on a counter, but it is not long before he raises it to his lips and drinks... He does not quaff deeply and does not detect the toffee that lies at the bottom... This pellet is still whole, yet its sweet coating will soon begin to dissolve in the liquid and when it has melted away, there will be released from this harmless lollipop a deadly poison."

He snatched his fist from his forehead and pulled the bandage from his eyes with the other hand. Then, with both arms outstretched, he cried out:

"Can such a sin go unpunished? No! An avenging hand will smite the murderer and he will be flung into the bottomless pit! Justice will prevail! Let him not think of repentance! Let him not plead for mercy! It is too late for both. His sins are known and there can be no escape for him. Soon all men will cry his name from the housetops—the name of a poisoner and the slayer of a defenceless lad! From heaven there shall come down—"

"Stop!"

There was another voice now, shouting above the voice of Desro.

"Stop! For God's sake stop! The lightning will strike me!"

Betty Collins screamed.

The green lime was switched off and the house lights came on. In the stalls a man was on his feet, his clenched hands pressed to his ears. It was Mr. Zephaniah Plumstead.

On the stage Desro was now standing in silence, looking down with a cynical smile on his face. Mr. Plumstead dropped his arms and stumbled out into the gangway. As he turned to hurry towards the exit, Inspector Charlton stood barring his way.

"I'd like a word with you, sir," said Charlton.

By now the theatre was in confusion. Everybody was talking at once. Among those who left their seats was Bradfield, who hastened to join his chief. Bill Goodwin came down off the stage and made for Betty Collins with long strides. She gave a little cry when she saw him and fled from a horrid world into the shelter of his strong left arm.

Then above the uproar there rose a strident feminine voice. Mrs. Hooker was shrieking across to Charlton from her box.

"Don't let 'im give yer the slip, mister! 'E's a cunnin'—. They call 'im Smarmy Joe in the Caledonian Road. Keep 'old on 'im. I'll teach 'im fer pois'nin' me ole man, the twicin'—! You ask the Islington cops abaht Smarmy Joe. They'll tell yer. Wait till I get rahnd."

She disappeared from view.

Ten minutes later, Charlton and Bradfield, with Mr. Plumstead between them, came away from the Grand Theatre. Shortly afterwards, with all the excitement over and the house restored to normal, the curtain rose for the first turn of the second half of the programme. It was the dancing act of the Eight Lawson Lovelies. Bradfield had missed them after all.

XXII.

Martin Has the Last Word

IT was the evening of the following Saturday. Charlton, Bradfield and ex-Detective-sergeant Martin were having a cosy chat round the fire in the green room in the Blue Boar Hotel. Nobody else was there to hear them, so the conversation had turned to the case on which Charlton and Bradfield had spent some anxious days.

"What put you onto this hot-gospeller?" Martin wanted to know as he put his tankard back on the table after a long draught.

"At first it was just a vague suspicion," Charlton answered. "He seemed too good to be true."

Bradfield said:

"He was more like a street-corner evangelist than any other street-corner evangelist I've ever seen."

"The question was," said Charlton, "how did he do it?—I mean the murder of Hooker. As far as I could tell, he had no opportunity at all, so I provisionally struck his name off my list of suspects. Then, while Peter and I were talking with the Super on the Saturday morning, a remark of Betty Collins suddenly came into my mind. She told us that Hooker always started the evening with a pint tankard and never let it run dry. There was the clue, if we'd only noticed it in time. Hooker started the evening, not in the hotel, but in the Shades. Tankards cost money, but Hooker was well known in here, and nobody stopped him from taking the tankard out of the Shades. He told young Bob Collins that he was going into the hotel, and that was good enough for Bob. A pity Bob didn't mention it to us. One important thing he did tell us, though: that during the short conversation between Hooker and Plumstead in the Shades, Plumstead placed his hand over

Hooker's beer. According to Bob, he said, 'This stuff will bring you nothing but grief and disillusion.' On the word 'This,' the cyanide passed from Plumstead's palm into Hooker's tankard."

He sipped his beer before he went on:

"In the conviction that that was what had happened, I sought round for some method by which the action of the poison could be delayed from just after quarter past nine until a few minutes before ten o'clock. That explains my reference to Fiddler's Wonder-working Pick-me-up, Peter."

"You had me foxed over that," admitted Bradfield with a rueful grin. "I can see it now, of course. When you first mentioned that marvellous elixir, I remember adding something about capsules."

"Yes, but this was no ordinary capsule. It had to be of some substance that would dissolve away in cold beer in less than three quarters of an hour and leave nothing behind—at least, nothing that Hooker wouldn't swallow without noticing it. When I went round to the Quentins' house last Saturday morning, I found in an aspirin-tablet bottle a couple of large-size pills of a light brown colour. I took them to Wallingtons' works at South-mouth and had a talk with young Stewart Marlow, their best research chemist, about them. It didn't take him long to decide that the thin coating over the cyanide centre was nothing more or less than ordinary toffee. He carried out a time-test for me under conditions similar to those prevailing in the Blue Boar on that Thursday evening. You'll remember that the hotel bar was very warm; there was a large fire in the grate. That helped the toffee to dissolve. The result of Marlow's experiment convinced me more than ever that Plumstead was our man.

"I could see that this was going to be difficult to prove. When I knew that he was going to be present at Desro's exhibition of magic, I had an idea. It was fantastic and unorthodox, yet the situation called for nothing less. Some weeks ago I was reading a book about the natives of Tierra del Fuego, who have—or had—their witch-doctors, as do most other primitive tribes. The author mentioned that it was a curious characteristic of these witchdoctors that, with the full knowledge that they themselves were frauds, they nevertheless went in terror of all other witch-doctors.

"It occurred to me that, human nature being what it is, Plumstead might hold the same views about his fellow charlatans as the Fuegian witch-doctors held about theirs. When the show at the Grand had started, I went backstage for a talk with Desro and his delightful daughter. They were only too ready to help. I had previously noticed the elephant charm on Plumstead's watch-chain, so I asked Joy Roberts to make a special point of getting hold of it and making it the last item for her father to be questioned about. I told her where Plumstead was sitting and rehearsed Desro in what I wanted him to say. He responded magnificently and in future I shall join issue with anyone who contests his right to be called the *Great* Desro."

He broke off to drink some more beer. Martin and Bradfield did the same.

"It was a devil of a risk I took," Charlton went on, "but the trick succeeded. Plumstead got scared at the uncanny powers of his rival witch-doctor, and panicked."

"'Ave you got any evidence against 'im?" Martin asked.

"He lived in a room at one end of the building in Highfield Road known as the tin tabernacle. Peter and I went along and searched it. We found close on three hundred pound-notes. We also found a vacuum jar."

"What's that?"

"A vacuum jar is on the same principle as a vacuum flask, except that it is larger and has no neck. The one we discovered in the tin tabernacle was the gallon size. It was fitted with a nest of metal dishes, which could be used for keeping three different kinds of food hot at the same time. Mrs. Winslake told us afterwards that Plumstead used it for outings of the religious group of which he had the damnable impertinence to appoint himself head. The butcher with whom he was registered confirms that he bought half a pound of liver on Thursday morning. Plumstead didn't know then, of course, the use to which circumstances would force him to put it. On the vacuum jar we found two lots of fingerprints—Plumstead's and those of the boy he murdered."

"Who was the boy?"

"His name was Cyril Preston—a wild Southmouth lad who was always running into trouble. His parents say he was so out of control that he often stayed away from home all night and refused to give any sort of explanation afterwards. The Southmouth police have had their eye on him for months. How Plumstead got hold of him on the Thursday night, we don't know. All we know is that he did.

"In addition to the notes and the vacuum jar, Peter and I discovered hidden in the room a glass tube containing two pills identical with those I found in Mrs. Quentin's sitting-room. Who actually prepared them is not yet clear. It may come out in the trial. I imagine Mrs. Quentin had more to do with it than anyone else. She must have got the cyanide from Winslake as a precautionary measure, in case anything went wrong with any of their little schemes, suicide being preferable to arrest. Alternatively, the necessity for a murder or two might crop up at any time.

"At the moment it's only an assumption, but I think we can take it that when Mrs. Quentin went back to Capri, it was to fetch a supply of pills. Meanwhile Quentin had hurried off to Highfield Road, where Plumstead was doubtless reading some improving treatise by the light of a guttering candle in his tiny cell, and persuaded him, in exchange for a sum of money, to carry out a little homicide on his behalf. When the fee had been decided upon, Quentin made for home, followed by Plumstead. The phial of capsules was handed over to Plumstead and he then made his way to the Blue Boar Shades, arriving there at approximately quarter-past nine.

"Plumstead used one of the toffee pills on Hooker and another for Winslake. It would have been a simple matter to dissolve it in warm water and then pour it on the porridge. Plumstead's one big mistake was over the porridge plate. Sergeant Peters took Plumstead's dabs and matched them with the finger-prints on the plate. This was afterwards confirmed by the Yard. Plumstead carefully wiped the top of the plate, but forgot the underside. There were no prints on the spanner used to fracture Cyril Preston's skull, but we found enough on the steering-wheel and other parts of the Ford V8 to connect Plumstead with that incident."

"'Ave they got this feller's partic'lars at the C.R.O.?" inquired Martin.

"No. He's always been clever enough to dodge conviction—at any rate in this country. His real name is Joseph Plumstead. He must have adopted the Zephaniah for business purposes; it has a pious ring. He used to be known to the ungodly as Smarmy Joe. Mrs. Hooker put me on to that. She knew him in the old days at Islington. I fancy he didn't know her—or has since forgotten. Otherwise he wouldn't have been quite so rude to her in the *foyer* of the Grand. In Islington, Plumstead made a handsome profit by putting religion on a commercial basis and persuading gullible people to subscribe to his so-called charitable organizations. His Boys' Club is still talked about in those parts; it was the nearest he ever got to prison. I've been up to see the Islington police. They say that, however much they suspected, they never got a chance to catch him at anything. Some years before the war, he ceased to be seen in the neighbourhood of the Caledonian Road. They believe he got a temporary job as steward on a liner bound for Bombay and stayed in India for a time. I've made local enquiries and found out that he's been in Lulverton about three years. Eighteen months ago he bought the tin tabernacle with money collected from his growing flock. If he hadn't been foolish enough to get himself mixed up with Quentin and his murderous designs, he might have gone on gaily mulcting the faithful of Lulverton for years."

Bert Martin finished his beer and wiped his mouth with the back of his hand.

"Well," he said, "all good things come to an end."

"Yes," Charlton agreed, "I suppose Plumstead had a run for his money."

"I wasn't meaning him," said Martin, looking pensively down into his empty can.

THE END

Catt Out of the Bag

How, where and why did a man disappear from a group of
carol singers on that cold December night in Paulsfield?
It hardly seemed likely that he had absconded with the
collection box. But the more Inspector Charlton found
out about the missing person, the less certain he became
that he would find him alive...

281pp   978-1-912916-375

Murder in Blue

John Rutherford, bookseller and sometime novelist,
discovers the bludgeoned corpse of a policeman one
evening while taking a stroll in a rainstorm. When
Inspector Charlton is called in to find the murderer, he
realises that the perpetrator of this crime may be prepared
to go to extreme lengths to cover their tracks.

276pp   978-1-912916-504

Measure for Murder

It is January 1940 and Mrs Mudge is busily occupied
cleaning the Little Theatre in Lulverton. But she's in for
an unpleasant surprise with her discovery of a corpse in
the box-office, stabbed in the back with a dagger — a
prop from the society's latest play, Measure for Measure.

281pp   978-1-912916-528